*Oh, my.*

Cecily's heart near climbed into her throat as she surveyed the wide expanse of Zach's naked chest, covered in dark curls. A flame flared, and its light danced across his bronzed skin, emphasizing his broad shoulders, muscular arms and the planes and hollows of his sculpted chest. He looked powerful, and dangerous, and very, very male. She swallowed the urge to turn and flee and made herself approach the fire. The flames did nothing to stop the heat spiraling through her entire body.

"I had to come. We leave after breakfast. I wanted to—I did not want to go without saying goodbye."

He stepped closer to the fire and hunkered down to feed in more wood, his attention focused on his task. She drank in the sight. Never had a man affected her like this—her heart twisted at the impossibility of even a simple friendship between them, at the width and the depth of the gulf between their positions in society. And yet she was here. She had come, despite knowing that visiting him here, at night, unchaperoned, would ruin her if it ever became known.

## Author Note

Although *Lady Cecily and the Mysterious Mr. Gray* is the final book in The Beauchamp Betrothals trilogy, it can be read as a stand-alone story.

This book is dedicated to the ADCs. It was during one of our monthly meetings that I had a "eureka" moment and realized that threading the mention of Romanies (or gypsies, as they were more commonly called in the Regency period) through *Scandal and Miss Markham* would help tie the story together. I had been wondering for some time who would provide the perfect (and yet totally imperfect) hero for Lady Cecily Beauchamp in the third book of the trilogy, and then I suddenly realized the perfect candidate—in the mysterious form of Absalom (Zach) Gray—was staring me in the face!

I researched Romany culture and beliefs as well as their history, which was absolutely fascinating and made me realize how easy it is to unthinkingly accept as fact all those commonly touted stereotypes. I just wish I could have shared more of my research—as ever, I use my research sparingly, to add flavor to my story, rather than allow it too much prominence.

Two books in particular were very helpful to me— *I Met Lucky People* by Yaron Matras and *We Are the Romani People* by Ian Hancock—but, needless to say, any mistakes in the story are entirely my own.

I do hope you enjoy reading about Cecily and her mysterious Mr. Gray.

# JANICE PRESTON

---

*Lady Cecily and the Mysterious Mr. Gray*

**HARLEQUIN®** HISTORICAL

Recycling programs
for this product may
not exist in your area.

ISBN-13: 978-1-335-52271-9

Lady Cecily and the Mysterious Mr. Gray

Copyright © 2018 by Janice Preston

Printed in U.S.A.

**Janice Preston** grew up in Wembley, North London, with a love of reading, writing stories and animals. In the past she has worked as a farmer, a police-call handler and a university administrator. She now lives in the West Midlands with her husband and two cats and has a part-time job with a weight-management counselor—vainly trying to control her own weight despite her love of chocolate!

### Books by Janice Preston

### Harlequin Historical

*Mary and the Marquis*
*From Wallflower to Countess*
*Regency Christmas Wishes*
*"Awakening His Sleeping Beauty"*

### The Beauchamp Betrothals

*Cinderella and the Duke*
*Scandal and Miss Markham*
*Lady Cecily and the Mysterious Mr. Gray*

### The Governess Tales

*The Governess's Secret Baby*

### Men About Town

*Return of Scandal's Son*
*Saved by Scandal's Heir*

Visit the Author Profile page at Harlequin.com.

To the ladies of the Anti-Doubt Crow (ADC) novelists.

Who'd have believed that within three years of our first meeting we'd all be published authors? Our monthly get-togethers keep me sane—thanks for the many, many laughs, the sympathy when the going gets tough and the sage advice when needed. Here's to more coffee and cake, and much more success.

xxx

# Chapter One

~~~~~~~~~~~~~~~~~

*Early June 1812—Worcestershire*

Lady Cecily Beauchamp's face ached with the effort of maintaining her smile. Not for the world would she reveal the sudden misery and doubt that assailed her as she watched her brother, Vernon, walk his new bride back up the aisle of the little country church where they had just made their vows. The happy couple were followed by Cecily's oldest brother, Leo, Duke of Cheriton, his new Duchess on his arm. In the space of four months both of Cecily's brothers had found love and wed, totally shaking Cecily's comfortable, settled world. She had spent her entire adult life in charge of the Beauchamp household and had raised Leo's three children from his first marriage with as much love and care as if they were her own.

But now...

Cecily stifled a gasp as a touch to her elbow almost catapulted her out of her skin. She glanced sideways into the face of a stranger and pressed her hand to her chest to quell the sudden thump of her heart as a pair of the darkest eyes she had ever seen captured her gaze. Black unruly locks framed his face, harshly handsome with chiselled cheekbones, skin the hue of dark honey and a hint of dark stubble shadowing his jaw, even though it was still before noon. A swift sweep of his body—tall and powerfully built—offered the solution to his unkempt appearance and tanned face. His clothing was clean and serviceable, but well-worn.

*No doubt he is a servant of the Markhams, invited to attend the wedding.*

Dismissing both the stranger and her own wayward twinge of regret—servants were servants, after all—Cecily smiled graciously and moved out of the pew to allow the man to pass.

She had arrived late at the church, very nearly missing the ceremony entirely after one of the carriage horses threw a shoe that morning, delaying the final leg of their journey. Rather than cause a disturbance, she and Dominic—Leo's eldest son, who had escorted her on the journey from London to Worcestershire—had slipped quietly into the back pew.

Her gaze swept the interior of the church. Dominic had already gone, as had the remainder of the small congregation. She had barely noticed the exodus, too caught up in her own sudden awareness of the changes that had rocked her world.

'Are you unwell? Should I fetch someone?'

The rich voice came from behind her. She turned. The stranger, his brooding gaze on her, stood by the open church door. Cecily felt a flush start low on her chest and rise to wash over her face, although she did not know why she should feel embarrassed by what a servant might think of her standing and wool-gathering when she should be outside, congratulating her brother and her new sister-in-law.

'I am quite well, thank you.' She walked towards the

door. 'There really was no need for you to wait or to be concerned.'

He filled her vision as she neared him and a glint caught her eye. She blinked. She was not mistaken. She felt her eyes widen. The man had a diamond in his earlobe.

How very…exotic.

Quickly, she wiped any hint of surprise from her expression. The stranger still watched her, his features impassive, but she got the impression he missed nothing with those ebony eyes of his. Sure enough, as her gaze locked with his, amusement glimmered in their depths before he swept a bow.

'After you,' he said.

Cecily stalked past him, her nose in the air. Her heels clacked rapidly against the flagstones as she continued through the church porch and outside, blinking as she emerged into bright sunlight.

'Cecily!' Vernon swept her into a hug and then kissed her soundly on the cheek. 'I'm so pleased you decided to come.'

Cecily thrust aside her troubles and doubts. This was Vernon's day. She loved her brother dearly and she would not cast a shadow by revealing her fears. She could not be that selfish.

'You gave us very little notice, Brother dear. We only just made it in time.'

'Did Olivia not accompany you? I have not seen her. Or Alex.'

'Unfortunately, Livvy took ill the morning we left.' Cecily still did not quite believe in her eighteen-year-old niece's sudden bout of sickness, but she'd had no choice other than to leave her behind. 'We decided it was best for her not to travel. And as for Alex—well—Alex is Alex,' she added, of Leo's rebellious younger son. She pushed all thought of her challenging niece and nephew from her thoughts and smiled up at her brother. 'Congratulations! I never thought I would see the day you trod this path willingly.'

Vernon grinned, and pinched Cecily's chin. 'You will understand when you meet her.' He caught Cecily's hand and tugged her over to where Leo and Rosalind stood with the bride. 'Thea! Meet your new sister.'

Cecily was immediately charmed by Vernon's new wife. She was tiny, with a neat figure and a vibrant face topped by a halo of copper-coloured curls. Her infectious smile invited everyone to share in her joy and she gave the impression of barely contained energy as she moved.

'I have heard so much about you, Cecily. I hope we can be friends.' Thea's voice was unexpectedly deep for a woman and endearingly gruff.

'I am sure we shall.' Cecily kissed Thea on both cheeks. 'Are your parents here?'

She would be staying at Thea's parents' home, Stourwell Court, for the next few days and it was only good manners that she should greet her hosts.

The spark in Thea's eyes seemed to fade. 'They have gone home. My father had a stroke six years ago. He is not strong and cannot walk. He insisted on attending the wedding in his wheelchair, but Mama took him straight home afterwards. You will meet them later.'

'I shall look forward to it.'

Vernon's letter had related the story of Thea's father's infirmity and the awful circumstances that were the cause of it. A swindler had courted Thea and then cheated her father out of a fortune before jilting poor Thea at the altar. Her family—not part of the aristocracy or even the landed gentry, but hard-working manufacturers of lead-crystal glassware—had been almost bankrupted and the shock had caused Mr Markham Sr's stroke. Thea and her younger brother, Daniel, had worked tirelessly to pull both the business and the family back from the brink of ruin.

Cecily glanced around the small group of people gathered outside the church. Apart from Leo and Rosalind, and Rosalind's grandfather, Mr Allen—all of whom had already been in the Midlands in order to collect Mr Allen's belongings from his Birmingham home—and Dominic, there were few others. Of the servant with the diamond in his ear, there was no sign and she supposed he had attended the wedding in order to help Mr Markham get to and from the church. A strange sensation stirred her insides at the thought of the man and his dark, unfathomable gaze. Irritated, she cast him from her thoughts.

'Allow me to introduce you to my brother,' Thea said and she drew Cecily towards a young man who was talking to Dominic.

Daniel looked nothing like his sister, being tall and dark, but there was little time to talk for Vernon soon ushered them all into motion, urging them ahead of him.

'Come now, it is time for the wedding breakfast. I intend to spend the rest of this day in celebration of my good fortune in marrying this gorgeous, perfect woman.'

He swept one arm around Thea's waist and pulled her close for a kiss. The sting of tears took Cecily totally unaware. To see her much-sought-after, handsome brother so utterly smitten with Thea, even though she was not of their world…that was true love. It had been the same with Leo and Rosalind. Almost from the first time Cecily had seen her powerful oldest brother—a duke from the age of nineteen—with Rosalind it had been clear he was besotted. Cecily ducked her head and blinked rapidly until she was sure her emotions were under control again and then she plastered another happy smile upon her face and allowed Dominic to hand her into the coach for the journey to Stourwell Court. She barely noticed the house as they drove up to it, so preoccupied was she. Then the carriage halted and they entered the house and were shown into the dining room where the wedding breakfast was laid out.

The first person she saw was the man from the church. And he was not a servant, as she had first thought, because Leo himself carried out the introductions.

'Cecily, my dear, this is Mr Gray, a very good friend of Daniel Markham. Absalom—my sister, Lady Cecily Beauchamp.'

Mr Gray bowed. When he straightened there was such a look of bemusement on his face that she almost—but not quite—giggled. And she never giggled. Ladies do not giggle, especially thirty-year-old spinsters who are sisters of a duke. But the giggle bubbled dangerously in her chest nevertheless.

'I am pleased to make your acquaintance, Mr Gray,' she said.

His dark eyes narrowed and she felt a whisper of caution deep down inside, but she could not fathom what it meant.

'Likewise, Lady Cecily.'

He moved away abruptly and they did not speak again, but her eyes were drawn to him again and again during the wedding breakfast. His stillness. His watchfulness. A quiver ran through her every time his dark gaze touched upon her and she deliberately looked away so she did not meet his eyes. Later, she questioned Thea—casually— about the presence of Absalom Gray and she learned that he was a gipsy—'or Romany, as he prefers,' whispered Thea—who had recently saved Daniel's life. Nothing much else was known about him. He was, Thea had confided, a man who guarded his privacy.

And then the diamond earring, which made him some-how mysterious and dangerous, and the faded, loose-fitting clothing—serviceable but not that of a gentleman—made sense. Cecily noticed that Mr Gray disappeared after the wedding breakfast and the toasts, and she felt at once relieved and disappointed: relieved in that she no longer needed to be on her guard against catching his eye and disappointed in that his brooding presence had at least diverted her from agonising over her own future.

She maintained her cheerful mask all through the afternoon and on into the evening, when neighbours and friends of the Markhams had been invited to share in the celebrations. Her life had prepared her for just this outward mien of calmness and grace, even when her insides were in tumult and even while her inner voice berated her ceaselessly for her mean-spirited response to both of her brothers' good fortune in finding love and happiness. She gazed around the drawing room, at the happy, champagne-flushed faces and, of a sudden, it all felt too much. She needed to get away. She needed a few minutes alone where she did not have to act a part.

She caught Rosalind's eye and gestured, indicating that she was going to relieve herself, before quietly leaving the room. Instead of heading to the ladies' retiring room, however, she found a side door that opened into the garden and she let herself out into the fresh air. She did not linger by the house, but followed a gravelled path that bisected a formally laid out garden, instinctively heading away from the laughter and the light to a place where, as twilight dimmed to dusk, she would be invisible to any other guest who ventured outside. As she walked, a breeze sprang up and she chafed her arms against its unexpectedly sharp bite, wishing she had thought to fetch her shawl before coming outside. She glanced back at the Court, its every downstairs window blazing with light, wondering if she should return to the celebration, but—just for the moment—she could not face it. The strange agitation that roiled her insides was making her nauseous. Inside the house, joy and congratulations continued to flow as freely as the champagne. And Cecily shared the joy and congratulated the happy couple with all her heart. Truly she did. But…

She needed time alone to sort through her thoughts and her emotions, which felt precariously balanced, as though the slightest nudge might result in a complete loss of control. And one thing Cecily prided herself upon was that she never lost control. She shivered, hugging her arms around her torso, and rubbed again at the gooseflesh on her bare arms, deliberately allowing her deepest fears a free rein as she continued to stroll along the broad path flanked by glorious roses in full bloom, intermingled with sweet-smelling herbs. The moon, brightening by the minute, was already high in the sky and the stars winked on, one by one, as the velvet cloak of the night shrouded the garden.

It wasn't that she begrudged either Leo or Vernon their happiness. She was thrilled to see them both so wonderfully, ecstatically in love. And she liked both Rosalind and Thea. Very much. But Vernon's marriage, coming so soon after Leo's, had left Cecily…where, exactly?

And now she could allow her innermost fears to float up to the surface and form into coherent thoughts, she could pin down the source of her greatest fear: these two momentous changes in the life of the Beauchamp family had left Cecily fast travelling down the road to that unenviable position: the unwed dependant.

The maiden aunt.

The recipient of pitying looks and the butt of snide jokes.

No longer mistress of anything, but a supplicant.

Her life had changed, through no fault of her own, and she had no power to prevent what would, inevitably, come. Her stomach clenched with resentment at the unfairness of the hand life had dealt her and she quickened her pace, as though she could outrun her shame at such mean-spirited and selfish thoughts and feelings. She reached the end of the path, turned a corner and thumped straight into a solid wall of flesh.

'Oh!'

Cecily teetered for a moment and two hard hands encircled her arms to steady her, the grip powerful and hot against her bare skin. Her heart thundered in her chest as she realised how reckless she had been, wandering around a strange place in the dark, with only the moon and stars to light her way, and she struggled to free herself. The man instantly released her, his hands falling to his sides, and her pulse steadied. She tipped back her head to see a pair of dark fathomless eyes set in a barely visible face, framed by a silhouette of straggling dark curls. The glint of a diamond in among those curls triggered recognition and her breath caught in her chest as her pulse rocketed once again.

## Chapter Two

'**M**r Gray. Good evening.' Cecily smoothed her hair back with hands that trembled slightly. 'I did not expect to see anyone else out here.'

'Nor I.'

'Yes. Well…' Cecily glanced back towards the house, her heart skittering in her chest. 'I really must be getting back.'

'Is that what you wish to do?'

'I…' She stared up at him. 'That is an odd question.'

'Is it? It is simple to me. Either you wish to return, or you feel you *must* return. They are different.'

Cecily's brows twitched into a frown. 'I shouldn't be out here alone with you.'

He ran his fingernails along his jaw, the rasp of stubble loud in the hush of the evening. 'You think you are in danger from me?'

'I… No. I did not mean that. It is not proper, however. I have my reputation to consider.'

His teeth gleamed in a smile and he gestured at the expanse of garden between them and the house. 'There is no one to see us. No one to question us. No one to condemn. And we are fellow guests, talking.'

Put like that…he was right, but she found his logic infuriating. Did he not understand? But of course he would not understand…he was a gipsy. What did he know of etiquette and the strictures of society?

'Let us walk a while. Tell me why you are troubled.'

Cecily gasped at such impertinence. 'Troubled?'

*Outrageous!* She should walk away. Now. She should refuse to engage with him. But instead she laughed. It was intended to be a dismissive laugh, but it emerged as a high-pitched squeak and her cheeks grew hot. 'I am not troubled.'

'Then why do you walk out here alone?'

'I needed some air. And you, Mr Gray?'

He tilted his head to the night sky and inhaled. Instead of a tight-fitting neckcloth such as the other gentlemen wore, a simple blue cravat encircled his neck and was loosely knotted at his chest. His neck as he looked skywards was thick and strong, his shoulders wide and straight, his chest broad. The power of the man was undeniable and yet… Cecily consulted her instincts. She had no fear of him. Her only fear—no, that was too strong— her only *apprehension* was being seen. Mr Gray's coat gaped open as his chest swelled with his indrawn breath, revealing an unbuttoned, brightly patterned waistcoat with a gold watch chain dangling loose from its top pocket and, beneath that, a pale shirt.

'I, too, needed air.'

He studied her once more. She saw again the glimmer of white as he huffed a quiet laugh and she suddenly felt rather breathless.

'It is one thing we have in common then.' His voice— warm and melodious—seemed to curl around her. 'I thought there might be…*something.*'

His eyes were fixed on her face and, her mouth dry, she moistened her lips.

'I... I do not know what you mean.'

He said nothing, but continued to watch her. Cecily shivered. She really ought to return. If her family realised she was missing, they would worry. She was jolted from her thoughts as Mr Gray shrugged out of his jacket and settled it over her shoulders. If she'd realised his intention, she would have refused the jacket, fretting about dirt, lice and fleas, and unclean practices. Her keen sense of smell, however, detected nothing more than the intermingled scents of woodsmoke, musky male and soap. She felt her tense muscles relax and she hugged the edges of the jacket across her chest as the warmth seeped into her chilled flesh.

'Thank you.'

'You are welcome, Lady Cecily.'

'You disappeared after the breakfast. Where did you go?'

'I am flattered you noticed.'

'I believe Mr Markham remarked upon your absence.' It was a lie, but she would not have him know she had been watching him. Or, in truth, been fascinated by him. 'Is your...er...tribe staying hereabouts?'

'No. I have come alone.'

'So where *did* you go?'

He stepped back. 'I am a free man. I go where I please.'

'Of course you are. I apologise. I did not mean this to sound like an interrogation.'

He inclined his head, but said nothing further.

Cecily frowned. 'You do not *sound* like a gipsy.'

'And how *should* a gipsy sound, in your vast experience, my lady?'

She stiffened, her chin lifting, irritated by his readiness to take offence.

'In my *experience*,' she said, haughtily, 'gipsies often speak with a foreign accent. I merely meant you sound as English as I.'

She swung his jacket from her shoulders and thrust it at him. 'Thank you. I am warm enough now. I must return to the party.'

He reached and in one smooth movement took his jacket and slung it over his shoulder. He then grasped her hand before she could withdraw it, his warm fingers closing around hers.

'I was born in England. And we prefer to call ourselves Romanies, or the Rom.'

It was not an apology, but she was mollified nevertheless. Mr Gray gave the impression of a man not given to apologies or explanations.

'I shall endeavour to remember that,' she said, by way of appeasement.

Although her brain instructed her to snatch her hand from his, she allowed it to remain—intrigued by the unexpected gentleness of his touch as he unhurriedly removed her evening glove, and strangely soothed by the caress of his thumb as it circled her palm.

'And is your mind now trouble free?' His intense gaze bored into her. 'I watched you. In the church.'

His words reignited her fears for her future as she had watched Vernon and Thea exchange their vows and her inner turmoil erupted anew. She pressed her free hand to her belly in a futile attempt to calm her nerves.

'And now I ask myself why the sister of a rich and powerful duke should have any reason to be unhappy.'

'Unhappy?'

He shrugged, his thumb still circling her palm in that spellbinding way, and by concentrating on that motion her inner chaos subsided again. His free arm slid around her waist and his hand settled at the small of her back. With a gentle nudge, he turned her to continue to follow the path and she found herself walking side by side with Mr Gray away from the house and deeper into the garden, even though his palm was no longer at her back and he had at some point released her hand. Cecily swallowed.

*I should not go with him. I really should not.*

'Walk with me. I will listen.'

He halted and so did she. He touched his finger to her chin…such a fleeting touch. 'I will not judge.'

Then he began to stroll along the path again.

And so did Cecily.

Yet again, all the precepts of her upbringing screamed at her to return to the house. To surround herself with… *normal*…people. To do and behave as would be expected of her and as she expected of herself, as she had done her entire life. But the urge to unburden herself was stronger. There was nobody in her life she could confide in. Not about this.

*Maybe…*

She stole a glance at the man by her side. His expression gave away nothing of his thoughts, but it was relaxed. Not tense, closed off, secretive or eager, just…he was just…

*He is present…neither planning tomorrow nor brooding over yesterday.*

The words whispered out of nowhere and she recognised them as the truth. He was calm and unhurried. Not impatiently waiting for her to respond, like most men of her acquaintance would be—wanting to deal with whatever she was fretting about so they could then get on with their more important lives.

*He is content to wait and for me to speak or not speak as I choose. What harm can there be? He is a gip—Romany— and in a few days I shall return to my normal life. Our paths will never cross again.*

And, somehow, that freedom to choose, the magic of the night, the scent of the roses and Mr Gray's calming presence combined to induce a trancelike state in which the normal rules by which Cecily always lived did not apply.

'I was thinking about my future.'

'And you see unhappiness ahead for you?'

'I... Yes.'

Silence reigned.

'My brothers' marriages...so close together... I did not expect...'

Her throat tightened, holding her words inside. They had reached the end of the path, arriving at an open area paved with flagstones, bordered on the far side by a stone wall as high as a man, with an arched gateway. Cecily crossed the area to a raised pool set in the middle and gazed into the still, black water at the reflection of the moon—a silvery sphere that, as she trailed her fingers in the water, shimmered and danced. She turned to face Absalom Gray. Here was her opportunity to sort out her tangled thoughts and feelings—to speak her concerns out loud and to think over her choices for her future. Mr Gray remained at the edge of the square, but the weight of his gaze upon her made him feel closer. Gave a feeling of intimacy. Cecily took a breath.

'I never expected my brothers to marry. Leo...he was married before and it was not a happy experience for him, although the marriage did give him two sons and a daughter.' She paced across the square, and back again to the pool. 'He is forty years old now and has been a widower for thirteen years. He has been pursued by endless females with the desire to be a duchess. I never...ever...'

'You never expected he would fall in love?'

There was no condemnation in his tone, but she felt her defences rise up.

'I am happy for him. I love my brother and I liked Rosalind from the moment I met her. We became friends. But...

I was seventeen when Leo's first wife died. I raised his children and I ran our household. And now…and now…'

Lady Cecily's voice faded into silence and Zachary Absalom Graystoke waited, content to allow her to unburden herself in her own time, knowing she would feel better once she had released whatever was troubling her. He was happy to help this duke's sister to face up to and resolve whatever was troubling her. Beyond that, he had no intentions. No ulterior motives. These people were as far removed from his life as it was possible to be. Facts were facts and a half-blood Romany was no more acceptable to the society in which the high-born Beauchamps moved than a full-blood Rom, no matter who his father had been.

Lady Cecily Beauchamp had fascinated him from the very first moment he set eyes upon her. She had arrived late in the church and had slipped into the back pew, next to him. Someone else had come in with her, sitting on her far side, but Zach had not the smallest interest in the young man, who was clearly related to the Duke. But the woman—he did not know her identity at the time—had captured his attention with her intoxicating scent and her tightly controlled emotions and her luscious curves. She sat there, next to him, all prim and proper and ladylike—a perfect lady—dressed in a gown the colour of bluebells, with a bonnet to match, and she did not see him. She had no concept of his presence until—with the need to move past her to go and help Daniel's father into his carriage—he had touched her elbow.

He had felt the jolt of connection deep in his gut: an emotional connection that continued to bridge the physical distance between the two of them even when they no longer touched, shimmering between them. And he had recognised then, and later at the wedding breakfast, the disquiet she was at pains to conceal from everyone around her, using her perfect, ladylike manners as a shield. And he had suffered another jolt, this time one of disappointment, when the Duke had introduced her as his sister, Lady Cecily. And although the distance between them had become a chasm, that connection lingered, even though Zach knew damned well he had nothing to offer *any* woman, given the way he had chosen to live his life.

'And now…' her voice as she continued drew Zach back to the present '…here I am, thirty years of age, and—as Vernon would say—at my last prayers.'

He had thought her a similar age to him, but she was the older by four years. Another gulf yawned between them, but it barely mattered—a hundred such gulfs could make no difference.

'I have never had a great ambition to marry, but then I thought I would always have the Abbey to run; I thought I would always be at the helm of the family, helping Leo.' Her voice shook and she sucked in a deep breath. 'I feel usurped. There. You asked why the sister of a rich and powerful duke should have any reason to be unhappy and now you know. You may see what a horrible person I am, beneath all this.' She indicated herself with an abrupt sweep of her hand.

'You fear the change your brother's marriage will bring?'

'Yes. And I know that is selfish. The strange thing is… Leo has been married a month already, so I knew everything had changed, but I pushed it from my mind. There was Olivia's come out to manage—'

'Olivia?'

'My niece. Leo's youngest. She made her debut into society this spring.' She perched on the low wall surrounding the pool and trailed her fingers through the water again. 'It was not until I saw Vernon and Thea together in the

church that the truth hit me…' She surged to her feet once
more and again she paced. To and fro. 'In my world—'
she halted in front of him, and he tamped down the urge
to touch her; to soothe her '—if a lady does not marry, she
eventually becomes…oh, I don't know how to explain it…
invisible. Unnecessary. She fulfils no useful function but
to run occasional errands or to carry out the tasks nobody
else cares to fulfil.' She fixed him with eyes that glinted
fiercely. 'I do not want to be that supplicant living in other
people's homes; tolerated rather than wanted or needed;
dependent upon others for her very existence.'

'Let us walk.' Movement would help him to resist her.

She nodded, once, and glanced back towards the house.
She turned, resolutely, and set off towards the archway in
the wall. Through there was an expanse of meadow and
a small ornamental lake that had been formed when a
stream was dammed.

'You believe that is what your future now holds?'

'It is inevitable, but I cannot talk to my family about
it. They would ridicule such fears—especially Leo and
Vernon. They will reassure me that I am loved and that
my home will always be with the family at the Abbey. But
Rosalind is the lady of the house now and she, like me, is
accustomed to being in charge, having raised her younger
brothers and sister. And I value our friendship… I do not
wish to clash with Rosalind over *anything* when we all return home for the summer.'

'Do you have choices?'

'Choices for ladies who do not wed are limited and they
are neither enviable nor easy.'

'But you would not have to earn your living?'

'No.' They strolled down the gentle slope of grass towards the lake. He heard her sigh. 'No, I would not. Leo
would give me an allowance. A generous one. And I am

fully aware that makes me sound ungrateful for my life of privilege.'

He sensed her eyes upon him, but kept his attention straight ahead, on the stretch of water ahead, gleaming in the light of the moon.

'I *am* aware of how fortunate I am.'

'Yes. You at least *do* have choices, unlike some.'

*Unlike Mama.*

His mother's face materialised in his mind's eye and a wave of grief rolled through him. He did not fight it, nor did he succumb to it. Grief was a part of life and living and he had learned to accept its appearance, knowing it would recede soon enough.

They paused at the water's edge.

'It may help you to decide what to do if you speak your choices out loud.'

There was a lilt of humour in her voice as she said, 'You mean you are not going to advise me what my choices are?'

'Should I?'

'You are a man. In my world, most men would fall over themselves to prove they know the best way for me to proceed.'

'I am not most men.'

There was a pause. 'No. That appears to be true.'

'So tell me then—in your world, what choices are there for an unmarried lady of your birth?'

'For a respectable lady with a need to earn a living, she might choose the role of a companion or a governess.'

'And for a respectable lady with no need to earn her living?'

She sighed. 'Nothing. There is nothing to look forward to but that slow descent into the role of dependent relative, as I said.'

'But if you have an allowance, does that not give you a choice?'

'Such as?'

'If you could choose your ideal life, what would it be?'

She laughed, but it turned into a sob, quickly choked off. He couldn't help himself. He put his arm around her shoulders, and smoothed his hand down the bare flesh of her arm. Her head tipped towards him and rested for a moment against his shoulder before she pulled away.

'And that proves how pathetic I am. You ask me about my ideal life and all I can think is that I want my life to continue as it has always been. I want to care for my family and I want to run a large, happy household. It is what I have always done and what I always expected to do. I want nothing else.' She bowed her head, pressing her fingers against her eyes. 'But that is the one thing I cannot have, is it not? My brothers are now married and our family has already changed, and I can only selfishly dwell upon how those changes will affect me and my life.'

He touched her nape and stroked, relishing the silky warmth of her skin and the delicate bumps of her spine.

'Change is like that, is it not?' His mind drifted back to his own past and he brought it swiftly back to heel. 'It is the nature of the beast; it can affect our lives in ways we cannot begin to imagine.'

She turned her head to look up at him. She was so close he could hear the quiet sough of her breathing, and her scent—reminding him of sweet apple blossom—mingled with the night air until he felt full of her. He forced his hand from her and crouched down, feeling around in the damp soil at the edge of the lake. His fingertips found the smooth surface of a large pebble and he picked it up, smoothing his thumb over it as he regained his feet.

'It is like the change a pebble makes when it is thrown

into a pond.' He tossed the stone high and long, aiming for the middle of the lake. 'It sinks below the surface to lie unseen on the bottom, but the ripples it causes touch every inch of the shoreline.'

'Yes. Yes, it is just like that. And I am on the shore, and the ripples are...oh, I don't know...unsettling...disturbing... and they force me to acknowledge that even good changes... wonderful changes...can have negative consequences.'

'And one of those negative consequences is how your brother's marriage will affect you?'

'Yes. No.' A sound of frustration, like a low growl, emerged from her and Zach hid his smile at the idea of Lady Perfect growling. 'I ought not to be talking to you like this.'

'But you wish to—*need* to—or you would not be doing it. Life is more content if we all follow what we choose to do rather than what we ought, should or must do.'

'If everyone did that, chaos would ensue. There has to be some discipline. Some law. Some obligation.'

'Of course there must, in wider society. I meant on a personal level. You are so bound by the etiquette and rules of your world that you cannot look beyond those boundaries.'

'That is easy for you to say.' Bitterness laced her words. 'But that is my—oh!'

Lady Perfect fell silent as a familiar ghostly shape swooped towards them. She did not scream as he feared she might. Rather, she watched, entranced, as the barn owl flew low across the pond, her flight silent, and landed on Zach's outstretched arm.

'What...?' Cecily's voice was a whisper, full of wonderment.

'Lady Cecily Beauchamp, meet Athena.'

## Chapter Three

Cecily had never been this close to an owl before. Athena stunned her, with her heart-shaped face and huge dark eyes and the contrast between the buff-coloured feathers on her wings and back with the snowy white of her face and breast. Mr Gray took Cecily's ungloved hand and raised it to the bird's breast. Her fingers sank into the soft feathers, more deeply than she anticipated.

'She is beautiful,' she whispered. 'Why is she so tame?'

Mr Gray touched the owl's head with his forehead, then lifted his arm high. The bird launched into flight and glided away as silently as it had arrived.

'I reared her from a fledgling.' His hands cupped in an unconscious gesture, as though he remembered the finding of her and as though he still protected her.

'How old is she?'

'She is nine now.'

'Do you keep other animals, Mr Gray?'

He rubbed his hand across his jaw. 'I do not keep them. They are free to leave if they so wish.'

'Will you tell me about them?'

'Another time. Maybe.'

He began to walk back across the grass towards the

garden and regret swirled through her. She followed him, hurrying to keep up with his long strides.

'I am sorry. I did not mean to pry. I should not have questioned you.'

'There you go again, with your *"I should not have..."*' he growled.

He slammed to a halt and pivoted to face her with such suddenness that she almost cannoned into him. Her feet, still clad in her satin dancing slippers, skidded from under her and she reached out, clutching his lapels to steady herself. His arms came around her, hauling her close, and she found her cheek pressed to his chest, the steady beat of his heart thumping in her ear...far steadier than her own erratic heartbeat which flittered, soared and swooped.

'Steady.'

His voice rumbled through her. His arms still held her captive, but they loosened a little, allowing her to tip her head back to look at him. His eyes flashed and a muscle leapt in his jaw as one hand slid lower and settled at the small of her back, fitting her snugly into the warm contours of his body. His breath caressed her skin as his free hand came up to cradle her cheek, his thumb drifting across her lower lip. Her breath quickened as his head lowered and, without volition, she rose on her toes to close the gap between them.

His warm lips were soft and smooth, exhilarating and yet soothing. She had only been kissed once in her life and the experience had been...forgettable. This...

*Oh, this...*

She pressed closer, slipping her arms around his waist, revelling in the sensual glide of his mouth on hers, lost in the moment. She tensed as his tongue probed her lips, but he murmured deep in his throat, a calming sound, and she parted her lips and let him in. Their tongues slid together as he entered repeatedly, exploring her mouth, delicately and without haste. An unfamiliar sensation gathered deep in her stomach, a growing ache of yearning...of desire. She settled deeper into his embrace, his male scent surrounding her as her pulse ran riot and her toes curled with pure pleasure.

It was he who ended the kiss, lifting his lips from hers and drifting them across her cheek. He nibbled her earlobe, then traced the outer rim with his tongue as she tilted her head to ease his access. Her wits were reassembling but, although she was shocked by her wanton behaviour, she felt no shame. His hands framed her waist and lifted her, setting her away from him. She resisted the urge to seek again the heat of his body, the security of his arms.

'That should not have happened.' The wicked glitter in his eyes belied his words.

'Should not?' she teased, even though he was right. Of course it should never have happened. But she challenged him nevertheless. 'Why not?'

He barked a laugh. 'That, my Lady Perfect, is a foolish question.' He raised his arm, gesturing at the night sky. 'Let us blame the magic of the moonlight and come the dawn we shall forget it ever happened.'

'Did you not enjoy kissing me?'

He reached for her hand, holding it in both of his, playing gently with her fingers. Then he raised it to his mouth and pressed hot lips briefly into her palm before folding her fingers over as though to hold his kiss in place.

'I did.' His voice was low. Sincere. 'But you know as well as I that a boundary was crossed. Until that moment, we were indeed fellow guests merely talking. Now...our consciences know the truth, but it can never be revealed to anybody else. Ever. It would be the ruin of you, were it known you kissed a Romany.'

She knew he was right and she still could hardly believe she—who prided herself on always being ladylike and correct—had behaved so out of character.

'Mayhap you are right and it was the effects of the moonlight,' she said. 'You were not thinking clearly. You were angry with me for prying into your life.'

Thea had already warned her that Mr Gray was a very private man. She should have taken heed.

He laughed. 'That, sweet dove, was not an angry kiss. It was not a punishment; it was self-indulgence. I have wanted to kiss you ever since I first set eyes on you in the church.'

Her insides lurched and heat washed over her face at the thought that such a virile man—such an intelligent and thoughtful man—could look at *her* in such a way.

'And I was not angry with you for prying,' he went on. 'You wanted to know something about me and you are entitled to ask. But, likewise, I am entitled not to answer.' He smiled, taking the sting from his words. 'I should not have walked away from you as I did.'

'Walked? That was very nearly a run.' She was desperate to lighten the mood. 'But I shall accept you do not wish to tell me about your life.'

'It is not—'

He stiffened, tilting his head to one side. Cecily listened, but could hear nothing.

'They are calling for you,' he said. 'You had better make haste.' He pointed at the archway that led back into the garden.

Guilt intertwined with the dread that her brothers would find her out. They would be furious, but with Mr Gray, not with her. They would blame him entirely. She would not allow that to happen. He had helped her and she would protect him in return. Somehow, she now felt better able to cope with the changes in her life.

She faced him, and held out her hand. 'Thank you for listening, Mr Gray.'

He stilled. He stared down at Cecily's outthrust hand for so long, she feared she had transgressed another of his unwritten laws. As she began to withdraw it, though, he grasped it and closed his fingers around it, saying, 'Zach. Call me Zach.'

His touch sent tingles racing up her arm and another flush to heat her cheeks. The memory of his lips on hers seared her brain.

'Zach?'

'Zachary. That is my name.'

'But…Absalom. They said you are Absalom Gray.'

She stared up at him. At the intensity of his expression.

'Absalom is my middle name. I should like to hear my given name on your lips, but I shall not insist. You must do as you wish.'

*As I wish…* It reinforced the message he had tried to convey about her future. She could choose.

She smiled. 'Zachary, then. Thank you for listening, Zach.'

He bowed over her hand, turned it and feathered warm, soft lips across the sensitive skin at her wrist and then, in that same calm, unhurried manner, he reached into his pocket, withdrawing her lace glove. He slid it on to her hand and smoothed it along her forearm. Tingles changed into sparks that radiated throughout her body and a feeling of nervy anticipation coiled in the pit of her stomach.

'You are welcome, Cecily.'

His voice, again, flowed around and through her, melting and comforting. Flustered, she snatched her hand from his and, grabbing at her skirts, she dashed through the archway and past the raised pool, towards the voices she could now hear clearly, raised in worry as they called her name.

She was out of breath by the time she met the first of the searchers, Leo, his brow creased and his eyes full of fear in the light of the lantern he held aloft.

'Cecily! Thank God! I thought… I thought…' His voice cracked. '*Where* have you been?' He raised his voice. 'It's all right. I've found her.'

He reached for her and pulled her into a tight hug. Guilt pressed on Cecily. She knew, better than most, how Leo worried about his family. How responsible he felt. His first wife had been murdered—in a summer house at Cheriton Abbey—and he had never forgiven himself for his failure to protect her.

'Leo. I am safe. I'm sorry. I wandered further than I realised. I did not mean to be gone for so long, but it is such a lovely evening and…'

She shrugged. She could say no more. She had wandered too far and forgotten the time. He would have to accept that.

The sound of feet running grew louder, then Vernon, Dominic and Daniel Markham burst into view as Leo released her.

'Cecily!' Vernon grabbed her by the shoulders and gave her a little shake. 'What happened? This isn't like you, going off on your own.'

She bit back the irritated riposte that threatened to burst from her lips. Her brothers would never see her as anything other than their little sister. Someone who needed their protection, even though she had been the one to keep the family strong when Margaret died, leaving three young children motherless.

'I was too warm indoors, Vernon, and I chose to come

outside and breathe the fresh air.' Her choice of words brought Zach's image into her mind: his dark, chiselled face with its straight nose and slashed brows. Those brooding eyes. That exotic diamond in his ear.

*Yes. I chose to go outside. He has a point...so many times I only do as expected and allowed.*

'The scent of the roses lured me into the garden,' she continued. 'There is no harm done.' Her gaze swept across the faces of the four men. Three of them looked mollified, to varying degrees. Leo, though—it was never an easy thing to fool her perceptive oldest brother. 'Come. Let us go indoors before you contrive to set everyone else into an unnecessary panic.'

Vernon slung his arm around her shoulders and pulled her close, dropping a kiss on to her hair. 'Pleased it was a false alarm, Cilly.'

Cecily shrugged his arm away. 'And *don't* call me Cilly.'

Trust Vernon; he never missed an opportunity to tease and he knew only too well how she detested that stupid childhood nickname. They had reached the terrace, then they were inside the brightly lit drawing room and Cecily donned her accustomed mantle of perfect society lady and mingled and chatted, but there was a tiny part of her that remained separate and secluded from the hubbub, and in her mind's eye she saw Zach's hands, cupped in that unconscious gesture of protection and that tiny part of her felt...safe.

Zach hunkered down as he fed sticks into the fire two mornings later. Shades of pink and orange brushed the horizon as dawn approached. Another restless night had seen him up even earlier than usual, intent on moving on. No good could come of lingering, of seeing her again. Cecily. Lady Perfect. The name he had dubbed her with sounded harsh, but it served a useful purpose. Its use whenever he thought of her—as he had frequently since their encounter in the moonlight two nights ago—kept the impossibility of anything other than a brief friendship to the forefront of his mind. It would help to stop him indulging in the fantasy of anything more.

He set a tripod frame over the flames and placed a skillet on top, adding a sliver of butter. When it melted, he swirled it around and cracked one egg and then another into the pan. He did it without thought. This had been his life for ten years. The life he had chosen.

As he ate the eggs, mopping up the yolk with a hunk of bread—Mrs Green, the cook at Stourwell Court, was nothing if not generous—he set his mind to the journey he must take to rejoin his family. He had left them camped on the outskirts of Worcester, but they had plans to move on, and he knew their path lay to the south and east, picking up harvesting work and odd jobs along the way.

*I must leave today...*

The same thought that had plagued him yesterday morning and throughout the day. He had glimpsed Lady Perfect from afar, with her family, but he'd deliberately stayed away from the house. Yes. He would be wise to leave; he *ought* to leave. He stilled. *Ought to...* He had chosen not to live his life by the conventions. To follow his heart, not the demands of his brain. How could he tell Lady Perfect to choose what she wished to do, rather than to slavishly follow the edicts of society or her family, and then ignore his own advice?

*Do I* want *to leave today?*

The answer was clear and strong. No. He did not want to leave. Not yet. He knew he *ought* to go, but he *chose* to stay. It was his way of letting the fates decide his future... and he preferred it to tossing a coin or throwing a dice.

Decision made, he unfolded his body, stood upright and stretched his arms high, arching back as his lungs filled. This would be a good day. He could feel it in his bones.

An eager whine caught his attention. Myrtle sat at his feet, gazing up with adoring eyes, tongue lolling. He reached down to fondle her ear and her eyes half-closed in ecstasy. Dogs were simple beings. Easy to please. Loving and faithful, although they did not always have cause to be. Zach walked to the cart and rummaged through the basket sent out to him by Mrs Green last night after he had declined to join the family and their guests for dinner. Sure enough, there was cold beef and Zach tossed a slice to Myrtle, who jumped awkwardly to catch it. His heart twisted as he watched her lurch away from the cart on three legs and he perched on the cart steps as the memories took hold.

He had found Myrtle a year ago, trapped by her hind leg in a snare in the woods, close to death. It was soon after his mother's death and caring for Myrtle had helped ease the pain of Mama's passing and given him a purpose. He hadn't been able to save her leg, but he had saved her. And, in a way, she had saved him, too, in the same way that caring for Athena had helped him cope with the catastrophic change in his life as he—at sixteen years of age—had struggled to adjust to life among his mother's people.

Sixteen years old. A boy. He and his mother cast out after his father's death, with nowhere to go and no one who cared. From that day forward, he'd locked the door on his past, changing his name from Zachary Graystoke to Absalom Gray. Even his mother had called him Absalom, the name of his Romany grandfather. And that memory led inexorably back to Lady Perfect and the question of why he had felt impelled to tell her his real name. Why it had been so very important to him to hear his name on her lips. And the only answer was that he wanted her to know something about him that was the truth. Not the half-truth known by everybody else in the non-Romany world. The *gadje* world.

Eventually, the swish of footsteps through long grass and the low murmur of voices interrupted his thoughts. His camp was close to a small copse, at the point where a brook entered the River Stour, and on the edge of a field which—Daniel had told him—would be cut for hay later in the season. Zach pushed himself upright and rounded his cart, to see Daniel, the Duke and his son walking to the river, fishing rods in hand. Daniel saw him watching and raised his hand in greeting.

'Morning, Absalom. Care to join us? We thought we'd take advantage of the peace while the ladies recuperate after another late night.'

The ladies… Lady Perfect… Without volition, he looked in the direction of the house, even though he knew it was out of sight. Was she awake? Did she think of him—wonder what he was doing—as he did her? He thrust down that thought. Of course she did not. She was a lady. He was a Romany. Why would she think of him? But maybe his listening, and his advice, such as it was, had helped to ease her mind. At least she had not succumbed to a fit of the vapours when he had so far forgotten himself as to kiss her.

With that he must be satisfied.

'Thank you, but no,' he replied to Daniel. 'I promised your sister I would look at her lame mare this morning.'

'Oh, good man,' Daniel said. 'Thea dotes on Star. She'd be broken-hearted to lose her and Pritchard seems at a loss to know what's wrong.' Pritchard was the Markhams' head groom. 'Absalom here is something of a natural healer, your Grace.'

'Leo. I told you to call me Leo. After all, we're family now.'

Zach could see by the pink that tinged Daniel's cheeks how pleased he was by the Duke's remark. He bit back a smile as he imagined the man's reaction if *he* were to have the gall to call him Leo.

'Well, enjoy your fishing,' he said. The sun was fully up now, revealing a cloudless, periwinkle sky. 'You have perfect weather for it.'

'Indeed we have.' It was the Duke's son who responded, with a grin. He slapped Daniel on the back as he continued, 'Markham's promised some great sport. He's boasting of barbel the size of seals.'

Daniel laughed. 'That's something of an exaggeration, but we do catch the occasional whopper.'

The three men continued to the river bank and turned to walk downstream, jumping across the brook. Zach watched them go with a touch of envy prompted by their sureness of their own places in the world: Daniel as comfortable with his own life as a manufacturer as the Duke and his son—his eldest son and therefore his heir—were with their privileged position. He swatted away that errant feeling. He might not belong quite as solidly to the life he had chosen, but it *was* his choice after all. Those other men…they had simply followed in their fathers' footsteps. He tidied his campsite and threw dirt on the fire to extinguish the flame, then, with Myrtle at his heels, he headed for the stables.

He followed the brook upstream to the point where, at some time in the past, it had been dammed to create the lake where he and Lady Perfect had talked the night before last. He skirted around the shore and then continued to follow the brook upstream, knowing it would lead him close to the stable yard. He could not help but glance over at the rear view of Stourwell Court—its three-storeyed, stuccoed block, topped with a hipped roof, visible on the far side of the flower garden—but he caught no glimpse of Lady Perfect. Or of anyone else. The curtains were still drawn at several windows on the first floor and it was likely she was still in bed.

How long had she remained at the party after she left him the other night? Had she danced? Laughed? Indulged in fascinating conversations with the other guests— conversations that would put their unlikely encounter straight out of her head? She had made no effort to seek him out yesterday. Had she even noticed him, in the distance, when he had seen her? His lips tightened. Such thoughts would help no one. Least of all him. He must let them go. He cut across the grass to the stables and rounded the outer wall to the yard entrance. And stopped short.

Her smile dazzled him. Her silky chestnut hair gleamed in the sun and her eyes—a glorious green, the colour of fresh, damp moss—sparkled. She was dressed for riding, in a riding habit that exactly matched her eyes, and she held a matching hat, trimmed with two curling ostrich feathers, by her side.

## Chapter Four

'Good morning, Mr Gray.'

Lady Cecily's gaze flicked to one side and Zach recognised Bickling—Lord Vernon's groom, whom he had met in Worcester—standing nearby. She was warning him to maintain the formalities in front of others, kindling a warm glow in his chest. She had not forgotten their conversation.

'Good morning, my lady. I did not expect to see anyone up and about so early.'

'I could not sleep once daylight came. I felt the need for exercise after two idle days so I thought I might ride around the estate. I can find no one to accompany me, however, even though I was told Leo and Dominic have already broken their fast.'

'They are fishing, with Daniel.' Zach pointed in the direction of the river. 'I am happy to accompany you, if Pritchard can supply a horse.'

The offer slipped out before he could censor his words. He sensed Bickling's uneasy stir, but ignored him.

'That would be splendid. Oh, Bickling, do wipe that disapproving expression from your face. Mr Gray is a guest here. There is no impropriety.'

'Milady, I was about to suggest *I* ride with you. It's not proper, you going out unchaperoned.'

She laughed and the sound trickled through Zach, awakening the strongest urge to hear her laugh again and again.

'Oh, Bickling! That is absurd. It is no more improper for me to ride out with Mr Gray than it is to ride out with only you as my escort. We shall not go far. Now, Lady Vernon said last night she was happy for me to ride her mare Polly, so please go and speak to Pritchard and ask him to saddle her and also one of Mr Markham's horses for Mr Gray.'

Bickling stalked off, grumbling beneath his breath.

'The Good Lord deliver me from protective men.' Cecily smiled up at Zach, tiny laughter lines creasing the outer corners of her lovely eyes. 'It is bad enough with two brothers and two nephews who all consider it their duty to monitor my every move without the servants joining in as well.'

'He is only doing as he thinks best,' Zach said. 'I need to speak to Pritchard before we go; I promised Lady Vernon I'd look at her favourite mare. She's gone lame.'

'Oh, the poor thing. Of course you must see to her before we go, Zach.'

Pleasure flared at her use of his name.

'I shan't be long. From Lady Vernon's description, I suspect the problem is in her back, not her legs. She might benefit from massage but she'll need the area warmed and relaxed first and that will take a while.'

He was soon back, having examined the mare and given instructions to Pritchard to rug her up using a lightweight blanket over a thatch of straw to help relax her. Cecily was crouching down, attempting to coax Myrtle to her. She looked up at Zach's approach.

'Look at this poor dog,' she said. 'Do you think she's a stray? How can she survive on only three legs?'

Myrtle lurched over to him and leaned against his leg,

nudging him with her head. He bent to fondle her ear as Cecily stood upright.

'She went straight to you. Is she yours?'

'I care for her.'

'Of course. As you told me, you do not keep animals. They are free to leave if they wish. That is correct, isn't it?'

'It is. Apart from Titan, that is.'

'Titan?'

'He pulls my wagon. I cannot allow him to wander off, or I would never be able to move on.'

'And is that important to you? The ability to move on?' She tilted her face to the sky. 'It sounds idyllic and uncomplicated in this weather, but it must be less pleasant in the rain and in the winter.'

He shrugged. 'It is what I have chosen.'

Bad choice of words. He knew it as soon as they left his mouth. Her eyes sharpened as she studied him.

'Chosen? You make it sound as though you do have an alternative if you wish it.'

The clip-clop of hooves announced the arrival of their horses—a pretty chestnut mare for Lady Perfect and a bay gelding for him—and Myrtle, wary of horses, slunk out of the yard to hide behind the stone entrance pillar. Zach was grateful for the interruption, but he answered Lady Perfect's comment anyway, hoping it would be enough to stop her probing further.

'Everyone has an alternative.'

Cecily eyed Zach thoughtfully. Did his comment have some deeper meaning? Wondering what alternative he had to his Romany way of life, she settled her hat onto her head and turned her attention to Polly, looking her over with a knowledgeable eye as she smoothed her gloved hand down the gleaming chestnut neck. Bickling laced his fingers to provide a step for her to mount and she quickly settled in the side saddle, waiting while Zach mounted the bay.

His loose trousers and short boots looked decidedly odd as riding attire, accustomed as she was to breeches and shiny top boots, but the loose fit did not detract from his sculpted thighs as he settled in the saddle. She averted her gaze and diverted her thoughts from a sudden mental image of Zach's muscular thighs clad in form-fitting breeches. An image that dried her mouth.

'We shouldn't be long, Bickling, so do not worry.' And with that, she touched the mare with her heel and they clattered out of the yard, her seat secure even as Polly shied away from Myrtle, still hovering by the entrance.

'I'll be back soon, Myrtle,' Zach said as he passed the dog, a brindled brown and white bull-terrier type, short-legged and stocky—the type of animal often used in dog fights.

Cecily suppressed a shudder at the thought—she loathed some of the so-called sports that even civilised men indulged in. Thankfully, her brothers did not enjoy dog fighting, cock fighting and the like, but... She cast a sidelong look at Zach as his horse ranged alongside hers as they followed a track that led away from the house, behind the stables. Did Romanys indulge in such sports?

'How did she lose her leg?'

'A snare. Set by a gamekeeper.'

'Oh. I thought... I wondered...'

His dark brows lifted.

'Well, she is the sort of dog used in dog fighting. I thought that might be how she was injured.'

His mouth settled into a tight line and she cursed herself for such clumsiness. He had demonstrated his love for animals in the short time she had known him and yet she had practically accused him of involvement in a horrid blood sport. How she wished she'd thought before opening her mouth.

'Why do you call her Myrtle?'

'Why not?'

Cecily tamped down the urge to snap at him for rejecting her olive branch. Her own mood was also a touch fragile this morning after a restless couple of nights, and she was tired and a little headachy with all the thoughts and—yes, alternatives—that had pounded relentlessly at her brain since their conversation in the moonlight. She had only reached a conclusion as this day dawned—a conclusion prompted partly by the memory of Zach's kiss—and she had imagined telling Zach all about her plans for her future the next time she saw him. Her decision to go for a ride this early had in part been to clear her head, but she knew, deep down, that she also had hoped to see Zach. And that had worked better than she imagined, although now she was well on her way to quarrelling with him and that would only ruin their ride.

Before she could say anything to smooth the conversation, Zach spoke.

'I call her Myrtle for the plant. When I found her, there was a lady who lived in a cottage on that estate who helped. She grew herbs and medicinal plants in her glasshouse and she made a poultice of crushed myrtle leaves to help heal the wound after we amputated her leg.'

'Thank you for telling me.' Cecily reached between them and touched his arm. 'And thank you, again, for the other night. You helped me more than you know and I am happy to have this chance to tell you of my decision.'

'You do sound less troubled today, although you look in need of sleep.'

'I have had much to think about.'

'And your decision?'

'You said earlier that everyone has an alternative and that is true for me, too. I can remain in my present circumstances and allow my life to dwindle and fade, or I can grasp my future with both hands. So I thought about what I truly want and that is my own household to run. I love the busyness and I love having family around and seeing the tenants and helping where I can, so the obvious solution is for me to marry. That way I shall get my own household and I will also avoid becoming a burden on my family in the future.'

There was a long pause, the only sound the occasional chink of a horseshoe against stone. His profile was harsh, his brows gathered in a frown at the bridge of his nose.

'You implied that wasn't an option when we spoke before.'

'I did not believe it was an option. Not then.'

'And what changed your mind?'

She could never admit the truth: that his kiss had awakened a delicious urge to experience more. Intimacy—it had never been a factor in her thoughts before. Her life had given her the domesticity and child-rearing aspects of marriage and she had been content with that. She had done her duty. That kiss had served as a reminder that there was a third element to marriage and the only way for her to experience more of that would be to marry. And she even had a candidate in mind. She had tried not to dwell on the suspicion that kissing Lord Kilburn might prove less enticing than kissing Zach.

'The deciding factor was that I know just the man.'

He faced her, his eyes turbulent with emotion. 'You have a sweetheart?'

'Not a sweetheart. But there is someone. He is a neighbour of my aunt in Oxfordshire, who I first met a few years ago, soon after his wife died. We met again earlier this year, in London. He proposed, but I turned him down because I was needed at home.'

She had been unable to fathom his lordship's feelings for her... There had been little of the lover in his court-ship—if that is what such a restrained pursuit could be called—and yet the flash of desperation in his eyes when she had refused him had made her wonder. She could not decide, however, if it was the loss of her or of her dowry that sparked that single glimpse of deep emotion.

'He is a widower with young children, so I shall be doing him a favour at the same time.'

Saying it out loud sounded a touch cold-blooded, but Lord Kilburn seemed a pleasant enough gentleman and surely would prove the perfect solution to her dilemma. She suffered no delusions—at the age of thirty there would be few options open to her. There was no queue of gentle-men clamouring to marry her and, having met his lord-ship again at various events during the recent Season, she knew he was still interested in her.

*Or, possibly, in my dowry.*

She dismissed that cynical voice. That was the world she lived in, and the old saying a bird in the hand is worth two in the bush could hardly be more apt. It would be fool-ish to expect love to find her as it had her brothers. It was different for women.

*Except Rosalind is the same age as you.* She *found love.*

She brushed her misgivings aside. The thought of leav-ing her beloved family brought an aching lump to her throat, but she forced it down, concentrating on the posi-tive aspects of marriage. She would have her own house-hold to run, stepchildren to care for and maybe even her own children. That, surely, would bring her happiness and contentment. It was the lot of many women in her position and, besides, what other choice did she have?

She could not bear to resign herself to life as the dependent relation.

'Marriage is not something to be entered into with the head. What about the heart?'

Zach's comment stung. Why should he care about her decision?

'On the contrary, in my world, marriage is often entered into with the head.'

*And Kilburn will make for a safe, steady, unexciting husband.*

She raised her chin. 'The Earl will be the perfect choice. We shall be perfectly content together.'

'An earl. Of course—the perfect choice for Lady Perfect.'

'Is that how you see me? Lady Perfect?'

'It is the image you present to the world.'

She stared at him. 'The image I present? You think me, somehow, false?'

He shook his head, his dark locks shining in the sun, and she had a sudden urge to run her fingers through those heavy, satiny curls.

'No. I do not think you false. Rather, I see you as dutiful and restrained, just as a perfect lady should be and who behaves just as she ought.'

'And shallow, I surmise.'

'Oh, no.' He turned his head to look at her and his eyes gleamed. 'You are not shallow, my lady.'

'And you deduce this from one brief encounter? You flatter yourself you know me because I was unwise enough to confide in you when I was feeling uncommonly low.'

'I hope you will look back upon our meeting with pleasure, my lady. And you are right. I do not know you. Not all of you. But I saw a different woman emerge in the moonlight when you allowed yourself to forget your status. That woman is still beneath, with her dreams and her passions, if you will only give her a voice.'

Cecily swallowed. She did not want more uncertainty. She had made her decision. His words rattled her... Was it really possible he understood more of what lay in her heart than she did?

'Heavens.' She forced a tinkling laugh. 'I do not believe I have ever heard such a lengthy speech from you, Mr Gray.'

'I limit my words to when I have something to say.'

'An admirable trait, I am sure.' They had reached a river. 'I should like to return now, if you please,' she said.

'As you wish. If we follow upstream, it will bring us close to the lake where we spoke the other night and that is not far from the stable yard.'

The lake...the moonlight...the touch of his lips. Her pulse quickened at the memory and she slid a sidelong glance at his impassive profile. Did he remember? Of course he did...it was an idiotic question. More pertinent— might he snatch this opportunity to kiss her again? And, if he did, would she allow it?

The sight of three figures on the bank ahead of them answered her question as to whether he might snatch a kiss. Zach had told her Leo, Dominic and Daniel were fishing and he must have known, by riding in this direction, they would meet them. He had no wish to prolong their private talk or to kiss her again, that was abundantly clear, and knowing that made her feel...deflated, somehow.

*And what did you expect? Have you given him reason to think you have enjoyed this conversation or his company this morning?*

'Zach.' The other men had yet to notice their approach and she must say this before it was too late. 'I should like you to know—I might not have shown it, but I *have* valued our conversations. They have helped me.'

He smiled. 'Thank you. I did not mean to annoy you, but please think about what I have said before you finally decide upon your future. You owe yourself that much.'

'I promise I shall. And I shall visit my aunt and meet his lordship again before making any commitment.'

The three men ahead had now caught sight of them and Cecily waved. She interpreted the reason behind Leo's frown so, to forestall any negative remark concerning her choice of escort, as soon as they were within earshot, she called, 'There you are! Mr Gray offered to show me where you were fishing. Isn't it a glorious day?'

## Chapter Five

Leo's frown lifted slightly, but he still looked stern enough to make Cecily anxious. Her brother was nothing if not protective and she would not have chosen to meet him in this way. She wished Zach had shown more discretion—a glance at his expression showed no apprehension. Did he not realise their social blunder?

*Of course he does not. He is a Romany.*

'I understood you said there was a horse needing your treatment, Gray.' Leo's voice was clipped with annoyance. His gaze flicked to Cecily and, to her chagrin, she felt her cheeks heat. 'I trust my *sister* did not distract you from your errand of mercy?'

He strode towards them. As he reached for Cecily, ready to help her dismount, a loud braying noise rent the air. Polly laid back her ears and skittered sideways, away from Leo. Cecily, her leg already lifted over the pommel and her foot free of the stirrup, was taken unawares and she lurched across the horse's neck, her hat falling to the ground. As her arms flailed in an attempt to grab the pommel, a strong arm wrapped around her waist from behind, plucking her from the saddle and onto Zach's lap. Before her brain could even register the sequence of events, Cecily felt her body relax back into the solid strength of Zach's as though she belonged, safe and secure in his arms. His lips pressed momentarily to her hair. Then he swung his right leg across his horse's neck, so he was sitting sideways on the horse, and he held Cecily close as he slid to the ground. There was no stumble as he landed—graceful as a cat—and he gently set Cecily on her own two feet. Only then did he release her, with a slide of his hand and a brief squeeze at the side of her waist.

Leo's face was like thunder but, before he could speak, Daniel said, 'Oh, well caught, Absalom. Lucky you were there, or Lady Cecily might have come a cropper.'

'My sister is an accomplished horsewoman.' The manner in which Leo bit out his words told Cecily of the effort it cost him to keep his temper in check. 'She would have recovered her seat without help, I assure you.'

Cecily cast an imploring look at Dominic, who ghosted a wink in reply to show he understood her silent plea to defuse the tension. He walked over, picking up Cecily's fallen hat on the way.

'Was that a *donkey*?' he asked, as he handed the hat to Cecily.

He gazed in the direction of the sound, as though expecting one to materialise from among the trees further along the riverbank and beyond a narrow brook.

'It was,' Zach said. 'He will—there he is.'

And, sure enough, a donkey emerged from the nearby copse and stared, ears stiffly upright, in their direction.

'Why is he not tethered? Does he belong to you?' Leo still scowled, his attention still locked on Zach.

'He is not tethered because he is free.' Daniel slapped Zach on the back. 'That's one of the first things I learned about my friend here.'

He emphasised the word 'friend' ever so slightly, and

Leo's gaze switched to him. With a barely perceptible nod, he signalled he had taken Daniel's point and Cecily breathed more easily.

'He can charm the birds out of the trees,' Daniel continued. 'Creatures love him and he allows them to stay or go as they please.'

The donkey—brownish-grey with ludicrously long ears and huge eyes—had crossed the brook and wandered over to them as they talked. He nudged his head against Zach, who scratched behind his ears. Cecily reached out and stroked his velvet-smooth nose.

'Does he have a name?'

'Sancho.' She caught the quick glint of humour in Zach's dark eyes—not black as they sometimes appeared, but the deepest, darkest brown she had ever seen. 'Sancho Panza.'

Dominic guffawed. 'Sancho Panza! Did you hear that, Father?'

Leo's lips twitched in a half-smile. 'And you see yourself as a modern-day Don Quixote, do you, Gray? You and your faithful squire on a quest to revive chivalry, undo wrongs and bring justice to the world?'

There was challenge and a hint of mockery in his tone, but Zach seemed not to notice. He stood, completely relaxed, the donkey by his side.

'I have yet to mistake a windmill for a ferocious giant,' he said, with a smile, 'but it seemed a fitting name.'

Leo acknowledged the comment with a tilt of his chin. 'Come, Cecily,' he said. 'I shall escort you back to the house.'

Before he could move, however, Zach was by Cecily's side, lacing his fingers for her to step into.

'Permit me, my lady.'

She stepped into his cupped hands and he effortlessly hoisted her on to Polly's back. Then he faced Leo.

'You may entrust Lady Cecily to my care, your Grace. The mare will be ready to treat by now, so it is time I returned. We'll leave you to enjoy your fishing.'

To Cecily's surprise, Leo accepted this with a curt nod, but the look he sent her warned she was likely to suffer a lecture on the wisdom of riding around the countryside accompanied only by a Romany. The hypocrisy of his attitude fired her sense of injustice. She knew only too well that Vernon and Thea had, prior to their marriage, spent several unchaperoned days *and nights* together on the road as they searched for Daniel, who had gone missing. Compared to that, a short morning ride around the Markhams' estate was completely harmless. She batted away the nagging voice that reminded her that the difference was that she was female.

*Thea is a woman, too. And Leo does not think any the less of her for* her *behaviour.*

'Your brother disapproves,' Zach said as they rode away, Sancho following behind at a trot.

They crossed over the same little brook and headed towards the copse from which Sancho had emerged.

'He is protective. It is who he is.' Cecily might find Leo's attitude exasperating, but she was *allowed* to criticise him and be irritated by him. He was *her* brother.

'My opinion of him would be less if he were not. He is a strong man and he cares for those he feels responsible for.'

'Do you have any brothers or sisters?'

His expression blanked and she cursed herself for asking such a direct question. Had she not already established that he did not respond well to curiosity? They rode along the edge of the copse until it gave way to a large hayfield. Between the edge of the uncut grass and the trees was a camp, with a tent and a cart. Standing next to the dead ashes of the fire was Myrtle, tail wagging so hard she was almost wriggling with joy.

'Why is Myrtle here? We left her at the stables.'

'She would not remain there on her own. This is her home. She will always return.' Zach turned his head and caught Cecily's eye. 'It is where she feels safe, where she is loved.'

Cecily's heart squeezed at Zach's words. Home. That is exactly how she felt about her home and her family—safe and loved. But hankering over the past was pointless. She accepted that now. Everything had changed and she was determined to find her new place in the world.

Zach leapt from his horse's back and crouched down to fondle the dog, murmuring, his voice too quiet for Cecily to make out his words. Then he sprang once more on to his horse and Myrtle settled down, her head on her outstretched paws, and heaved a sigh. As they rode away, Cecily looked back, seeing that the donkey, too, remained at the camp, cropping at the grass.

'What did you say to Myrtle?'

He sent her a sharp glance. 'You think it odd that I talk to her?'

She did, a bit. But she did not say so. 'I have never had a pet dog. Rosalind—the Duchess—she has a dog. He is huge, almost up to my waist, and she talks to him all the time. He lives with us now.'

'You are a good horsewoman. Do you not talk to your horse?'

'Not really. Only if they need calming down.'

He shook his head. 'I find that odd.'

'Is it because you live alone, do you think?'

He laughed, tilting his head to the sky and breathing deeply, as he had the other night. 'I am not lonely, if that

is what you wish to know. I am content. I enjoy this life
and being outdoors. I love nature. I am a fortunate man.'

A picture of his campsite formed in her head. He had
so little, compared to the riches and the opulence she and
her family took for granted: the huge, sprawling Cheriton Abbey in Devonshire, minor estates scattered around
the country, each one of them with a house at least as big
as Stourwell Court, and a full contingent of staff to keep
them in readiness for family visits, plus a magnificent
town house in Grosvenor Square in London. And yet he
was content, and she...she...

*I have done nothing but complain. Poor little me: my
brother got married and I am no longer the mistress of
the Abbey and all his other properties.*

Zach's attitude was humbling.

'You are fortunate to be so content. I hope to be as settled and as happy as you in the future.'

'True contentment comes from following your heart
and in appreciating what you have, not hankering after
that which you have not.'

She pondered his words. 'That is true, but only to an
extent.'

She pictured Leo's bleak expression as she had ridden
away with Zach. She knew her brother well enough to
know he used his anger to mask his concern, as well as any
hint of weakness, and she also knew she had upset him by
following her own inclination—her heart—and returning
to the Court with Zach rather than with Leo.

'What if, by following your heart, you cause pain to
someone you love?'

Zach's mouth twitched. 'Then you have a choice to
make about which is more important to you.'

'Mayhap that is why you are so content. You only have
yourself to please.'

Pain flashed across his face and was as quickly gone. 'What is it?'

'My mother—she died last summer.' He raised his hand to the diamond in his ear.

She touched his arm. 'I am sorry. Is...is your earring a traditional Romany adornment?' Her fascination with that glinting diamond prompted her to risk the question.

'It was part of a wedding gift from my father to my mother. She had to sell her jewellery after he died.' Bitterness lit his eyes. 'But she gave me the ring and I had the stone made into this.'

Diamonds? Cecily hid her surprise that a Romany could lavish such an expensive gift upon his bride, but she felt the poignancy that Zach's mother had been forced to part with such a treasured gift. 'It is a lovely memento of both of them.'

They had arrived back at the stable yard and a groom emerged to take charge of the horses.

'I shall see you later,' said Zach after he had helped Cecily to the ground. His dark gaze roamed her face, then drifted down her body, conjuring heat wherever it lingered. Her corset grew tight, restricting her lungs. 'I am invited to dinner. I refused the invitation last night, but I shall accept tonight.'

The news pleased her. She longed to learn more about this enigmatic man and watching him interact with the others at Stourwell Court would hopefully allow her to do so.

'Are you going to treat Thea's mare now?'

'Star? Yes, I am.'

'I should like to watch.'

He held her gaze. 'Your brother will not approve.'

She smiled. 'But my heart is telling me I wish to see how you help her even though my head tells me I *ought* to return to the house.'

\* \* \*

And he could not argue with that, because it was how he had encouraged her to think. Zach shook his head at her, smiling, then strode into the stable, where Star was tethered in a large pen at the far end, rather than in one of the stalls. The heels of Lady Perfect's boots rang on the cobbled floor as she followed behind.

'Wait outside,' he said, hoping she would not chatter and distract him while he worked.

He stripped off his jacket, rolled up his sleeves and entered the pen, where he was joined by Pritchard, the head man, and an older groom called Malky, who went to the mare's head to hold her. Zach stripped the blanket from her back and brushed away the wisps of straw, listening to the low murmur of Malky's voice as he kept Star calm and replied to Lady Perfect's question about what was wrong with her.

First, Zach felt gently along either side of the mare's spine, probing the tension of her muscles. He tried hard to keep his full attention on the mare, but found it wandering all too often to Lady Perfect who—to his surprise—now stood quietly on the spot he had indicated, doing nothing to distract him… It was his own visceral awareness of her presence to blame for that. He began to gently massage the knotted muscles either side of her spine.

A shadow fell across him and he looked around. It was the Duke, his countenance even more forbidding than before. Zach returned his attention to his task.

'Leo!' Cecily spoke in a hushed voice behind him. 'Thea's horse is lame, but they can't find out which leg it is. Bleeding and purging have failed to help and so they have asked Mr Gray to try and help her.'

Zach watched Star's ears closely for signs of pain. 'There is no heat in her legs or hooves,' he said, sparing a glance at the Duke, who stepped closer, his interest unmistakable. 'The pain appears to be in her back—it is making her tense and she naturally restricts her stride to protect herself.'

'Thea will be very grateful if you can help her, Absalom,' Daniel said. 'Star is her favourite...the horse she rode when she and Vernon set out to search for me.'

Zach listened to the murmured conversation with half an ear as he continued to massage Star. Then he took a carrot and a knife from his pocket. He cut a chunk and crouched by her foreleg, holding the carrot beneath Star's nose, just out of her reach. As she followed the carrot, Zach lowered his hand, bringing it back between her forelegs. When he judged she had stretched sufficiently, he rewarded her with the carrot.

He straightened. 'If it is done slowly and steadily, it will help to stretch her back,' he said to Malky, who nodded. 'Lead her out, then. I'd like to see her walk.'

The onlookers moved aside as Malky led Star from the pen and out of a rear door in the barn that led straight out on to the stretch of grass between the stable and the lake. Admiration glowed in Cecily's mossy eyes as Zach passed her, sparking a flame of awareness and need deep in his gut. Then he caught the Duke's eye and that smothered the flame more effectively than a shovelful of earth would extinguish his campfire. She was Lady Perfect. Sister of a duke. And the warning in his Grace's silvery eyes promised dire retribution if Zach forgot his place.

He concentrated on keeping the churn of anger and resentment deep inside, letting nothing of his feelings show. There was no point in provoking such a man when his own conscience told him there was no future for him and Lady Perfect, no matter how fascinated he was by this prim and proper lady. No matter how she called to his soul.

'That'll do.' After five minutes, Zach motioned to Malky to return Star to the stable. 'Walk her in hand several times a day, just five minutes at a time to begin with. I'll bring down some belladonna salve for her and massage her again this afternoon. And I'll look in on her again before I go up to the house for dinner tonight.'

As he spoke, he happened to glance at the Duke, whose lips thinned at Zach's words. His clear disapproval prompted an urge to tweak the man's tail, despite Zach's earlier resolve not to provoke such a powerful man needlessly.

'I will update you on her progress when I see you tonight, my lady.'

He smiled directly at Cecily, noting both the flare of her eyes and her flicker of unease. He felt, rather than saw, the Duke's irritation.

'It is time we returned to the house.' The Duke took Cecily's arm and began walking. 'I am sure Thea will be eager to hear how her horse fares.'

Cecily accompanied her brother without protest. Daniel let out a low whistle.

'That is a high-risk strategy, my friend.'

Zach raised his brows and Daniel grinned.

'No point in playing the innocent with me, but do take care. You might not realise it, but Cheriton is one of the most powerful men in the country. Cross him at your peril.'

'If he is as powerful as you say, he can have no fear of a humble Romany.'

'Humble?' Daniel laughed. 'I could describe you in many ways, Absalom, but humble ain't one of 'em. If I didn't know any better, I'd say you're every bit as high-born as most of the nobs I've encountered. Not Cheriton and his family, of course. They're a breed apart.'

His words—although spoken in jest—jabbed deep at

Zach. If only Daniel knew... He schooled his expression as he saw his friend's eyes sharpen.

'I've never known a man so reluctant to reveal anything of himself,' said Daniel. 'I'm willing to bet you have a colourful past, but...' he held his hands up, palms out, as Zach frowned '...have no fear. I know better than to probe further.'

'I see no point in revisiting the past. It is best left behind, that way it can wield no power over you.'

Daniel slapped Zach on the back. 'If you say so, my friend. If you say so.'

## Chapter Six

That evening Zach was the last to arrive for dinner. He found the Markhams and the Beauchamps—including Lady Perfect, who stood closest to the door—gathered in the salon. Thea squealed as soon as she saw him, jumped up from her seat on the sofa and rushed across the room to grab his hand—earning her a glare from her mother and a look of loving indulgence from her new husband. She pulled him further into the room.

'Thank you, thank you,' she exclaimed breathlessly. She halted next to Cecily, who appeared to look at him, but did not meet his eyes. 'Cecily told me what you did for Star and Malky said you have showed him how to massage her and she already seems a little better. I wish I had been there, but we were—'

'We were catching up on our sleep,' a deep voice interjected. Vernon had joined them, sliding his arm around Thea's waist. 'You have my gratitude as well, Gray. If there is ever anything I can do in return, you only have to say the word.'

'It gives me pleasure to help a creature in pain,' said Zach. 'I need nothing in return. I have hopes she'll make a complete recovery, although she won't be fit to be ridden for several weeks.'

'Several *weeks*? But Daniel told me you will leave soon.' Thea sounded horrified.

Zach smiled. 'I shall work with her again in the morning and continue to do so until I leave, but Pritchard and Malky are more than capable of caring for her.'

The newlyweds soon lost interest in him and wandered hand in hand over to the window, leaving him alone with Cecily.

'Well, my lady. Have you had a pleasant day?'

'Most pleasant, Mr Gray.' His keen eye detected the note of constraint in her well-modulated tones. 'As did you, I trust?'

So formal. So upright and ladylike, clad in a gown the colour of beech leaves in the autumn, its delicate fabric clinging provocatively to her curves. He took a moment to savour her, she looked so luscious—temptation personified. Pain stabbed his heart.

*Not for you. Never for you.*

Apart from that touch of restraint in her voice, there was no further sign of tension. Her hands—clothed correctly in elbow-length evening gloves—were loosely clasped at her waist. The perfect society lady. Not for her the enthusiasm and joy that Thea did not hesitate to display. How long would it be before life with the Beauchamps, and mixing with those in the highest level of society, depressed Thea's bounce and turned her into yet another perfect lady?

Cecily raised her brow, prompting him to respond to her question.

'I did.'

He regretted his brusque reply as a delicate flag of colour lit Cecily's cheekbones. What else could he expect of her? She had told him she was thirty years old. Twenty-plus years, then, of being schooled to behave in precisely the way she was behaving now, conforming to the mores of her class.

Polite. Dutiful. Restrained.

The perfect lady.

*Do not blame her for what is not her fault.*

'I carried out some repairs to my cart and cleaned Titan's harness.'

He caught the flash of something else in those glorious green eyes. Some deep emotion, held tightly in check.

'Where shall you go when you leave here?'

He smiled, and shrugged. 'I have not yet decided. Where the wind blows me, if you will.'

He would set Titan's head to the south-east and, sooner or later, he would catch up with his family.

'I am sure that has disadvantages, but it also sounds so very—free.' She ended on a wistful note. She had started to relax, her shoulders dropping, her eyes softening.

'Have you told your brother of your plan to marry yet?' He had grappled with that knowledge all day and yet… why? His common sense told him it was not his business what this perfect lady chose to do with her life. That connection between them was undeniable, but it was also unrealistic. Impossible. And he was not a man to hanker after the impossible.

'I have not told him, so I should appreciate it if you do not mention it. I am not certain I shall confide my entire plan to my brothers—I shall simply experience a sudden urge to visit my Aunt Drusilla.'

Mischief sparked in her eyes and her full lips twitched, coaxing a smile from him, and triggering a sudden craving to taste her again. He thrust that urge aside, along with the idle conjecture as to how her brothers might react were he to act on that impulse. Hung, drawn and quartered sprang to mind. His smile widened and she eyed him curiously.

'You say that as though there is a joke in there somewhere,' he said, by way of explanation.

'You would have to meet my aunt to appreciate the humour. Even her sons—my cousins—avoid visiting Leyton Grange as much as possible.'

In his peripheral vision, Zach noticed the Duke lean down to murmur into his wife's ear, before straightening and turning purposefully towards Zach and Cecily. Zach easily interpreted his thoughts: his sister had talked to the gipsy for long enough and it was time to put a stop to the conversation. He obviously took his role of head of the family seriously. It was no wonder she behaved in such a restrained manner in his presence. How well did he—or the rest of her family—know the real Cecily that existed beneath this perfect outer shell? Had they, like him, ever sensed the wealth of passion simmering deep inside?

The Duke had joined them. 'Gray.' He nodded a greeting.

Zach nodded in reply. 'Duke.'

He was damned if he would continue to 'your Grace' the man.

'Might I borrow my sister? My wife would like a word with her.'

What could he say? Cecily threw him a tight smile, then crossed the room to sit with the Duchess. The Duke remained.

'I am conscious we as a family are in your debt, Gray, but you would oblige me if you avoid being alone with my sister again.'

There was no anger or threat in his words, merely an arrogant assumption that Zach would do as he was bid.

'Alone?'

Zach cast his gaze around the salon in an exaggerated manner. The Duke's jaw firmed.

'Your sister is in no danger from me.'

Silver-grey eyes bore into him. Zach stood his ground, holding the man's gaze.

'Do not wilfully misunderstand me.' The menace was there now. Soft and assured. 'You must be aware of the ways of our world and how easily a lady's reputation can be damaged. The Markhams are our hosts and I am conscious of my obligations as their guest. *They* vouch for you and I therefore acquit you of any criminal intent, but be aware I shall be watching you. Very closely.'

Anger roiled deep down in Zach's gut.

*He thinks it is about money. He thinks I might blackmail him. Label the gipsy a scoundrel, a thief.*

It should not be a surprise. Since living as a Romany, he had encountered many such prejudices towards his kind. The injustice of painting every member of an entire people the same criminal colour—merely due to the actions of a few rogue individuals or families—still burned within him. He longed to wipe that superior look from the Duke's face, but he must be satisfied with knowing the truth in his own heart.

'Watch as much as you please, Duke. You will soon grow bored.' Zach leaned closer and lowered his voice. 'I have no interest in your money.'

He had more than enough money of his own to live very comfortably if he so wished. He simply did not choose to live his life among people such as the Duke, who peered down their noses at him as though he was not quite a real man.

A muscle leapt in the Duke's jaw and his fingers curled into a fist. Zach held his gaze until, finally, with a curt nod, the Duke stalked away.

*Typical arrogant, cold-hearted nob.*

His conscience then reared up, calming his anger and allowing his common sense to reassert itself. The man was

Cecily's brother and she clearly loved and respected him. As she was a product of her upbringing, so was the Duke a product of his. The kinder part of Zach understood the Duke merely sought to protect his family. After all, he too had a protective streak as wide as the sky. But the resentful part—the part he tried so hard to control, the part that would wallow in past injustices and past betrayals if he allowed it to—wanted nothing more than to make the Duke and every unfeeling aristocrat like him *pay* for their blind acceptance of the privilege of their birth.

And the wild part—the part that clamoured to challenge and to seduce and to take risks merely in order to *show* them—that was the hardest to control of the lot.

At the breakfast table the following day, Cecily eyed her brothers and her nephew with growing resentment. She understood *why* one or other of them had stayed close by her side throughout the previous evening—at least until Zach had left—but that did not soothe her exasperation. What was wrong with simply talking to the man? She ignored the whisper of her conscience, reminding her of their kiss. Her brothers did not know about that. They could have no valid excuse for treating her as though she were unable to exercise self-control when she had never given them any cause to doubt her.

She bit into her toast and marmalade, and chewed absent-mindedly as she considered ways in which she could see Zach again. All too soon they would all go their separate ways and, before then, she wanted—*needed*—to talk to him, to feel his solid support, to hear his quiet belief that she was capable of her own decisions and that it was not wrong for her to put her own needs first for once.

'Thea?'

Thea looked up and smiled. 'Yes, Cecily?'

She hesitated. If she asked to go with Thea to look at Star, for certain Vernon would find an excuse to accompany them, even though the men were currently planning to ride around the estate with Daniel, to advise him on agricultural matters. Mrs Markham, as usual, would spend much of her time with her husband in his bedchamber and Mr Allen, Rosalind's grandfather, would no doubt join them after a late breakfast. He had struck up a friendship with Mr Markham and they spent much time together happily exchanging stories of the old days.

That just left Thea and Rosalind, which suited Cecily perfectly.

'I thought I might stroll in the flower garden this morning, before it grows too hot, and I wondered if you might care to accompany me?'

Thea's eyes lit up. 'That will be fun.' She turned to Leo and her freckled cheeks fired red as they often did when she spoke directly to him. 'Do you think R-Rosalind would like to join us, yo—Leo?'

Thea was still uncomfortable being on familial terms with a real duke and the entire family found her uncharacteristic shyness around him completely endearing.

'I am sure she will.' Rosalind had not yet put in an appearance that morning and Leo rose to his feet. 'I have finished here. If you will all excuse me, I shall go and ask her.'

He left the room and Cecily released her held-in breath. It was not easy to fool Leo, but at least the first part of her plan had worked. She hoped neither of her new sisters-in-law would behave *quite* so stuffily as the male members of her family—surely they would suspect nothing if she suggested a visit to the stables to see how Star fared?

'I,' said Rosalind, pausing to breathe in the scent of a blush-pink rose, 'am under the strictest of instructions not to allow any…um…the word used, I believe, was *intercourse*—singularly inappropriate under the circumstances, I would suggest—between we delicate members of the fairer sex and Mr Gray.'

Cecily laughed, relief loosening the tension that had gripped her ever since the three of them had ventured out into the garden. She had watched from her bedchamber window as the four men clattered past the front of the house and down the carriageway earlier, and only then had she joined her sisters-in-law in the salon. Her fear that Rosalind would capitulate to Leo's edict was unfounded…it appeared her sister-in-law had lost none of her spark since becoming a duchess.

Thea gasped at Rosalind's words, looking stunned as her gaze swivelled between Rosalind and Cecily.

'Are you shocked, Thea?' Rosalind smiled and took her hand. 'I did warn you before you married Vernon that it takes a strong woman to cope with a Beauchamp. It is merely a case of choosing your battles wisely, I find.'

'You would dare to defy Leo? But he is a *duke*.'

'He is a man first and foremost. And my husband.' Rosalind strolled on, following the path Cecily had taken three nights before. Cecily hooked her arm through Thea's and urged her on to catch up with Rosalind. 'I support him as any obedient wife should…*unless* I think he is being unreasonable. And then I reserve the right to make my own decisions. And in this case—' her hazel eyes glowed green in the sunlight as she turned her head and grinned at Cecily '—I find myself unconvinced by his rationale.'

They reached the square with the raised pool at its centre and there they paused.

'And I have to say,' continued Rosalind, 'I am more than delighted to discover that our sister Cecily is more of a Beauchamp than I ever imagined.'

'What do you mean?'

Uncomfortable with being the centre of attention, Cecily perched on the low wall that surrounded the pool and stirred the still surface with her fingers. She had always been in the background: the mortar that held the bricks of the family together, unnoticed and taken for granted.

'Merely that you and I have been friends since my arrival in London and yet this is the first time I have glimpsed the steel beneath the ladylike exterior. Do not misunderstand my meaning. I am not encouraging anything, shall we say, *untoward*—but I cannot for the life of me see why you should be barred from even *speaking* to the poor man.'

It was true. Why indeed should her brothers dictate whom she might speak to? What was the harm in simply conversing with Zach?

'Thank you, Rosalind. It does appear harsh, when Mr Gray's only sin is being born a Romany.'

'Indeed. From my own viewpoint, I have found him interesting to talk to, friendly and intelligent, and I like that he does not gabble. He only speaks when he has something to say, unlike so many. Plus, there is the matter that he saved your brother's life, Thea, and for that reason alone I believe we owe him the courtesy of trusting him.'

'I agree and I like him a lot,' Thea declared in her gruff little voice, 'and Vernon does, too. Or he did. But now he seems to disapprove.'

'They are being protective,' Cecily said. 'I do not blame them… To them I shall always be their little sister. But I cannot help wishing they would *trust* me.'

Rosalind patted Cecily's shoulder. 'Do not worry, my dear. Thea and I will continue to re-educate them. I am certain they will begin to understand that females are quite

as capable of intelligent thinking and responsible actions
as men.'

Cecily laughed. 'If not more so.'

'Do you realise, this is the first time we have all three
had a chance to talk privately together?' Thea looked from
Rosalind to Cecily and back again, causing her copper
curls to spring free and bounce over her forehead. 'I am
so happy to be part of your family.'

Cecily stood and hugged Thea. 'And we are happy to welcome you, too. Now—' she looked at the other two '—shall
we go and see how Star is getting on?'

Her first sight of Zach—walking along beside Star, his
concentration completely and utterly upon the horse—sent
Cecily's heart soaring and her pulse skipping. He looked
strong and confident, dressed in his customary loose trousers and shirt, a red neckerchief knotted at his throat and a
faded red and green embroidered waistcoat that hung open.
Her determination to defy her brothers, not to mention her
belief that her only interest in Zach was in his conversation, faltered as she took in his long, loose stride and the
blue-black sheen of his curls. The urge to slip her fingers
through those silky locks coiled deep in her stomach.

Zach halted and Star did, too, even though she was not
constrained—her halter rope was looped over her neck.
He smoothed her neck, his lips moving as he talked to her.
His hand continued along Star's back, pausing occasion-
ally to circle. The mare stood calmly, her head turned as
she watched the man. He in turn watched her, reacting to
the slightest flick of her ear.

'He is so good with animals,' Thea said. 'They really
seem to trust him. Vernon says he has a natural gift with
them. It is as though they become enchanted.'

*Enchanted...*

A shiver coursed down Cecily's spine. Was she enchanted by this man? She did not have to think about the answer...

*Yes. The question is: Does it change anything? Is it a reason to stay away from him?*

They would go their separate ways soon enough and, in the meantime, if she wished to talk with him—even kiss him again—why should that matter? The path of her future was laid out before her—she would not deviate from that.

Zach had seen them and he raised a hand in greeting before continuing with his treatment on Star. After a few more minutes, he rubbed her cheek and turned to walk towards the watching women. Star followed. As he approached, Zach swept one hand through his hair and his diamond earring flashed as it caught the sun.

'That diamond...' Rosalind murmured. 'I wonder if I could persuade Leo...' She directed an impish smile at the other two. 'Hmmm. Probably not. But there is something deliciously dangerous about such an adornment, do you not agree?'

Cecily did agree, but she would never admit to such a thing out loud. She was surprised—and a little irritated—by Rosalind's indiscreet comment.

'Rosalind,' Thea hissed. 'You are not—*attracted*—to Mr Gray?'

Rosalind gurgled with laughter. 'Thea! I am shocked. The attraction is not to Mr Gray, but to his choice of jewellery. Leo is the only man for me. I knew that from the first moment I set eyes on him, even though we had a few ups and downs along the way.'

'I am relieved to hear it,' Cecily said. 'I admit, for a second, you set me wondering as well.'

## Chapter Seven

'Good morning, ladies.'

Zach stopped before them, a half-smile on his lips. His dark eyes moved from Rosalind to Cecily to Thea, and Cecily could not help but imagine his gaze lingered a little longer upon her.

'Good morning, Absalom.' Thea held her hand out to Star, who stretched her neck forward and snuffled at Thea's outstretched palm. 'What is your verdict on Star's back?'

Zach smiled fully. 'She will fully recover. I am sure of it. She needs time, that is all.'

'Oh, I am so relieved.' Thea put her hands either side of Star's face and kissed her soundly on the nose.

Cecily glanced at Zach. His eyes warmed as they met hers, prompting a smile to curve her lips.

'I could not bear to lose her,' Thea went on. 'I know I cannot take her with me when we go to Vernon's estate, but Pritchard will send her down as soon as she is well enough.' She slid the halter rope from Star's neck and turned to Zach. 'Is it safe for me to lead her back?'

'Of course, my lady.'

Thea's cheeks glowed. 'I still cannot get used to that. Did it take you long to get used to being called "your Grace," Rosalind?'

Thea started back towards the stable yard and Rosalind went with her in order to reply to her question.

'Your brothers and your nephew rode out with Daniel earlier.'

Cecily began to follow the others. Slowly. 'Daniel asked for their advice on agricultural matters.'

She glanced sideways in time to see him nod. 'You are here because they are not?'

She caught her lip between her teeth. 'I have enjoyed our conversations. My brothers can be...'

'Protective. Yes. When they are not here, you do what you enjoy. When they are present, you do what is expected of you.'

They were close to the yard now, where Thea had handed Star over to a groom.

'It is not as simple as you believe. Not in my world.'

'I understand.'

'No. You do not. I love my family. I do not enjoy dissension or arguments and neither do I wish to cause them anxiety. *That* is why I behave as I was brought up to behave, not because I fear repercussions. Leo is not an ogre, but he worries about me, about the whole family.'

'I doubt he loses sleep with his worries. He is a powerful man, accustomed to obedience at every turn. Noblemen can rule their fiefdoms in accordance with their own rules, no matter how self-serving.'

An uncommon bitterness had entered his tone, but they were too close to the others for Cecily to question his statement.

She simply had time to say, hurriedly, 'Leo might be a duke and hugely powerful in many ways, but that does not stop him caring. Or fretting, although he tries very hard to hide it.'

They joined Rosalind and Thea and, very soon afterwards, the three women made their way back to the house. As they did so, the mournful bray of a donkey rent the air. Rosalind stopped dead, her hand to her chest.

'*What* is that infernal racket?'

'It is Sancho Panza. Absalom's donkey,' Thea said, with a grin. 'He's very loud, is he not?'

'I thought I made my position clear?'

Leo's voice always grew quieter the angrier he became and his voice was at this moment so low Cecily had to strain to hear him.

'Your position?'

'I warned you about speaking to that gipsy again—'

'He is a *Romany.*'

'But Bickling tells me that you—all *three* of you—were hobnobbing with him earlier, in the paddock and then in the stable yard.'

'*Hobnobbing?* Leo. Be reasonable—the man is treating Thea's favourite horse. We went to see how she was and we held a brief conversation.'

'So it was Thea's idea?'

Warning bells clamoured in Cecily's head. If Leo blamed Thea, Vernon would leap to her defence and then there would be trouble.

'It was *my* suggestion and a perfectly innocuous suggestion at that. And once I mentioned it, Thea was eager to go and, although Rosalind did suggest it was unwise...'

She let her words drift into silence, hoping they would mollify her brother and forestall any blame for his wife.

'It is time you returned to London.' Leo paced the room. 'No doubt Olivia is running rings around Lady Glenlochrie and Freddie, not to mention leading Nell astray. Heaven knows what mischief she has been up to since you've been away.'

When Cecily left London, she had left both Olivia and Rosalind's stepsister, Nell, in the care of Rosalind's younger brother, Freddie—recently appointed as Leo's secretary—and Nell's formidable aunt, Lady Glenlochrie.

'Time *I* returned to London? Do you not mean it is time *you* returned? Olivia is *your* daughter and Rosalind will presumably be keen to get back to Nell. *And* Susie.'

Rosalind had been very reluctant to leave Susie—a runaway child rescued by her and Leo—in the first place and it had taken some persuasion by Leo to convince her that being cooped up in a carriage to Birmingham, merely to collect Mr Allen's belongings, would prove scant fun for a lively six-year-old. They had already been away from London far longer than anticipated.

Leo's jaw set and his brows lowered, but Cecily saw no reason why her life should continue to be bound by duty now Rosalind was available to take the reins of family and household. She waited, brows raised.

'We shall *all* leave tomorrow,' he bit out. 'Vernon and Thea will be leaving shortly in any case.'

The newlyweds planned to visit the Lake District on honeymoon before returning to London in July.

Cecily knew what Leo planned. The Season was nearing its end. They would return to London for a few weeks, then Beauchamp House would be packed up and they would all adjourn to Brighton for a few weeks, to enjoy the sea air and to coincide with the Brighton horse races, following which they would return to the Abbey. Leo's arrogant assumption that she would merely fall into line, as she had always done, reassured her that she was making the right decision to attempt to secure her future elsewhere.

'As it happens, I am not returning to Town.' She tilted her chin in an unconscious gesture of defiance.

'What do you mean?'

She took some comfort in seeing her normally un-shakeable brother taken aback.

'I plan to visit Aunt Drusilla. I shall ask Dominic to take me to Leyton Grange on his way back to London.'

'Aunt *Drusilla*?' Leo shouted with laughter, but sobered as Cecily continued to stare at him. 'You cannot… Are you serious?' He took her hand. 'Cecy—my dear—there is no need for you to endure that old harridan just because you're in a fidget with me.'

'A *fidget*? Am I not entitled to be a touch annoyed when you treat me like a pea-brained young miss in her first Season?'

'Cecy.' He placed his hands on her shoulders and sighed. 'I know you are not pea-brained, but do give me credit for having a little more experience than you. I recognise the signs. Absalom Gray, I grant you, is a fine-looking man but he is a g—a *Romany*. You heard what Daniel said yesterday—he can charm the birds and the beasts, and I make no doubt the man can charm the fairer sex as well. *That* is why I warned him off and why I shall continue to do so. He is dangerous, my dear. You think you are up to all the tricks men can employ and that may be true of the civilised men you meet every day. But who knows what tricks and wiles a man like Gray has up his sleeve?'

Cecily bit her tongue. Yes, she was fascinated by Zach, but she was completely confident he had used no *tricks* or *wiles* to capture her interest.

'I still intend to call upon Aunt Drusilla. Quite apart from the fact it is at least two years since I last visited her, it will give Rosalind and the staff at the Abbey a chance to grow accustomed to one another without me getting in the way.'

She was aware their staff—many of whom qualified as old family retainers—would find it hard to adapt to a new mistress of the house and especially so if Cecily was still there.

Leo's silver-grey eyes softened. 'Is that what this is all about? Cecy—my dearest sister—you know you will always have a home and a place at the Abbey.'

She tried to pull away from his grip, but he pulled her into a hug. 'It wouldn't be home without you there.'

A lump swelled in her throat, which ached with sudden tears. She had no idea when she would see him again... So much depended on what happened at Leyton Grange and whether or not Lord Kilburn renewed his offer. But she knew she would not return to the Abbey, at least until Christmas. If her plan did not succeed, she thought she might pay an extended visit to their cousin Felicity, Lady Stanton, in Hampshire. The Stantons' first baby was due next month and she knew Felicity would be glad of her company.

But further plans and arrangements could wait for now.

'I still intend to visit our aunt.'

She freed herself from his embrace and hurried from the room before her tears could betray her.


'What worm have you got in your brain now, Cilly?'

Cecily glared at Vernon. He had knocked on her bed-chamber door with a request to 'talk to her' shortly before it was time to go down to dinner. She had no doubt he had been sent by Leo to 'talk some sense into her'.

'Do *not* call me by that dreadful name.'

'Oh...very well.' Vernon sighed in an exaggerated fashion. 'Cecily, then. But why on earth are you so set on visiting that old dragon?'

'Duty.' She smiled sweetly. 'Is that not what well-brought-up ladies are trained to consider above all else? Particularly above personal preference?'

'Hmmm. You might have a point there. But…really? Aunt Drusilla?' He sauntered across the room to peer out of the window. Then he stiffened and spun round to face her, his expression suddenly hard. 'Promise me it's not because Gray is travelling in that direction. Have you arranged to meet up with him?'

She stared, aghast. 'How *dare* you suggest I would do such a thing?'

'Then why? Tell me. Convince me.'

'I want to get married.'

'To *him*?'

'Don't be ridiculous, Vernon. He is merely a friend and I am more than aware of the fact he is a Romany, so please do not insult my integrity. I *know* what is due to our family name.'

Vernon's brow furrowed. 'But—what has Aunt Drusilla got to do with you finding a husband? Surely—in London—' His brow cleared. 'Oh, no.'

In two long strides he was standing before her, an expression of utter incredulity on his face. Cecily cursed beneath her breath. She had forgotten. Vernon was the only member of her family she had told about Kilburn's proposal.

'Cilly. You cannot be serious.'

Cecily folded her arms across her chest. 'I am deadly serious. It is for the best.'

'For the best? That pompous ba—? He's higher in the instep than Leo at his most ducal. And there are rumours of debts. *Big* debts. For God's sake, Cilly…if you want to get married I know any number of decent fellows who would jump at the chance. I only have to give them a nudge in the right direction.'

She glared into her brother's eyes—green like hers. 'Don't you *dare*. At least Kilburn *wants* to marry me—

or he did—and *he* won't need coercing into making an offer.'

'*You* were the one who suspected he only offered for you for your dowry. Or because he wants a mother for his children.'

She shrugged. 'What sensible man does not consider the value of a potential bride's dowry? And as for needing a mother…the children are very young still and it is right and proper for a father to think of their needs. I wish for my own household to run. I shall stay with Aunt Drusilla and discover if his lordship wishes to renew his offer.'

'And that's another thing—Aunt *Drusilla* as your neighbour? Dear God…there'll be no bearing it.' Vernon paused, then inhaled and changed tack, his tone now wheedling. 'Cecily—dearest—there's no need to rush into anything. Give it some time. I thought you and Rosalind were friends? Why can you not—?'

'It is precisely because we *are* friends that I cannot remain there. I have made up my mind.'

'No. Look, Cilly…if you need a respite from the Abbey, you can come and live with me and Thea at Woodbeare for some of the year. And then, if Livvy ever finds a man brave enough or foolhardy enough to take her on, you will have them to visit as well.'

He beamed, as though he had solved all her problems, but his words sent a chill shimmying down her spine. If she needed confirmation she was following the right course, this was it. The thought of being passed between the various members of her family like an unwanted parcel was too much to bear.

Better to be married—even to a man she did not love—than that.

She straightened, her chin jutting forward. 'This is what I have decided, Vernon. I shall speak to Leo after dinner and explain it to him properly. I hope you can support my decision but, if you find you cannot, I should appreciate it if you would stay out of that conversation.'

Cecily sped through the moonlit garden, expecting at any moment to be summoned back to the house by a shout. None came. She slowed at the paved square, but still headed with purpose for the archway that led to the parkland beyond, to the lake where she and Zach had talked, where Athena had skimmed, ghostly and silent, across the surface of the water to land on Zach's outstretched arm.

Zach had not joined them for dinner. Nothing was said of his absence and she did not ask, preferring not to know if it had been at Leo's behest. She prayed he had not already left Stourwell Court. She wanted to say goodbye. She had pleaded a headache and retired to bed early. As soon as Anna, her maid, had left her she had swiftly dressed again—donning just her shift and a simple round gown—and wrapped a shawl around her. Heart pounding, she had sneaked along the corridor to the back stairs, praying she would not bump into any of the servants. She was fortunate. She reached the side door she had used before and slipped outside without being seen.

They were leaving in the morning. She had no other chance to say goodbye; to say thank you. She didn't stop to debate the rights or wrongs of her choice—she followed her heart.

At the shore of the small lake, she turned to her right. As she followed the shoreline there, in the distance, she saw a flame flicker. Her heart—until now clenched in anxiety—softened and expanded. He had not gone. She walked slower now, smoothing her hair back and readjusting her shawl. Steadying her breathing.

At the site, she paused. Beyond the fire, burning steady and low, she could make out the dark bulk of his wagon and the rounded hump of his tent. And the figure of a man.

'Why are you here?'

He moved forward, his face still in the shadows, but his body highlighted by the warm glow of the fire. Loose trousers rode low on narrow hips and above...above...

*Oh, my.*

Her heart near climbed into her throat as she surveyed the wide expanse of his naked chest, covered in dark curls. A flame flared and its light danced across his bronzed skin, emphasising his broad shoulders, muscular arms and the planes and hollows of his sculpted chest. He looked powerful and dangerous, and very, very male. She swallowed the urge to turn and flee and made herself approach the fire. The flames did nothing to cool the heat spiralling through her entire body.

'I had to come. We leave after breakfast. I wanted to... I did not want to go without saying goodbye.'

He stepped closer to the fire and hunkered down to feed in more wood, his attention focused on his task. She drank in the sight. Never had a man affected her like this—her heart twisted at the impossibility of even a simple friendship between them, at the width and the depth of the gulf between their positions in society. And yet, she was here. She had come, despite knowing that visiting him here, at night, unchaperoned, would ruin her if it ever became known.

He looked up and captured her gaze, studying her, revealing nothing of his feelings or his thoughts about such a shocking indiscretion on her part. She fought to keep her own emotions hidden.

'And your brothers?'

'What about them?'

'Are they aware you are here?'

That startled a laugh from her. And the tension in the air softened somewhat as one corner of his mouth lifted.

'The answer is no, then.' He stood and rounded the fire to her. Loosely clasped her hand and led her to a log, set on its end. 'Please. Take a seat.'

She did, lowering herself carefully. No sooner had she settled than something nudged under her hand and she found herself stroking Myrtle's ears. Pleasure, pure and simple, fanned through her.

'She would not come to me yesterday,' she said in delight.

'This is her home. She is more confident here. She can sense you are no threat now, but the bustle of the stables scared her.'

He sat cross-legged on a pallet of bedding, across the fire from Cecily.

'So you leave tomorrow?'

Sorrow dispelled her pleasure. 'Yes.'

'And you are still set on visiting your aunt? And on marrying your earl?'

'Yes to the first. As to the second…possibly.'

He propped his elbows on his knees and rested his chin on his hands. 'Tell me.'

He said no more, but waited. Where should she start? But she knew the answer to that, for what had he been telling her all along? She would speak from her heart.

'I have been thinking about what you said.'

'I have said a great many things.' His teeth gleamed as he smiled. 'More to you than to anyone since my mother died.'

The thought pleased her, that she had not just taken from him, but given something in return.

'You said I should give myself more time to consider my

plan to marry and I agree. There is no need to rush into it.
I shall visit my aunt and when Lord Kilburn returns to his
estate I shall visit him and meet his children again and I
shall listen to my heart.'

'*Kilburn?*'

## Chapter Eight

Cecily had expected approval that she had listened to his advice and would listen to her heart. Zach's exclamation of horror took her by surprise. She had never seen him so perturbed.

'You say that as though you know him.'

Zach scowled. 'We have met.'

'And what, pray, is your objection?'

There was a lengthy pause. 'He is too dull and self-important for a woman like you.'

'Like me? I should have thought I was perfect for such a man. I am hardly a giddy girl any longer. If I ever was.'

The silence stretched as his gaze roamed her face and her body, coaxing trails of fire that sizzled along her veins.

'That word again. *Perfect.* On the surface maybe,' he said eventually. 'But deep down lies a different woman and Kilburn is not the man to satisfy *her*.'

Those sizzles of fire erupted, flaming her skin and firing her temper. 'And you are?'

Their eyes clashed and Cecily battled to hold his gaze. One kiss did not give him the right to question her decision. Or to think he knew anything about her.

'I did not say that,' he said, quietly, 'but Kilburn is not the man for you.'

She jumped to her feet, her insides churning with anger. 'It is time I went. You might be wise in some ways, Zachary Gray, but you know nothing of my world.'

He did not move. He continued to stare at her, a deep groove etched between his brows as though he were waging some internal battle.

'I know more than you imagine,' he said eventually. 'And Kilburn...there is a darkness at the heart of him.'

'Then tell me what you know of him. Convince me.'

He dipped his head to stare into the flames, his shoulders stiff. 'I have said enough.'

She stamped her foot. 'You *cannot* malign a man's character like that and not elaborate.'

'I am asking you to believe me. Trust me. You will be unhappy.'

Frustration and anger bubbled together. The man was infuriating. There was enigmatic and there was just plain stubbornness. What could Kilburn have done to set Zach against him? Why would he not tell her? Clashes between landowners and Romanies setting up camp on their property were common.

'Did he drive your people from his land? I should have thought you would be accustomed to such things.'

She flinched as Zach surged to his feet, anguish etched on his face. She stood her ground as he stormed around the fire to confront her even though her insides quaked. He halted in front of her, hands fisted at his sides. Then he hauled in a deep breath. His shoulders dropped and his fingers uncurled as he exhaled, shuddering.

'I did not mean to startle you. I'm sorry.' He held her chin, tilting her face, his dark eyes searching hers. 'Please, heed my warning, dove. Go if you must, but watch him carefully. Take note of his actions rather than his words. He is not a kind man. Probe his character.' His words grew ever softer, his eyes more intent. He placed his other hand against her chest, covering her left breast, with exquisite pressure. 'And hear your heart.'

'I—'

Her voice hitched as his gaze lowered to fix on her mouth and his fingers curved around her breast. Heat flared from the smouldering fire deep in her belly, flickering through her entire body until her veins, her nerves, the entire surface of her skin scorched hot. His other thumb moved then, slowly and deliberately, dragging her lower lip gently sideways as his warm breath danced across her skin. Without volition, her hands rose to his chest, her fingers splaying through crisp curls, and a moan escaped from somewhere deep, deep inside her. She followed the powerful contours of his chest up to his shoulders where her fingers curled into firm, hot flesh.

His arms came around her, one hand settling at the small of her back, the other between her shoulder blades, fitting her body into his, soft curves against hard muscle. She tilted her face, seeking, and his lips grazed over hers, gently nibbling, soft and persuasive; she twined her arms around his neck and pressed closer still, pushing her fingers among those heavy, silken curls that so fascinated her. His tongue parted her lips as his hands skimmed down her back to the swell of her bottom and he cupped her, lifting, as he angled his head and deepened the kiss, the hard ridge of his arousal pressing into her stomach.

Strange sensations spiralled through her—she could barely believe how one kiss made her feel…or the effect she was having on this gorgeous virile man. Her entire being was focused on him and on this dizzying pleasure. Nothing else—not one single thing outside his arms—

mattered. He swung her off her feet and carried her to his pallet, following her down, his body half-covering hers. Only then did he break their kiss, raising his head and sweeping her face with his glittering gaze. He stroked her hair back and then clasped her wrists, loosening her hold and easing her arms from around his neck. Still holding her wrists, he splayed her arms. As her hands touched the blanket on either side of her head, he changed his grip, lacing his fingers through hers, holding her in place.

With lips and tongue he explored her face and her neck, her shoulders and her arms, murmuring his appreciation and endearments, soothing her even as her skin heated and tingled wherever he touched. His head moved lower, his mouth caressing the slope of her breast. She tipped her head back, arching her back, as a moan escaped her lips. Her breasts felt excruciatingly tight and her nipples ached. She moved restlessly and tried to pull her hands from his, longing to touch him. *Needing* to touch him. He tightened his grip.

'Zach—?'

'Hush, my dove. Allow me…'

He shifted position and her hands were now above her head, together, her two wrists pinioned by just one of his hands as the other cupped her breast, the thumb rubbing her nipple, creating the most delicious…the most tantalising… She raised her head to peer down at him. His mouth was on the curve of her breast, tasting, licking, and then with one swift tug, he tugged her neckline, and her breasts sprang free. He drew one nipple into his mouth, his tongue swirling, teeth nipping oh so gently.

*Oh, heavens!*

She could not bear to lie still. She thrashed her head from side to side as her body bowed, but then he shifted again, bringing more of his weight on her so, once again, she could not move. She watched as he gazed down at her exposed breasts. When he looked up, the heat and the fierce desire in his eyes sent her senses reeling as her insides turned molten.

'Zach—?'

She could only watch, helpless, as he lowered his head again, turning his attention to her other breast, gently tugging and suckling. Her eyes closed in ecstasy and her head sank back to the ground as she gave herself up to his lips… his tongue…his teeth…and moan after moan sighed from her until, finally, he released her wrists and he took her lips in a long, soothing kiss as he gathered her to him and rolled on to his back, taking her with him.

'Did that please you, little dove?'

'You know it did,' she breathed, taking in the wicked glint in his eyes as she leaned over to kiss him.

This time she took control and he lay still as she stroked and kissed, licked and nibbled, fascinated by his bronze, hair-roughened skin and the shift of his muscles as she explored. The only time he stopped her was when her fingers strayed too close to his waistband as she explored his flat stomach.

'Not wise, my dove,' was his only response when she raised a brow.

She knew he was right. She appreciated his restraint. Had the decision been left to her, she wondered, would she be so controlled? She ought not to play with fire. To-morrow she would be gone and she would—surely—soon forget this sexy, enticing Romany and the wild cravings he conjured forth.

When at last she snuggled close, Zach settled her into the crook of his arm, her head on his shoulder as he stroked her hair. She nuzzled into his neck, tasting him, savouring his unique salty maleness, and she ached—a hollow, yearning ache for what she could not have, deep in her core.

She twirled his chest hair with restless fingers.

'You are…an unusual man,' she said.

'I have been called worse.' He began to sing, low and musical, in a language at once foreign and soothing. When he finished, she stirred.

'Was that a Romany song?'

He pressed his mouth to her hair. 'Yes.'

'What is it about?'

A laugh rumbled in his chest. 'It is a song for a man to sing to a woman.'

'What does it say?'

He tilted her face to his and kissed her—slowly, sensually, as though he were savouring every single moment, his lips soft and smooth and oh so tempting. Then he lifted his mouth from hers.

'That.' He settled her head against his shoulder once more and she made herself relax, controlling the urge to continue…to kiss him again…to take more…to…to…

'Where shall you go when you leave here?' Anything to distract herself.

She felt his shrug. 'You have asked me that before, dove.'

'Will you rejoin your family? Are they still camped at Worcester?'

'They will have moved on by now.'

'But…how will you find them?'

She worried about him. The countryside was vast.

He flicked her nose. 'Don't you worry about me, dove. I will find them. I know their direction and where they will camp.'

'It is a strange way to live. At least, to someone like me.'

'It must appear so.'

'You said—the other day…' She paused. She did not wish to anger him, but her curiosity was fierce. 'You implied that you had *chosen* your way of life. That you had an alternative.'

He shifted position, as though uncomfortable. He was silent so long she feared he would simply not answer.

'Every Romany has the choice to change if they so wish. They can choose to find a job and somewhere to live. But they are born to travel. It is in their blood. They do not hanker after roots to anchor them to one place, or a roof to shut out the sky. They live beneath the sun, the moon and the stars.'

His use of 'they' rather than 'we', and the care with which he spoke, suggested there was more—a secret he did not wish to reveal, not to her. She was, after all, a stranger to him—a *gadji*, as he termed non-Romany women—and they would probably never meet again. She must respect his desire for privacy even though she longed to probe the bitterness she had glimpsed in him that morning at the stable yard.

*'Noblemen can rule their fiefdoms in accordance with their own rules, no matter how self-serving.'*

Had he been thinking of Kilburn? The Earl was surely not the sort to attract such vitriol from a man who otherwise appeared content to accept life, and people, as they were. She recalled Zach's warning—*there is a darkness at the heart of him*—and caution whispered through her.

Time passed and her heart grew heavy in her chest as she accepted the inevitable. She forced herself to pull away from him.

'I must go.' She smiled at him, at the tenderness in his dark eyes. 'And, yes, this is one of those times when I shall follow what I *must* do rather than what I should like to do.'

'And what is it you should like to do, my lady?'

'That which I cannot—stay here, like this, until dawn breaks.'

His throat rippled as he swallowed, but his expression revealed neither regret nor relief. He stood up. 'I will walk with you.'

'There is no—'

'There is *every* need. Do not argue.'

He reached out and she placed her hands in his. His fingers folded around hers and he pulled her gently to her feet. Then he released her and strode to his cart to grab a shirt, which he tugged over his head. Cecily watched, committing him to memory. This was not reality. She knew that. It was but an interlude in the play of life: a very short interlude. She did not—*would* not—delude herself. But, oh, how she regretted... Tears clogged in her throat and stung her nose and her eyes.

Yes. How she regretted.

She turned away and waited for him to join her.

Zach tucked his shirt into his trousers, taking his time, until he was certain his emotions were again securely boxed. What was it about this woman that touched him? And made him wish for the impossible—that he was not who he was? It was as though she had reached deep inside him and taken possession of his soul.

Her sort had never interested him: prim and proper ladies hiding their disdain for more lowly born folk behind their exquisite manners and their perfect behaviour. Even as a child, he had recognised the truth in their eyes. They had looked down upon his mother. They had ignored him, the son of the gipsy woman. And as a man he expected no different from their sort. His father's sort. *Kilburn's* sort.

But Cecily—and Thea and the Duchess, if he thought about it—were different. Thea, he could understand. He had helped her brother. She was grateful. The Duchess— her attitude had puzzled him, until he had met her grandfather and learned of her father's humble beginnings, and then her lack of highhandedness had made more sense. But a duke's sister—*never* had he imagined she would be so…non-judgemental. And neither would he have believed such passion smouldered in her depths or that she would reveal that side of herself to a man like him.

As a man, he had avoided gentlewomen, let alone a lady of her breeding. In the years since he and his mother had made their home with her family, he had preferred to dally with the local servant girls at the various places near which they had set up camp. Those girls—fun and uncomplicated—understood the game for what it was: a bit of fun not to be taken seriously. He had taken care not to dishonour any of the Romany girls he met by showing interest in them. With a father who was a *gadjo*, even his mother's family did not consider Zach as true Rom, yet all the non-Romany world saw of him was a man who was a gipsy.

He belonged nowhere, to neither world.

Cecily, though…how he yearned to belong with her. To love her, to bury himself inside her, to claim her and to never let her go. But to think like that was fantasy. For her sake he must let her go but—to Kilburn? Fury scorched his gut.

*Kilburn.* Of all men.

The shock of hearing that name, after all this time, still reverberated through him: picking open the old wounds, shining a light on the past he had tried so hard to forget, reminding him once again of his misery at his half-brother's rejection and of the humiliation and the torment to which he and his friend, Kilburn, had subjected Zach throughout his boyhood.

How could he persuade Cecily to heed his warning about Kilburn without revealing both the identity he had renounced a decade ago and the wretched truth of his past? Even he found it hard to believe Kilburn would treat a lady—his own wife—with the same barbaric cruelty he had employed against a sixteen-year-old half-Romany boy. Every fibre of Zach's being rebelled at the thought of exposing *that* particular shame to such a perfect lady.

He battened down his thoughts, and returned to where she waited by the fire. *His* Lady Perfect—it meant something different now to when he had coined the phrase. She was the perfect lady for him—but he could not have her.

'Come.' He took her hand. 'Let us go.'

They walked to the lake and crossed the parkland to the archway into the garden. In silence, they trod the pathway to the side door into the house. The door she had left by. Quietly, Zach tested the door; it was still unlocked.

As one, they faced one another and Zach raised her hand to his lips and breathed in her scent as he kissed her skin. He stroked her hair back, framing her face with his hands, then pressed his mouth to hers, tasting her sweetness for the very last time. His heart was a solid mass of aching, brimming with black despair.

'Farewell, my perfect lady.' His voice barely audible. He kissed her cheek, the saltiness of her tears on his lips. He folded his arms around her, pulled her close to his chest and put his lips to her ear. 'Please. Trust me. Kilburn has a cruel streak—watch him carefully. Do not rush to a decision. Wait. Give yourself time. Consider. Your heart will tell you.'

She leaned back in his arms and cradled his face, one soft hand against each cheek. 'I will.' A choked whisper. 'I promise. Goodbye, Zach.'

And she was gone.

## Chapter Nine

Three days later, Zach caught up with his family in the beautiful Vale of Evesham. They were a smallish group. His grandfather—the Absalom he was named after—was the head of the family. His aunt, married to the oldest of his uncles, was the heart. For ten years, his home had been with them. They had taken him and his mother in after his father—a *gadjo*—had died and they had nowhere else to find refuge. He steered Titan around the perimeter of the camp and drew him to a halt at the far side, at a distance from his uncle's tents. His mood lightened at the sight of his family—uncles, aunts, cousins—as they gathered to greet him.

Perhaps now, in the midst of his family, he could cast Lady Perfect from his thoughts. And his dreams.

'Well, Absalom.' His uncle spoke the Romany language, deep, thick and musical. 'You have returned? You did not stay?'

'As you see, *kako*.'

Come.' His aunt urged him from his cart. 'The boys will see to the animals. Come and eat.'

Myrtle had leapt down as soon as the cart halted and was hopping around on three legs, and Zach hoped she would remember her training. Dogs were considered unclean by the Rom, due to their habit of licking their genitals, and Zach had trained her not to come too close to where the food was being prepared or eaten, or to venture inside his bender tent when he erected it but, since being alone, he had been less strict, remembering the canine companions of his boyhood and the pleasure he had derived from them when his older half-brother had rejected him.

His grandfather sat by the cooking fire, a blanket around his shoulders. Zach sank down on his haunches next to him.

'Are you ill, *purodad*?'

Saggy eyes in a seamed face studied him before his grandfather shook his head. 'Just old, Son. But thankful for the sun that shines. We wondered if we would see you again.'

His words shocked Zach. They were the same with which his uncle had greeted him.

'You thought I might just disappear? Without a word?'

His grandfather shook his head. 'No. That would not be your way. But your aunt—she sensed your image fading. She says your father's blood still speaks in your veins.' He smiled, revealing gappy teeth. 'There is no shame in that. Your father's world could still be yours, if you choose.'

*If I choose...*

Zach's thoughts turned inwards, picturing Cecily: her skin, soft and delicate as a butterfly's wing; her gentle eyes, the colour of moss; her lips, the pink of a cloud brushed by the evening sun as it dips below the horizon. His pulse leapt at the thought of her, pumping the blood to his groin, and he grew hard with pure desire. For Cecily. But his heart and his soul, they were bleak. Empty. He clenched his jaw, staring into the flames, willing his body back under control.

His thoughts moved on.

To Kilburn.

And the unease he had tried so hard to ignore erupted, firing his blood and pounding through his body. A husband had absolute dominion over his wife and Zach could not rid himself of the gut feeling that he should go after Cecily and, somehow, *make* her listen to him.

His grandfather was watching him, narrow-eyed.

'There is no shame in feeling torn.'

'Torn?'

'The two halves of you. I see it, as your aunt saw it. You battle against yourself, inside here.'

He put his hand on his chest, over his heart, and then paused as Zach's aunt brought him a plate of rabbit stew. She smiled as Zach thanked her. Grandfather waited until she was out of earshot before continuing.

'A lusty man like you needs a mate and you have returned here today with the memory of a woman in your eyes. A woman who haunts you.'

Zach frowned. 'Have I? I have only just arrived. How can you know?'

His grandfather shrugged. 'I have lived a long time. I know people. I know *you*. I saw that same look in your mother's eyes when she met your father. A mix of shame and of longing. She told me she was happy with your father. Happy until he died.'

'She was. We *were* happy.'

His grandfather shrugged. 'Then go back and find your woman.'

He made it sound simple. And, probably, to him it was. But to Zach it was anything but. A man marrying a Romany—she would be elevated to his status even though she might—and his mother *had*—face disapproval and ostracism. A woman, though—she would be relegated to her husband's status. In his case, that of a Romany. And

Cecily was the daughter of a duke. The sister of a duke. Their positions in society could hardly be further apart. She would face losing everything, including her beloved family. He could never ask her to choose. She would never be happy. He could never make her happy.

*Neither will Kilburn.*

That truth clawed at him. Was it enough to hope she would heed his warning? Should he have tried harder? But how, without revealing his past and his shame? Pride. It was a powerful force... Could he bear to humble himself in front of a lady like Cecily? But, on the other hand, could he bear to continue his life without ever knowing what decision she had reached?

'She intends to marry another.' He unfolded his body, rose to his feet. 'She is too highly born for me.'

His grandfather tipped his head back to look at him. 'Your father was high-born. You are his son. You have land and a house—what else would this *gadji* need or want?'

*Her world, her family's love and respect, her perfect life.*

No point in voicing that to his grandfather.

'The man she intends to marry—he is cruel. I can stop her from making *that* mistake, even if I cannot offer her an alternative.'

Grandfather's brows rose to disappear under the brim of his old hat, but Zach would not explain further. He had said enough. His gut instinct told him—had been telling him for days—that he could not just leave Cecily to her fate. He must do everything possible to help her see the truth of Kilburn's character.

'I shall leave in the morning.' He remembered the countryside around Leyton Grange—Lord Derham's country estate, where Cecily's aunt lived—and he instinctively knew the direction to take and how far he must go. Two days' travel. Maybe a touch further. Cecily had promised to take her time and not to rush her decision. He must hope he would be in time.

'We head south when we move on,' his grandfather said to Zach the following morning as he was leaving. *'T'aves baxtalo.'*

Good luck.

'Cecily!'

Cecily put aside her book and rose to her feet, stifling a sigh. She had yet to turn a page—she had read the words, but their sense had eluded her as her mind's eye had cast back in time to a campfire in Worcestershire. She was already fatigued by Aunt Drusilla's constant demands. She had been at Leyton Grange almost a week now and her first action had been to pack Miss Fussell—Aunt Drusilla's long-suffering companion, an impoverished cousin on the late Lord Derham's side of the family—off to her bed. Miss Fussell had a cold which, having been neglected in favour of running around after Aunt Drusilla, had since developed into a chronic cough. Cecily had found herself in the unenviable position of filling Miss Fussell's shoes, expected to cater to her aunt's every whim in the days following, until Miss Fussell had re-emerged from her sickroom this morning, insisting she was much better.

Cecily crossed the room to her aunt's side, sparing a searching look at Miss Fussell as she passed her by. The poor woman appeared to have diminished in stature since her illness—and she had not been large to begin with—but Cecily was pleased to see a touch of colour back in her cheeks. Experiencing the life that loomed in her future had only strengthened Cecily's determination to avoid such a fate at all costs. And, in the absence of any other likely suitors, Lord Kilburn appeared to be her best hope. Or a nunnery. And, after those delicious kisses she had shared with Zach, that thought had been summarily dismissed—with a wry, inner smile—the instant it had popped into her head.

If only Kilburn would return to his estate. She was impatient to meet him again, conscious of Zach's warning, but she could not assess the character of a man who was not there. As soon as she could decide her way forward, she could leave here—a prospect that grew in appeal by the hour.

'Why do you not read to me, Cecily?' Her aunt—large-bosomed and purple-turbaned—fanned her face vigorously. She suffered from frequent hot flushes and yet still insisted on the fire in the salon being lit and drawing her chair close in the belief that draughts were fatal. 'It is exceedingly selfish in you to sit on the far side of the room instead of next to me, where you might make yourself useful and entertain me. Heaven knows, I see little enough of my dear, departed brother's family as it is. There can be no excuse for such neglect. I am the last left of my generation of Beauchamps, but am I afforded the respect I deserve? No, I am not.'

'I am here now, Aunt,' said Cecily hastily, aware she might prose on for an age. 'I shall read to you if you wish, but you told me you were about to take a nap. I did not wish to disturb you.'

'Well! I should have thought it was obvious I was not asleep, if you'd cared to look, Niece.'

Miss Fussell struggled to her feet and held out her hand. 'That book does not appear to hold your attention, my dear Lady Cecily,' she said. 'My throat is much, much improved. Allow me to read to Cousin Drusilla.'

She cast a worried look at Aunt Drusilla as she spoke

and Cecily's heart went out to her. The poor woman had nowhere else to go. She had no home and the Derhams were her only family. She lived in a state of constant anxiety lest Drusilla decided to turn her away.

'Well, I must say, Minnie, at least you have dispensed with that awful croaking sound when you speak. I could not stand to listen to such a noise for more than a minute at a time. And that cough—*how* it irritated my poor nerves.'

Aunt Drusilla plucked at the shawl covering her legs and plied her fan vigorously to her pink, shiny cheeks. Cecily swallowed the retort she longed to fling at her aunt. Instead, she smiled at Miss Fussell.

'Are you certain you are strong enough to read aloud? I should not like to be the cause of more damage to your throat.'

'Ridiculous notion, Cecily. Really, you young things— you have no stamina. Of course Minnie is strong enough. The very idea. Why, she has done nothing but lie abed this past week or more. She must have stamina to spare by now and I know her pride will not allow her to neglect her duties any longer.'

Miss Fussell all but snatched the book from Cecily's hands at those words. 'Yes, yes. I am certain, thank you, my lady. Cousin Drusilla is right. I have neglected my duties of late. I must atone for it.'

Cecily's heart went out to her. 'If you are sure, Miss Fussell, then I shall go for a walk. I am need of some fresh air. With your permission, Aunt?'

Cousin Drusilla waved a dismissive hand. 'Yes, yes. Go if you must. But be sure to close the door properly against the draughts. I do not want to catch a chill at my age.'

Cecily's eyes met those of Miss Fussell and they exchanged a speaking glance. As Cecily left the room, she heard Miss Fussell begin to read.

Cecily, as had become her custom since the day of her arrival, left the Grange via a side door and strolled in the direction of Chilcot Manor, Lord Kilburn's home—a mere twenty minutes' walk from the Grange. A well-worn pathway linked the two great houses and it was this pathway she followed through a wide belt of ancient woodland that still grew close to the Grange, affording shelter from the east wind. The now-familiar track forked within the wood and Cecily took the left path—the right fork led, eventually, out to the road—until she reached the edge of the wood. Here a rough wooden fence marked the boundary between the two estates. A weathered stile made crossing the fence easy and she then followed the still-visible path across a meadow to a small copse. She skirted round the copse and the medieval Chilcot Manor, set in a sweeping vista of landscaped parkland—complete with ornamental lake—came into view.

Her pulse quickened as she saw clear signs of activity at the house: two maids were on hands and knees scrubbing the steps, a gardener was raking the gravel forecourt and what looked like a footman, in his shirt sleeves, was up a ladder, washing windows. Even at a distance, there was an undeniably frenetic quality to their movements— it appeared that the master's arrival was imminent. Cecily recalled Vernon's comment about his lordship's debts, but the number of servants and the pristine condition of both Manor and grounds surely belied those rumours?

She turned to go. Kilburn's servants were already aware of her presence at the Grange and she had little doubt they would convey that piece of news to Kilburn and that he would call upon Aunt Drusilla the following day to pay his respects.

She followed another path that wound down towards the ornamental lake. When she had first met Kilburn—

two years before, during her last visit to her aunt—Kilburn had taken great pride in informing her that the parkland at Chilcot had been designed by Humphry Repton. There was no denying it was spectacular, with plentiful walks and artfully contrived vistas, and Cecily usually took great pleasure in wandering around the immaculately kept grounds and discovering new delights. Today, however, as she approached the lake—the shoreline punctuated with clumps of the yellow flagged flowers and sword-shaped leaves of irises—there was an inexplicably tight ball of nervousness lying heavily in the pit of her stomach.

There was barely a breath of wind today and the lake's surface was like a mirror, reflecting the few fluffy white clouds in the sky. She gazed across the water, her mind whirling. On impulse, she looked down, searching the ground until she found what she was looking for. She removed her glove, stooped and picked up a flat, smooth pebble, caressing the warm surface, the slightest ache in her throat signalling the emotions she battled to hold at bay. Zach's face materialised in her mind's eye—tanned skin, dark eyes, wild curls. And that diamond...

*No!*

She leaned back and sideways, positioning her arm as her brothers had taught her, long ago in her carefree childhood. Her arm swept around, and she released the pebble with a flick of her wrist to skim it across the water. It bounced. Once...twice...three times in all. Not bad, considering how many years it had been since she had done such a thing.

She watched the ripples radiate out from the three spots where the pebble had touched the water. They spread to the shore, dissipating among the clumped iris swords which barely seemed to register the disturbance. She eyed the clumps. How solid and unmoving they seemed, yet a man with a spade could easily break the clump apart if it became overcrowded, and move the resulting portions to wherever he chose. Even to another part of the country.

She tried to apply that thought to her situation—as though her family were the existing clump and she was an offshoot that could be removed and set down, to grow and thrive elsewhere. But—what if she were transplanted to the wrong spot? What if, instead of thriving, her roots withered and shrunk, and she shrivelled? What if...?

But her thoughts were too random—fluttering hither and thither, like butterflies around a lavender in full bloom—and she could not think through the analogy to a conclusion. With a *hmmph* of disgust, she spun on her heel and marched back to the Grange and to the never-ending demands of Aunt Drusilla.

'Lord Kilburn has called to pay his respects, my lady,' Parker, Aunt Drusilla's butler, bowed as he announced his lordship's arrival the following afternoon.

Cecily pursed her lips against a smile as her aunt straightened in her chair, tucking stray strands of hair under the lace cap she wore that morning.

'Minnie! Take this,' she hissed as she tore the blanket from her lap. 'Make haste.'

Cousin Minnie scrambled to gather the blanket and then scurried to conceal it behind the floor-length curtain.

'Do show his lordship in,' Aunt Drusilla said, as she adjusted the neckline of her morning gown, tugging the lace fichu to conceal any hint of bosom, 'and send in refreshments.' She eyed Cecily up and down. ''Tis a pity you chose that particular gown this morning, my dear. The colour draws attention to your age. I have advised you before that you should wear more white, to honour your unmarried status. Kilburn is just the sort of man—hush. He is here.'

Cecily bit her lip, now struggling to contain a laugh. Her aunt had been extolling the virtues of her widowed neighbour ever since Cecily's arrival. Little did she realise that was the precise reason for Cecily's visit. The door opened again and Kilburn walked in and bowed. He slid a look at Cecily as she rose to greet him, his interest in her still apparent even though she had refused an offer from him not four months since.

'Lady Derham, your servant,' he said. 'Lady Cecily—a delight to see you again. Miss Fussell, you are in blooming health, I see.'

Cecily tamped down her irritation. Could he not see how pale and frail poor Miss Fussell looked? She set a polite smile on her face and joined in the conversation.

Twenty minutes later, Aunt Drusilla announced that Kilburn would be leaving now.

'You may walk to the door with his lordship, Cecily, dear,' she said. 'I am certain you have much to tell him about your brothers' weddings. I am sure *I* shall be unable to satisfy any curiosity on his part, as neither of my nephews saw fit to inform me of their plans.'

Aunt Drusilla lost no opportunity to complain that she had not been invited to either wedding, even though—often with the next breath—she would lament that the state of her health precluded her from travelling any further than to the local church for Sunday services.

'Would you care to walk with me a short distance?' Kilburn's horse had been brought round from the stables. 'I am in no great hurry to return to the Manor. I dine alone tonight.'

'That would be most pleasant, sir.'

Here was an ideal opportunity to learn more about his lordship. They fell into step, Kilburn's horse plodding along behind them.

'You must visit us at the Manor, my lady—the children will be delighted to see you,' Kilburn said as they strolled down the main carriageway, his hands clasped behind his back as he matched his long stride to her shorter one. 'It will have to be within the next few days, however, as I plan return to London shortly.'

Cecily glanced at him, taking in his tall, lean figure and his aristocratic profile, with its hooked nose and deep-set eyes. His brown hair was already receding although he was but a few years her senior and, despite his gaffe when he complimented Miss Fussell on her healthy appearance, he had given her no cause to view him with caution, either today or during their earlier meetings.

'Thank you. I shall enjoy renewing my acquaintance with the children. It is an age since I have seen them. No doubt they have grown since I last set eyes upon them.'

'Indeed.' She could hear the pride in his voice. 'Thomas is growing tall and straight and his manners, though I say so myself, are exemplary.'

Cecily waited, but he added nothing to his statement. 'And the girls?'

'They also thrive.'

Cecily frowned at that throwaway remark about his young daughters, but took care to smooth her expression as he turned his head and caught her eye.

'They are in need of a mother's guidance.' His voice was loaded with meaning and the smug satisfaction in his eyes suggested he had an inkling of the real reason behind Cecily's visit to her aunt.

She swallowed.

*Probe his character*, Zach's voice whispered in her memory. *He is not a kind man.*

Kilburn's intended early return to London had removed some of the urgency from Cecily's decision. She, too, would return and she would make it her business to get to know him better.

'Might I visit the children tomorrow, then, sir? For I, too, plan to return to Town very shortly. I have been here—'

Her jaw snapped shut and they both halted as a familiar shriek arose—ebbing and flowing—from the road beyond the gatehouse.

## Chapter Ten

Kilburn's horse raised his head and stared intently in the direction of the sound.

'What on earth was that?'

'It sounded,' said Cecily, her heart beating a rapid tattoo as anticipation prickled along her spine, 'like a donkey.'

Cecily's stomach churned as they resumed their walk. It was, surely, ridiculous to be excited by the braying of a donkey, but she could not deny her reaction. All she could think—hope—was that it was Sancho. And Zach.

*And then what? What difference will it make?*

As quickly as her spirits soared, they crashed to the ground. It made no difference whatsoever. He was still a Romany. Whatever feelings he aroused in her, any relationship was impossible—even simple friendship, given what had already passed between them.

They reached a point where a track branched off from the carriageway, towards the belt of woodland that defined the boundary between the Grange and the Manor. This track culminated in a narrow gate rather than a stile, allowing riders to pass between the two estates. Cecily had intended to accompany his lordship as far as the edge of the wood, but she now changed her mind. She had come to the Grange with the intention of encouraging him to renew his offer, but Zach's warnings had shaken that resolve. She still wanted to marry, but was Kilburn the right choice?

She could risk walking with him no longer, for what would her answer be were he to grasp this opportunity to offer for her again? The gleam in his eye spoke of rekindled hopes and she now realised it might prove tricky to discourage him from renewing his offer too soon, before she was ready to accept or refuse him.

She needed more time: to observe him; to prepare herself; to come to a decision.

And neither could she deny her impatience to be rid of Lord Kilburn so she might investigate that sound.

'I must return, sir,' she said. 'Will it suit you if I visit the children tomorrow afternoon?'

'You will not walk further with me?'

Kilburn looked around. They were standing in the open and Cecily knew that, even if he had thought to try and woo her with a kiss, he would not do so where they might be seen. He had never behaved towards her in any manner other than that of a gentleman. And that in itself made her wonder anew at his motives for his original proposal. His conduct had never been that of a man consumed by tender feelings, let alone passion.

'Not today,' she replied.

He looked searchingly at her, then nodded. He raised his hat.

'Until tomorrow, my lady.'

He mounted his horse and set off down the track at a canter. Cecily waited until he was out of sight, then hurried towards the gatehouse. She could see Walker, the old retainer who manned the gates between dusk and dawn, working in his garden beyond the house. Out on the road she looked right and left, but there was no sign of anyone, human or animal. Her heart—uplifted in hope—sank down to its rightful position.

*Foolish, foolish, foolish.*

She trudged back through the imposing stone pillars that flanked the entrance to Leyton Grange.

*I should be grateful, for what does it say about me that I was so excited to think it might be Zach?*

She must put him from her thoughts and her heart.

Must.

His words whispered in her memory: 'Follow your heart, dove.'

*I cannot, for my heart will only lead me to ruin.*

But she halted nevertheless. Suppose…just *suppose* it was him? Where would he camp? She spun on her heel and ran back out on to the road, where she turned left, heading towards a stretch of common land on the opposite side of the road. Known locally as the Wedge, it was where the villagers grazed their livestock and she had ridden across on her previous visits.

She turned on to a faint path worn by sheep and deer through the coarse, tussocky grass and clumps of bramble and gorse. The land rose before her, obscuring her view of the whole area, and she found herself holding her breath and treading softly as she approached the top of the rise. On the far side, she knew, the land dropped away to a stream. What better place for a travelling Romany to set up camp? She stopped. The skin on the back of her neck prickled with awareness and she spun around.

Nothing.

Her heart raced and her mouth went dry as she slowly turned a circle, searching every clump of bushes, and the more distant trees, for any sign of life. There was no sound. Not a breath of wind. No birdsong.

Nothing.

She moistened her lips and swallowed, silently berating herself for such a ridiculous attack of nerves. She was country born and bred—she had never been a girl who clamoured to go to London every Season. She had been content at the Abbey, visiting London seldom, and had only gone there this year because it was time for Olivia's come out. The countryside was familiar territory for her, so why were all her instincts screaming at her to beware? She scanned the area again. Slowly. Meticulously.

Still nothing.

She glanced in the direction she had been heading. She had not even reached the top of the rising land, had no idea what lay beyond. But her curiosity had disappeared, to be replaced with a strong sense of self-preservation. Her mind made up, she started back towards the road. The aged gelding Aunt Drusilla used to ride was still at the Grange. She would ride him over here tomorrow, and have a good look round. She would feel safer on horseback.

As she neared the road she sensed rather than saw a movement off to her right. She whipped round to face whatever it was, her heart in her mouth. At first, she could see nothing. Then a bushy clump of hazel jerked, even though there was still no wind. She was not so very far from the gatehouse now. Walker would hear if she called for help. She could not walk away without knowing what was there. What was it that had roused her fears and sent her scurrying home like a frightened rabbit?

'Who is there?'

There was no answer, but the hazel shivered again as one branch was pulled out of sight and then sprang upright again. Her pulse steadied and a nervous laugh escaped her lips. It was some animal, browsing. A deer or some such. That was all.

'I thought you intended to return to the Grange?'

Her heart rocketed into her throat again as she whirled to face Kilburn, who was close behind her. She had not even heard him approach.

'Wh-where is your horse?'

He gestured behind him. 'Back there. Tied to a tree.' His brow darkened. 'What are you doing?'

Her cheeks scorched, but she raised her chin. 'Why are *you* spying upon me?'

His brow arched as he looked her up and down. His supercilious air only served to infuriate her more. 'I was curious as to why the sound of a donkey appeared to set you into a spin.'

'It did not.' She was confident she had hidden her surge of excitement from him.

His grey eyes narrowed. 'I beg to differ. You masked it well enough until you believed yourself alone, but the erratic behaviour that followed suggests otherwise. I watched as you paced up and down the driveway as though you could not decide what to do. And then you disappeared in the direction of the Wedge. So I followed.'

'Why did you not make yourself known? I sensed something—someone—watching me. You should have spoken.'

He grasped her arm, his fingers biting into her flesh, and steered her in the direction of the gatehouse. 'Allow me to escort you home.'

She had no choice. If Zach had made camp in the area, the last thing he would want was Kilburn paying him a visit. She could not doubt that whatever dislike Zach felt for Kilburn would be mutual. Besides—she glanced up at Kilburn's harsh profile—marriage was still her goal and it would not help her plan to openly defy him. His spying on her angered her, but she could not deny that, in his eyes, he was protecting her.

'You are right, in that I was somewhat agitated,' she said, swallowing her irritation at having to humble herself. 'I—I have much on my mind and I could not face returning to the Grange quite yet. I longed for some peace and quiet in which to order my thoughts.

'I knew I should not venture off the estate on my own, but then I told myself it would only be for a few minutes. Then I sensed I was being watched.'

They halted opposite the entrance to the Grange. The disapproving set of Kilburn's mouth softened.

'You were frightened,' he said. 'I hope that has taught you a lesson. There is a reason ladies should not wander around unaccompanied.'

She bit her lip and cast her eyes to the ground. He was—infuriatingly—right. She had an example in her own life—Leo's first wife had been murdered as she walked in the Abbey grounds. The culprit had never been caught…it was thought to be the work of a passing vagrant. But knowing Kilburn was right did not stop Cecily from wishing she could wipe that condescending smirk from his face.

'Wait there while I fetch my horse.'

Cecily did as he bid, but looked back along the road, picking out the bush that had been moving—the one that had frightened her so. And there he was. Sancho Panza. Even at this distance she could recognise his distinctive brownish-grey colour and those ridiculously long ears that flopped back and forth as he again tore a mouthful of leaves from a branch. She quickly looked away, focusing her attention on Kilburn. If Zach had come—if he had followed her—then he would still be here in the morning. She could be patient.

Cecily awoke at dawn. Her heart raced as she slipped from her bed and dressed in a simple butter-yellow muslin gown. It promised to be another glorious day, but she put on her spencer as it was bound to be chilly this early in the morning and tied the ribbons of the matching bonnet beneath her chin. She walked down the main staircase, head high. She would not stoop to creeping around like a criminal, even though she prayed she would meet no one. If she saw a servant, she would simply tell them she was going for a walk. She saw no one. Anna would not enter her bedchamber until summoned, so nobody would realise she had gone. Rather than stride openly down the carriageway and mindful that the entrance gates might still be closed this early in the day, she left through the side door that would give her access to the path she normally followed to Chilcot. Once she reached the woodland she would be hidden from prying eyes and could follow the right fork of the path, which would lead her out on to the road opposite that tract of common land.

Twenty minutes later, slightly breathless, she crossed the road. Again, all was quiet and still, including the bush that Sancho had been browsing. She had changed her mind about where Zach might have set up camp. The ground down near the stream was very open and more likely to be damp, plus the access for his horse and cart would be awkward. A flat clearing closer to the road was more likely, even if it was further from a source of fresh water. With that in mind, she walked on along the road, her eyes skimmed for any sign that a vehicle had been driven on to the Wedge.

It was not long before she saw the wheel tracks. She paused to tuck any stray hair back under her bonnet, even as her inner voice chided her for wasting time. She realised the truth. She was nervous. What reception might she expect? And what—oh, dear God—*what* did she think to achieve with such a scandalous visit?

The camp was silent, the fire unlit. Zach's skewbald cob, Titan, was tethered a short distance away, dozing: head down, lower lip drooping and one hind leg cocked. Cecily stood stock still and gazed around, disquiet threading through her. Then a low moan reached her ears. She hurried across the site to Zach's tent, built of bowed lengths of wood stuck into the ground, with a tarpaulin slung over and secured with rope and wooden pegs. As she pulled aside the flap, a snarling growl sounded from the dim interior.

'Myrtle, do not growl, it is me.'

The dog eased towards Cecily, her head outstretched, wariness in every line of her barrel body. Cecily petted her as her eyes grew accustomed to the gloom. She could make out a large hump on the ground and a sour smell of sickness pervaded the tent.

'Go away.' The voice was rough and laced with pain.

'I will not.' Cecily tied the flap so it remained open. 'You are not well.'

'I'll be all right if I'm left alone.'

She dropped to her knees and crawled into the tent. 'What is amiss?'

Zach propped himself up on one elbow, his breathing harsh and shallow. 'I mean it, Cecily. Go away. You must not see me like this.'

He flopped back down, as though his strength was spent by that one small effort. His body curled as his knees drew up and he moaned again. Then he hauled in a rasping breath.

'It will pass.'

Cecily shuffled closer and put her hand to his forehead. It was hot and damp.

'How can you know?'

Her mind darted around, seeking solutions. She must do something. She could not just leave him. She had nursed sickness many times, but always with the help of a houseful of servants and, where necessary, medical help from a physician.

'I know,' he said, the words sounding as though they were forced through gritted teeth. 'It is the result of something I have eaten.' She felt the power of his glittering gaze on her. 'Please. Go. There is nothing you can do. The sickness will run its course.'

'I shall make a fire.'

His lips parted—more of a grimace than a smile. 'Do you know how?'

'Have you a tinderbox, or do Romanies spurn such artificial help?'

He gasped a laugh. 'Of course we do not. We are pragmatic, if nothing else. It is in the cart, along with dry kindling.'

'And I shall fetch water,' Cecily declared. 'It is important to keep drinking.'

He sighed. Then groaned again as he curled again around his stomach. 'If you can find some rhubarb root, that will help.'

'I will ask the gardeners for some. But let us see if you can keep sips of water down for now.'

She began to back out of the tent, but he grabbed hold of her wrist.

'Will you not be missed?'

She smiled. 'No. Do not fret. It is early yet. I shall do what I can for now and then return later.'

Worry gnawed at her as she carried a pail down to the stream to collect water. What if it was more serious than he thought? He was in pain, his stomach clearly cramping. Should she send for a doctor? But would a doctor condescend to treat a Romany? She knew the prejudice many people had for Romanies. She might be delaying the inevitable, but she would wait and see how he was later today. Her main worry was how she could take care of him without anyone else knowing.

She came up with only one answer: she must feign illness herself—to account to Aunt Drusilla for her absence—and she must take Anna into her confidence. Anna had been her maid for fifteen years and Cecily did not doubt her loyalty. But would that loyalty allow her to aid her mistress in an endeavour of which she would strongly disapprove? But care for Zach she would, until he was well enough to forage for firewood and hunt for food, and fetch water for himself. And if that meant she must light the fire and learn to cook for him and care for his animals, then that is what she would do. It was what she *wanted* to do.

She carried the water back up to the camp, switching it from hand to hand as her fingers cramped and her arm ached.

*Heavens. How heavy it is.*

She thought of the scraps of housemaids in wealthy households up and down the country, who lugged water upstairs for their masters and mistresses to bathe in, and felt shame that she had never really given thought to the labour involved.

Back at camp, she dipped a tin mug into the pail and returned to the tent. Zach's eyes were closed and his breathing was soft and heavy. She placed the mug where it could not be knocked over and left quietly. Myrtle nudged at her hand and she looked down at the dog.

'Are you hungry, Myrtle?'

The terrier's ears pricked and she tipped her head to one side, panting. Cecily rummaged through the cart, but could find nothing edible. No doubt Zach had planned to catch a rabbit or some such, but the illness had overcome him. Cecily bent to stroke Myrtle.

'I shall bring you some meat from the Grange, Myrtle. I promise.'

She smiled as she pictured Zach's likely reaction to her talking to his dog. It had not taken long for her to succumb to that habit, even though the thought of it had been so strange before. The other animals, presumably, could forage for themselves, but poor Myrtle, on three legs, was unlikely to be an effective hunter. Titan—a true cob, with a heavy mane, long tail and thick feathers around his huge hooves—had woken up, shaking himself vigorously before walking to the limit of his tether and straining to reach the grass just beyond his reach. He had already nibbled bare a perfect circle around his stake.

Cecily went to him and bent to tug at his iron stake. It did not budge. She tried again. Still no movement—she huffed a sigh before kneeling down and taking hold of the stake. She alternately leant back, pulling, and then pushed forward, trying to loosen the stake by wiggling it. She had seen the men working at the Abbey remove posts in just that way. After several minutes, during which she feared she might have to give up, she had finally worked the hole big enough to pull the stake free.

*Now what?*

She walked to a fresh patch of grazing, Titan lumbering behind her. He began to graze and Cecily pushed the stake a few inches into the ground. She eyed the giant horse doubtfully. He was a powerful animal. One tug and he would dislodge his stake, and then where would Zach be? He would, rightly, blame Cecily. She cast around, and found a rock. She picked it up and bashed at the stake— missing it as often as she hit it. But the stake sank further into the ground and she felt the thrill of success.

After that, she tipped some water into another bucket she had found—she made a mental note to carry two half-full buckets from the stream next time—and put it within Titan's reach. Her gloves, she saw with a rueful look, were ruined. They were cotton gloves, perfect for summer, but never made to carry buckets and hammer stakes. She returned to the tent.

'Why are you still here?' The growl this time was from man, not dog.

'I have brought you water. Here. Let me help.' She crawled again into the tent and alongside Zach. He was on his back and she slipped her arm under his shoulders and helped him to half-sit. She reached for the cup and held it to his lips.

'Just a few sips,' she said.

After he lay back down, she felt his forehead again. Surely it was a little cooler? Less sweaty?

'How do you feel?'

'Not as ill as I did.'

'When did it start?'

'Yesterday, not long before I arrived. I managed to set up the tent, but nothing more.'

'I have to go now, but I promise I will be back later this morning. I'll bring food and rhubarb root and any other remedies I can find.'

'I do not want you to come. You risk too much and—what if I am wrong and it was not something I ate, but something catching? I cannot be the cause of you falling sick. I will manage. I have before.'

She stroked his hair back from his face. 'You do not need to manage. I want to come. I will take care—no one will know I am here, so there is no risk. And I have a strong constitution. I helped nurse my nephews and my niece through any number of childhood complaints and caught nary a one.'

If she thought he would be grateful, she was wrong. He scowled at her.

'I do not want you to see me like this, woman. Weak. Dirty. What must you think of me? Of the sort of a man I am?'

She tried to contain her laugh at his disgruntled tone, but she could not prevent her lips stretching in a smile as she shook her head at him.

'That is your male pride talking.' She'd seen that often enough in her brothers and her nephews—that hatred, almost a fear, of being seen when they were at their most vulnerable. 'And as to what kind of a man you are—you are a *normal* man. All this—' she gestured at him '—has proved to me is that you are more human than I feared.'

His brows twitched upward. 'Human?'

She felt a little foolish, but she said it anyway. 'When we met, I saw you as almost a magical being, with the special rapport you had with animals and with nature. You seemed to understand my deepest fears without even knowing me. And part of me feared you had bewitched me. But seeing you like this...'

She hesitated. She picked up his hand—so strong, so capable, and yet, at this moment, in need of help. Her help.

'You are human. And all humans, no matter how strong, need help from others from time to time. To admit that—to *allow* it—is not weakness. It shows courage.'

His throat rippled as he swallowed. She leant over him and stroked his hair back from his forehead again.

'Be happy I am here, Zach. You might as well accept my help, for I will not turn my back on you when you have need of me.'

## Chapter Eleven

Zach's head pounded like the devil and his mouth felt—and tasted—like a stagnant pond slowly fermenting in the heat of the sun. But the stomach cramps that had so debilitated him had eased—and he just thanked God that, through the preceding night, he had managed to drag himself out of his tent whenever necessary. The thought of Lady Perfect discovering him this morning in soiled bedding—he shoved that thought aside with a shudder. He could think of nothing worse.

His bender tent was hot and airless. It must be close to midday. He reached for his cup, only to find he had drunk all the water. And kept it down. That, surely, was a good sign. But knowing there was no water drove his thirst until, unable to bear it any longer, he pushed aside his blanket and sat up. His head spun, red-hot spikes torturing his eyes and brain. He screwed his eyes shut, but remained sitting by the force of his will. After what felt like several hours of agony, the pain dulled to a throb. Teeth clenched, he carefully manoeuvred himself on to hands and knees and, remembering to grab his cup, he crawled out of the tent.

The bright sun stabbed at his eyes and it took several attempts before he could blink away the tears and actu-

ally see anything. A pail stood outside the tent, a couple
of inches of water in the bottom of it. He dipped his cup
in and drank greedily. His mouth and throat were soothed
but, as the water hit his stomach, it roiled violently, cramping again. Zach rolled to one side and retched. He groaned,
spat and wiped his mouth with the back of his hand.

'Is this yours?'

He lifted his head, squinting as he peered in the direction of the voice, trying hard to focus. A man stood some
twenty yards away, holding Titan. He had a shotgun under
his arm and two dogs at his heels. Further back stood another man, holding two horses. Zach's first thought was
for Myrtle. But, surely, he would have heard if the dogs
had attacked her. She was likely hiding somewhere, waiting for them to leave.

'Well?'

Zach eyed the man again. Too well-dressed for a groom
or a gamekeeper, and there was something about him...
He blinked again, gradually recognising the man he had
not seen for more than a decade. Kilburn. He blanked out
the memories. Time to think about them later. After Kilburn left.

'He is mine.'

'I found him wandering on my land. I will not toler-
ate it. If he strays again, I will have him shot. And if you
know what's good for you, you'll move on. Your sort aren't
welcome here.'

Kilburn threw down Titan's rope and stalked off in the
direction of the road. Titan turned his head and gazed after
him, stoking fear in Zach's gut. If Titan had tasted better
grazing... Urgency gave him strength. He pushed himself
to his feet and staggered over to his horse. Once he had
hold of Titan's rope, he felt he could breathe again and he
sank to the ground. He must stake him but, for now, he

could do nothing but lie there, panting as though he had run a mile. He felt extraordinarily vulnerable, out in the open instead of inside his tent, but he could do no more.

A cold nose touched his cheek. He forced open one eye. Myrtle grinned at him, her tongue lolling. He could feel his senses swimming; he wrapped Titan's rope several times around his hand for safety, then closed his eyes.

'Oh, good heavens!'

Cecily dropped her basket and ran to Zach, who lay in a heap out in the open, with Myrtle tucked up against him and Titan dozing over him, his huge hooves mere inches from Zach's head.

'Zach? Zach! Can you hear me?'

Cecily crouched by his side, her hand on his forehead. He was burning up, his shirt drenched with sweat, his lips cracked and dry.

*Oh, dear God. What do I do? Think! Think!*

Myrtle had hopped to her feet and stood a little distance away, eyeing Cecily uncertainly. Titan had roused.

*I must get him away. What if he stands on Zach?*

'*Horses never willingly tread on fallen riders, same as they'll sometimes shy away from shadows or holes in the ground.*'

Vernon's words of advice from years ago echoed through her head, calming her. Alex had fallen from his pony and Cecily had panicked. She swallowed and forced herself to take deep breaths as she unwound Titan's rope from around Zach's hand and led him away. Then she looked around, feeling helpless again. Nothing in her upbringing had prepared her for this. Titan must have pulled his stake from the ground and Zach had, somehow, realised and come from his tent to capture him before he wandered away. She knew the horse was vital to Zach. It was her failure that had caused him to relapse.

'Milady! Here you are. I *warned* you not to come, but would you listen?'

Never in her life had she been so relieved to be on the receiving end of one of Anna's scolds.

'There is no time for that, Anna.' Cecily thrust the rope at her maid. 'Here. Tie him to a tree or something for now, then come and help me move Mr Gray back to his tent.'

Anna held up her hands in horror and backed away. 'I can't, milady. Please don't make me. I can't abide horses, great snorting things.'

Cecily had forgotten Anna's fear of horses. She led Titan to a nearby sapling and tied the rope around it and then, between them, she and Anna managed to half-drag, half-carry Zach over to the tent. Cecily stooped to peer inside and wrinkled her nose. It was unbearably hot in there and it smelt stale. She straightened and looked around the site. The sun was still high in the sky, but the spreading canopy of a nearby oak provided welcome shade.

'Come. Let us move him under the tree.'

After they had settled Zach, Anna dusted her hands off and gazed around the camp with a look of determination.

'Why did you follow me, Anna? I told you to stay at the Grange.'

'If you think I am going to sit in your bedchamber a-twiddling my thumbs while you run all manner of risks, you have another think coming, my lady. And it's a good thing I did come. How would *you* manage this on your own?'

Cecily bit her tongue against the barely concealed scorn in Anna's final comment, knowing the maid had a point and grateful for her presence. The task of caring for Zach would be much easier with two of them.

'What if you are missed?'

'I told Mr Parker you needed to sleep. That I would sit with you and no one was to be allowed to come to your room. How we shall stop your aunt from sending for her physician, mind, I do not know. I heard her carrying on when I sneaked out.'

Cecily grimaced. 'We can only take each day as it comes. Let us sort out here first. And, Anna—' she squeezed Anna's shoulder '—I *am* pleased to see you.'

Anna's cheeks went pink. 'Oh, go on with you, milady.'

'Can you light the fire, Anna? I need to move that basket out of the sun.'

Cecily fetched her discarded basket and placed it on the cart bed. She delved through the various packages and found what she was looking for.

'Myrtle,' she called. 'Here, girl.'

Myrtle hopped over to Cecily, her eyes hopeful. Cecily tossed her the large bone Anna had spirited from the kitchen and watched as the dog settled down to gnaw at it. Then she went to the tent and dragged out all of Zach's bedding, shook it out and draped it over nearby bushes to air. The fire was lit and flaming well. Anna picked up a pot and looked around.

'Where did you get the water, milady?'

'A stream. Over there.' Cecily pointed. 'I shall go.'

'No, you will not. That's not a fitting task for a lady. Just watch the fire. I shall fetch the water.'

After she had gone, Cecily went to Zach. His fiery colour had calmed and his breathing was easier. She lifted his hand and placed it on her lap, gazing down as she idly caressed his fingers.

'Lady Perfect.' A hoarse whisper.

She started. 'Oh! I thought you were asleep.'

'Thirsty.'

'Anna has gone to fetch water.'

'Anna?'

'My maid.'

'She is here?' He struggled, trying to sit. 'Dangerous.'

'Hush.' She pressed him gently back to the ground. 'All will be well. She followed me, but she will help us. No one will find out.'

He closed his eyes, his forehead deeply furrowed. Then he opened them, and captured her gaze. 'Kilburn. He was here.'

Horror clawed at her. *Kilburn? Here?*

'But...why? How? Did he recognise you?'

He opened his mouth, but no sound emerged. He shook his head, frustration in his dark eyes.

'Hush. Wait until Anna returns. It will be easier when you've had a drink.'

As soon as Anna returned, Cecily helped Zach to sip some water. He sighed, then coughed. 'Better.'

'Good. I have brought rhubarb root—can you tell us how to prepare the remedy?'

'Boil a small piece in water for five minutes, then leave it to cool.'

Anna set about boiling a can of water while Cecily bathed Zach's face.

'Tell me about Kilburn. What did he say?'

'He brought Titan back. He'd strayed on to Kilburn's land.'

'Oh.' That did not sound so ominous. 'I'm sorry. That was my fault. I moved his stake so he could graze, but it was harder than I anticipated to hammer it back into the ground.'

Humour crinkled the skin around his eyes. 'Lady Perfect hammering? I'd like to have seen that.'

'Well, I did not do a very good job of it, if Titan escaped that easily.'

'No.' Worry replaced the humour. 'He must not stray again.'

Cecily patted his hand. 'I know how important he is to you. Between us I am sure Anna and I can stake him securely.'

He looked away. 'I can't bear this,' he muttered. 'Lying here helplessly while you risk everything.'

'*Everything?* That is an exaggeration, surely?'

He clutched her hand. 'You must not allow Kilburn to see you here.'

'Did his lordship recognise you?'

Zach snorted. 'Of course he did not. He looked at me, he saw a gipsy and he looked no further.' He shook his head, his brow furrowed. 'And that is how it must stay,' he added in a mutter.

'I am sure there is no danger of him recognising you,' she said, soothingly. 'And you must not trouble yourself about me, for even if Lord Kilburn should find out I am here, he can hardly—'

'No!' His grip tightened, almost painfully, as he half-rose. 'Promise me. Promise—' He collapsed back, beads of sweat dotting his forehead and upper lip. 'Your maid— now she knows about me, she can come.' Pain knit his brows. 'I want you to—go. Stay away.'

It might be the most sensible solution, but she would not do that. She wanted to be here, to care for him and to make sure he got well and strong again. There was little to be gained in arguing the point, however. It would merely agitate him to no purpose.

She said nothing, but bathed his face again.


'Milady! Milady!' A hand shook Cecily's shoulder. She tried to bat it away…she'd been having a wonderful dream and she was loath to be disturbed. *Milady!*

'Wha—? What is it?'

She winced. She'd been sitting on the ground, leaning back against something hard, and her muscles grumbled as she straightened and prised open her eyes. Anna's round face was close to hers, her eyes huge.

*Zach!*

Cecily jerked fully awake. 'Anna? What is it?'

She looked around. Zach was asleep, by her side, breathing peacefully. She placed one hand on his forehead. It was cool. Hopefully he was on the mend.

'That horse, milady. Galumphing great thing. It's gone.'

Titan! Cecily scrambled to her feet and grabbed Anna by the shoulders. 'Did you see him go?'

The maid nodded, her eyes tearful. 'I tried to stop him, I swear I did. But he just kept going.' She held out her hands, red with rope burn, and the tears spilled. 'He was too strong, milady.'

'Which way, Anna?'

The maid pointed towards the road. Cecily did not hesitate, but ran after the cob, cursing herself for not properly attending to him earlier. She'd intended to tie him somewhere where he could graze, and to give him water, but she'd been so focused on caring for Zach she'd forgotten all about poor Titan. Both Myrtle and Sancho roamed free, but Titan needed proper care and she'd failed him. She reached the road and saw Titan immediately—grazing happily on land belonging to Chilcot Manor. She walked towards him. At the last minute, just as she was about to pick up his rope, he walked on. Once out of her reach, his head went down and he tore again at the grass.

After several futile attempts to catch the infuriating animal, Cecily stopped and pondered her dilemma. The sun blazed out of the midsummer sky and she untied her bonnet ribbons—grimacing at the clamminess beneath her chin where the bow had been tied—and used her chip-straw hat as a makeshift fan. Every failed attempt had driven Titan further from the road and closer to Chilcot Manor. Ergo, she must try to catch him from the other side. She plopped her hat back on her head, leaving the ribbons dangling, and circled wide until she was between Titan and the house. He lifted his huge head and eyed her as she once again walked towards him. With a disdainful flick of his head, he turned and lumbered back towards the road, but only far enough that she could not grasp the rope. Patiently, she repeated the exercise until, finally, he was at the roadside. At least they would soon be back at the camp and, between them, surely she and Anna—

An unladylike curse escaped her lips as Titan threw up his head, swished his tail and trotted in a wide circle around her. On the heels of that spurt of anger came tears of pure frustration. Why was he so difficult to catch? Other horses weren't as awkward as this.

*How would you know? You've always had grooms to carry out such tasks.*

She felt like screaming, but she bit it back.

Then the braying began. She'd not seen Sancho since she'd arrived at the camp—she'd barely spared him a thought, knowing Zach allowed him to roam free. She gazed in the direction of his haunting cries as they rose from the vicinity of the camp and echoed through the still summer air like a harbinger of doom. He was nowhere to be seen. She was torn. Should she return to the camp to make sure everything was all right, or should she continue the seemingly futile task of catching Titan? She looked back at the escapee. The massive cob stood to attention, his head high, ears pricked. Then he trotted up the field towards her, the ground vibrating beneath his feet. He did not stop, but went straight past her, over the road, and a disbelieving laugh burst from her as he disappeared in the direction of the camp.

Stunned, she followed.

Zach was now propped in a sitting position under the tree. Anna tended the campfire and Sancho and Titan were touching noses as they greeted one another. Angry, feeling an utter fool, Cecily marched over to the two animals and picked up Titan's rope.

'He would not allow me to catch him,' she announced.

'That is good. I have trained him well.'

Zach grinned, sending Cecily's indignation soaring anew. He looked much improved from earlier, but that was no excuse for him to mock her.

'That appears to me to be a remarkably silly trick to teach an animal.'

'Not silly at all. That way he cannot be stolen.'

'But Lord Kilburn caught him, you said.'

'He was on horseback and there were two of them. Titan isn't built for speed.'

'No. He's built for mischief.'

Zach's grin widened.

Cecily stuck her nose in the air. 'I have caught him now, at least.'

'He only allowed you to do so because he is in camp.'

*'Hmmph.'*

She swept her hat from her head and again fanned her face, conscious of her sweat-damp skin. No doubt she was brick red, too. What a sight she must look. She jammed her hat back on her head, pulling the brim down over her forehead to shield her face from the ferocious glare of the sun. Before worrying about her appearance, she must deal with Titan.

'I shall have to tie him more securely. I do not know how he got free this time.' She looked across at the sapling she had tied him to. 'Oh.' The slender young tree had been near uprooted and half the leaves stripped off.

A muffled snort reached her ears. A glance at Zach revealed merry eyes above a mouth that quivered. Dratted man. Laughing at her. She'd done her best. She glared at him, but then started forward as he pushed himself to his feet.

'No, Zach!' He swayed precariously as soon as he was upright, propping his other hand against the tree trunk as Cecily grasped his arm. 'You must not! You will—'

'Yes. I must.' The words were gritted out as he removed the lead rope from her hand. 'I have to make sure he is secure.' He paused, grimacing, then added, 'Did anyone see him?'

'Please. Sit down.' She tugged at his arm, but he snatched it away. 'Zach, please. You are ill. I will make sure he is tied properly this time, I promise.'

A low growl vibrated in his throat. 'Like you did last time, Lady Perfect?'

'I did my best.' There was no need for him to snap at her. 'It is not my fault your horse is such a brute. Look what he did to that poor tree.'

She glared at Zach, then hesitated, feeling a frown gather on her forehead as she recognised the worry in his dark eyes. She touched his hand. 'What is it?'

'You did not answer me. Did anyone see Titan?'

'I do not believe so. Why do you ask?'

'I cannot risk losing him.'

'I know, but I am sure he would not stray too far. You will not lose him.' She tried a smile, hoping to lighten the mood. 'Sancho can always summon him home.'

He huffed a bitter laugh. 'It is not the straying that worries me. Landowners have a habit of objecting to Romany animals grazing on their land.'

'But…Lord Kilburn would not deprive you of your horse. He might be angry, but—'

'Nevertheless, *I* shall stake him this time.'

Zach pushed away from the tree and crossed the camp, supporting himself by clutching a handful of Titan's mane. Cecily watched him pause by the wagon and pick up a stake and a mallet, fighting the impulse to rush to his side and to support his slow steps, instinctively knowing he would spurn any further offer of help.

'He is proud, that one,' Anna said from her seat by the fire, where she was tending a pot of chicken broth, prepared by the cook at the Grange to tempt Cecily's fictitious loss of appetite.

Cecily watched as Zach—his grimace showing the effort it cost him—slowly hammered the stake into the ground. 'He is.' She glanced up at the sky. It must be late afternoon. 'We should return to the Grange, Anna. Mr Gray appears much improved and we must not linger.'

Anna got to her feet. 'I'll fetch more water before we go, milady. That should see them through the night.' She cast a scathing look at Titan. 'That monster sinks half a bucket in one mouthful.'

Cecily waited until Zach had finished securing the horse. His forehead was beaded with sweat, his face grey with exhaustion and it was a sign of how weak he felt that he allowed her to support him back to the shade of the tree without protest.

'You have not yet taken your rhubarb-root remedy,' she scolded.

A smile flickered at the corners of his mouth. 'Nor will I, not while you are here to see the effect it will have.'

'Oh! I… Yes, of course. It is a purgative, then?' She felt her cheeks heat. 'Yes. I see.'

He closed his eyes then and she sat next to him and

stroked his hand until Anna returned with the water, placing one bucket within Titan's reach.

'Zach, we must go now.'

He opened his eyes.

'Is there anything else we can do?'

'No.' He tipped his head back against the trunk and sighed. 'Thank you, Lady Perfect.' His ebony eyes roamed her face and she had to fight the instinct to tidy her hair. 'I mean it… I don't know what I would have done without you.' He closed his fingers around her hand and squeezed gently.

'Should I come back later to check on you?'

'No. You have risked enough.'

'Promise me you will take that remedy.'

'I promise. The sickness has passed so I should keep it down.'

'We shall return tomorrow to see how you fare.'

She could not resist pressing her lips to his forehead before regaining her feet.

Anna argued with her all the way back to the Grange, but Cecily would not give way. She would not be easy until she was certain Zach was fully recovered and, no matter the risk, she would return to the camp in the morning.

## Chapter Twelve

The subterfuge continued and the following morning, once breakfast was cleared and Aunt Drusilla and Miss Fussell were settled in the morning room, Cecily and Anna managed to slip unnoticed down the main stairs and out through the side door, across the lawns and into the shelter of the nearby belt of trees. Anna carried a basket of provisions for Zach, even though she made no secret of her disapproval of all these *shenanigans*, as she put it. Cecily only listened with half an ear, knowing that, beneath her bluster, Anna was desperately worried about this unusual behaviour in her mistress. As was Cecily, if the truth be known. Common sense—not to mention her upbringing and the knowledge of the correct conduct expected of a lady—warned her she should allow Anna to visit Zach and report back. But she could not. She had to see him. She needed that reassurance.

The fire was burning under a pan of water when they arrived at the camp and Zach was seated nearby—in the shade, she was pleased to see. His smile, when he saw her, squeezed her chest until she felt she could not breathe. How had he become so very important to her in such a short time?

'Good morning, Zach.' She had given up calling him Mr Gray in Anna's presence. Let her maid make of *that* what she pleased. 'How do you feel today?'

'Much better. Thank you.'

She put her hand to his forehead—no heat, no fever. She could breathe again.

'What can we do to help?'

'Nothing. I can manage.' Stubbornness swirled in his dark eyes.

Cecily canted her head and raised her brows. She was rewarded by a reluctant smile.

'I have not recovered my full strength yet, so the food you bring is welcome. Thank you.'

Cecily left him and inspected the camp. There was little water left and she saw that Titan was still tethered in the same spot as yesterday. He and Sancho dozed nose to tail in the sunshine. Myrtle—panting hopefully—sat at Anna's feet as she unloaded her basket on the cart bed.

'Anna will fetch more water directly and I shall help you move Titan to a fresh patch of grass.'

'No.' Zach pushed himself to his feet. 'I managed him yesterday. I shall do so today.'

He reached for Cecily's right hand and, before she realised his intention, he stripped off her glove and examined her palm. Her stomach turned a slow somersault as his thumb stroked along the base of her fingers, where two blisters had developed.

'I thought as much.' His voice was gravelly. 'You should not have—'

She snatched her hand from his and placed her fingertips to his lips, silencing him. 'Should not have what? Helped you when you were in need? Do not say that to me, Zach. I *wanted* to help and, if ever you have need in the future, I will help you again. Please remember that.'

'Obstinate woman.' The smile in his eyes belied his words. 'Now, I must move Titan. I was about to do so when you arrived.' She started to follow him, to help, but he stopped her. 'No. I can do it.' His lips quirked into a quick smile. 'A bit slower than normal, but I can do it.'

'Very well.' Instead, she went to the fire and fed more wood on to it. She would make coffee. They had brought some ground beans with them.

'Cecily?' She jumped, startled by the angry exclamation. 'What the d—! What are you doing here? I understood you to be indisposed.'

Her heart rocketed, then thumped tangibly in her chest as she identified that voice. She hauled in a deep breath, straightened, smoothed her palms down her skirts, rolled back her shoulders and turned to face Lord Kilburn. He bowed, even though his expression was thunderous and, biting back a sudden urge to giggle, Cecily bobbed a curtsy in reply. How ludicrous to observe the niceties like this, especially when the man looked about to rip up at her. She squared her shoulders.

'Good morning, my lord. I apologise. You have caught me out in my white lie.'

'What are you doing here, in a *gipsy* camp?'

His lip curled in a sneer and Cecily's fingers clenched involuntarily into a fist even as she cautioned herself to take care. Zach, for whatever reason, did not wish to be recognised and it did not bear thinking about the consequences should Kilburn suspect her interest in Zach was anything other than purely altruistic.

'Mr Gray has been very ill.' She indicated Zach, who had just pushed Titan's stake into the ground and was watching with narrowed eyes. She was relieved to see that Sancho had wandered off and was nowhere to be seen—at least seeing him wouldn't remind Kilburn of her agitation the other day at the sound of a donkey. 'My maid and I have come to assist.'

'Ill?' Kilburn was across the campsite in three paces. He grasped Cecily's arm, his fingers biting into her soft flesh. 'And what concern is that of yours? He is a dirty, common gipsy—you should have nothing to do with him.'

Cecily tried to free her arm, but he tightened his grip.

'My lord! Unhand me this instant.'

Rage lent him strength. Zach strode over to where Kilburn held the struggling Cecily and wrenched the other man's fingers open. The Earl was no match for him, even in his weakened state. He thrust his face into Kilburn's, even as a corner of his mind screamed caution.

'You heard the lady,' he snarled. 'Take your hands off her.'

Kilburn's face mottled with rage. 'I'll have you horse-whipped, you damned scoundrel,' he spat. 'You dare to touch me? Touch a *lady*?'

He barged Zach aside with his shoulder. Taken by surprise, Zach staggered back several paces, but managed to stay on his feet. He hauled in a deep breath, and another, filling his lungs with fresh air, willing his temper under control and his mind to stay sharp.

'Come, Cecily.'

Kilburn placed his hand at the small of Cecily's back, turning her, and then it slid lower, to rest on her bottom, as he steered her out of the camp. Black rage swirled through Zach at the sight of the man daring to touch her with such an intimate gesture, but he stayed back in response to Cecily's silently mouthed *No* as she shot a quick glance over her shoulder. Remaining a bystander went against every instinct he possessed, but he accepted now was not the time for a confrontation. For Cecily's sake, he could not risk Kilburn believing there was anything more than compassion to account for her presence here.

'I shall escort you home to the Grange and you may explain to me and to your aunt precisely *what* you think you are about—'

Cecily slammed to a halt. She sidestepped, away from Kilburn's hand, and drew herself up to her full height. Zach could not tear his eyes from her. She was magnificent. He might have known she would not need his help.

'How *dare* you?' Her tone was icy, her eyes flashed and two angry spots of colour highlighted her cheeks. She was every inch the Duke's daughter, as haughty as though she stood in the middle of a society ballroom rather than in a Romany camp. 'I have no obligation to explain myself to you or, indeed, to my aunt and you have no right to assume authority over me, sir.'

She gestured to Anna, standing open-mouthed by the cart. 'Please go and fetch some more water for Mr Gray, Anna. Another two buckets should be sufficient to see him through until this afternoon.'

Anna, reluctance in every line of her body, left the camp. Cecily turned her back on a clearly shocked Kilburn and returned to Zach, smiling.

'Now, Mr Gray, you must not overtax your strength.' She urged him under the shade of the oak. 'Please oblige me by sitting down and staying out of the sun.' Then she added a hastily whispered, 'Please do not intervene and risk recognition. I can manage him.'

Out of the corner of his eye, Zach saw Kilburn approach.

'Take care,' he muttered, then continued at normal volume, 'Thank you, my lady. I promise I will rest soon, but first I must tether my horse securely.'

'And that is why I have come,' Kilburn growled. 'That

animal was seen on my land again yesterday, despite my warning to you. My men now have orders to shoot him on sight.'

Cecily rounded on him. 'My lord, such unpleasantness is uncalled for.'

His eyes narrowed. 'Again, my lady,' he said in a soft voice, 'what is this heathen to you? Why are you here? This is conduct unbefitting a lady. I am surprised at you.'

Zach stiffened, but by the slightest movement of her hand, Cecily stayed him.

'Mr Gray happens to be a friend of my brother's. How could I leave him to struggle alone when he was so ill?'

'Your brother?' Scorn sharpened his tone. 'And which brother might that be? The Duke? You expect me to believe he would countenance his sister associating with a vagabond?'

'As it happens, Mr Gray is a friend of my other brother.'

'I might have—'

*'Although—'* and it was a miracle her icy tone did not freeze Kilburn solid as she faced him down '—you should be aware that it was his *Grace* who introduced us, at Vernon's recent wedding.'

Kilburn appeared somewhat nonplussed by that titbit of information and admiration for Cecily filled Zach as she proceeded to take full advantage.

'It was *my* fault the horse broke free. And perhaps, my Lord Kilburn, as you are so concerned about him, you might finish hammering in that stake?' She indicated Titan, standing docilely where Zach had pushed his stake into the ground. 'Then if he strays you can blame no one but yourself.'

Kilburn scowled and Zach held his breath, praying the other man wouldn't question why Zach had turned up here, in the same place as Cecily, so soon after having met her at Vernon's wedding.

'Very well,' Kilburn said. 'But, once he is secure, I shall escort you to back to the Grange. You must see it is entirely inappropriate for you to be here with a gipsy, whether or not he is your brother's friend.'

He stalked across camp to Titan and picked up the discarded mallet.

'He's right, my lady.' Zach was eager now for the man to leave his camp, for how long would it be before something triggered Kilburn's memory and he recognised Zach as the youth he had known? 'With the water Anna brings, I can manage without further help. Thank you. For everything.'

'Very well.' Cecily's green eyes clung to his. 'We will bring further provisions tomorrow, however, if only for the reassurance you have fully recovered.' She smiled. 'Would you tell Anna to follow us to the Grange when she returns with the water, please?'

Her lashes swept down, veiling the raw longing in her gaze. That glimpse of her true feelings fired his blood and he could not stop imagining the two of them. Together. He yearned to kiss the satin-soft skin of her neck—to feel her pulse leap under his tongue—to kiss her soft, succulent lips until she throbbed with desire. Any more than that—he swallowed a self-deprecating laugh. He was not a man to indulge in fantasies—and yet here he was, fantasising about making love to Cecily—Lady Perfect, a duke's sister—and teasing out the passion he knew simmered deep inside her and showing her the pleasure life had to offer. But a fantasy it was. An impossible fantasy.

Or...was it?

He stared at Kilburn's hawkish profile and whip-lean frame as he wielded the mallet. He had told himself he had come to Oxfordshire to stop Cecily throwing herself away on such a cold, heartless bastard—after all, who knew better than he what Kilburn was capable of, beneath the civilised veneer he presented to his peers? Deep down, though, he knew he had hoped to find a way for them to be together.

If he followed his heart, he would fight for her, even though he had so little to offer. He was unlikely to ever be accepted in society with his mixed blood—unless by some miracle her brother championed their cause—but might *Cecily* accept him?

Kilburn had finished. He flung the mallet on the ground, stalked back across camp to Cecily and, without so much as a glance at Zach, he took her by the elbow and propelled her towards the road, collecting his horse on the way. Cecily submitted to him, but Zach could read her outrage in every line of her body. He settled down in the shade, leant back against the trunk of the oak and brooded. Was what he longed for even feasible? A woman—a lady—like Cecily could never embrace this life he had chosen. But the alternative was unappealing. To him. He had chosen his Romany heritage above that of his father. It was simple. And honest.

*And tough*, a voice whispered in his head. Too tough for a woman raised in a duke's household.

The clank of a bucket caught his attention and he looked up as Anna returned with the water. She put down the buckets and walked over to stand over Zach, her hands planted on her hips.

'Lady Cecily has gone with Lord Kilburn,' Zach said. 'She said for you to follow them back to the Grange.'

'What do you think you are about? Why have you followed my mistress here? She doesn't need your sort of trouble, believe you me.'

'Why do you believe I want to cause trouble for your mistress?'

She shot him a look brimming with scorn. 'You don't fool me. *Neither* of you fool me. And, believe me, if you cause problems between my lady and his lordship, you'll have *me* to deal with.'

He pushed himself to his feet. His head still felt woozy and his lids had begun to droop, but he could not have her hovering over him like some kind of avenging angel.

'What do you know about Lord Kilburn, Anna?'

Anna's eyes widened. 'Well—nothing.' Then she rallied. 'But he is an earl. A gentleman. Not a low-born gipsy like some.'

'Kilburn will not make your lady happy, Anna.' Weariness wrapped around him, but he needed to warn the maid. 'He may have been born a nobleman, but he is no gentleman.'

He sat, abruptly, and closed his eyes in a bid to stop his head spinning. When he opened them again, she was gone.

Cecily did not trust herself to speak. Fury pumped her blood through her veins, but caution prompted her to keep it hidden. She walked silently beside Kilburn—at least he had relinquished his hold upon her arm once they reached the road—and waited to see what he might say. Cecily indicated they should return along the path through the wood and Kilburn raised no objection. He did not speak until the road behind them was lost to sight.

'Your compassion does you credit, Cecily. But I do not understand why you did not simply send your maid to aid the gipsy. You had no need to attend in person.'

'Mr Gray is a *Romany*. And Anna was with me the entire time. There was no impropriety and no danger.'

He glanced sideways at her and a frown stitched the skin between his brows. 'That is not what I asked.'

'I—well, the truth is—' She caught her lip between her teeth. She could in fact think of no valid reason, but her thinking time had made her conscious of the very real danger that Kilburn might wonder at the coincidence of Zach turning up here, in Oxfordshire. Glimpsed through the trees, the Grange loomed larger with every step.

*Oh, heavens. Whatever will Aunt Drusilla say?*

But that thought spawned an idea.

'The truth is—and I am ashamed to admit it—' She halted, facing Kilburn. 'The truth is that my aunt is a demanding tyrant and I grabbed the opportunity to escape her for a few hours. I feigned illness so she would not know I had gone out. There. *That* is the shameful truth.'

He searched her expression and she maintained her guileless expression until his frown cleared, although there was still doubt in his eyes. Nevertheless, her pent-up breath released and she felt her shoulders relax.

'As usual, Lady Cecily, you show excellent judgement. I have known your aunt my entire life and any person who must endure her company for longer than half an hour has my sympathy.'

'Like poor Miss Fussell?'

In one accord, they began walking again.

He shrugged. 'At least she has a roof over her head and she is no doubt grateful for it.'

'But *she* cannot escape the constant demands. Even when poorly, she dragged herself from her bed to satisfy my aunt's every whim.' She couldn't resist the opportunity to goad him, 'That is why she looks so frail—although you did not seem to notice it when you called.'

She sensed his quick glance at her.

'Oh, but I did notice it,' he said, after the briefest of pauses.

'But you specifically commented on how well she looked.'

'I could hardly say I thought she looked ill. That would be unkind, would it not?'

Cecily did not quite believe him. She suspected a mere companion would be beneath his notice, but did that make him a bad man or was it the typical reaction to be expected of a gentleman in his position? Instead of seeking his faults, mayhap she should try to appreciate his good points if she wished to keep her plan of matrimony alive. She cast her mind back over the events of today. Kilburn had been concerned for her, behaving as any gentleman might in the circumstances—removing her from an inappropriate situation and delivering her back to her aunt's house. But the *manner* in which he had done it—no matter the circumstances, there was no excuse for him to manhandle her. And as for his threat to shoot Titan… She glanced at him. Was it an idle threat, made to scare Zach into keeping his animals from straying? Or, more disturbingly, did he mean it?

She had come to Leyton Grange with the hope of encouraging a further offer from Kilburn, but she was more confused than ever. Could she trust this man?

She did not allow herself to think of Zach. He was an impossible dream.

'What will you say to your aunt, when you go inside?'

'I still hope I might return to my bedchamber unseen, unless you intend to accompany me inside and expose my deception?'

Kilburn stopped walking again and took her hand, pulling her around to face him. 'I am unhappy you have risked your reputation so thoughtlessly, but I shall not tell your aunt—or anyone else—upon one condition.'

She resisted the urge to tug her hand free. 'Which is?'

'I heard you tell that gipsy…*Romany*,' he amended in response to her frown, 'that you would bring him more food in the morning. I want your promise that neither you nor your maid will do so. You have done enough.'

'But Mr Gray is still not recovered enough to hunt for food. He needs to eat to regain his strength.'

'Your finer feelings do you credit, my dear, but you worry needlessly. His sort do not suffer in the same way as people of our breeding. However, if it will set your mind at ease, *I* shall undertake to take him supplies in the morning. And I shall take the opportunity to send him on his way. We do not want his sort loitering around here.'

What could she say? She could hardly refuse, even though his arrogance infuriated her all over again. How dare he dictate to her like this? Except—if she was honest she could not deny that, again, in his eyes, he was protecting her from herself, as her brothers had always done. At least he had offered to take provisions to Zach.

'I promise.' Speaking the words brought home the enormity of their meaning. She would never see Zach again.

A faint smile curved Kilburn's mouth. His grey eyes were confident as he tipped her chin with his fingers. Nerves knotted her stomach, setting her pulse racing, but not in a good way. Not in the glorious surge of anticipation that had seized her in the seconds before Zach had kissed her. Now, the nerviness and the quickened pulse were urging her to take flight. She swallowed, and relaxed her tight jaw as his head lowered to hers. Cool dry lips settled on her mouth and she did not fight it, but endured, praying he would not prolong the kiss. She had chosen to walk home this way so she would not be spied from the windows of the Grange. She had overlooked the possibility that he might take advantage of their invisibility.

He gathered her to him as his tongue probed her lips and entered her mouth. And still she allowed it, forcing herself to remain compliant. If he were to be her husband she must become accustomed to him kissing her. And more. She directed her thoughts elsewhere, wondering what her family were doing at this moment.

Finally he was finished. He raised his head and smiled with smug satisfaction.

'Now, I shall allow you to slip discreetly back into the house,' he said. 'And I shall, with your permission, call upon you this afternoon and escort you to the Manor to become reacquainted with the children.'

'Yes. Thank you.'

He stepped back and bowed his head. 'Until later, then, my dear.'

She watched him ride away, a dismal void inside her. Mayhap a nunnery would be the better solution to her quandary after all? Intimacy with Kilburn held nothing of the appeal and excitement that Zach's kiss had aroused. Once more, she determinedly switched her thoughts away from Zach. That way lurked madness indeed.

## *Chapter Thirteen*

He hadn't dared to hope she would come, but he heard the whisper of her footfall through the grass even before the prick of Myrtle's ears warned him of someone's approach. The stir of the dog's tail confirmed it was friend, not foe. He rose to his feet and stared into the darkness beyond the campfire, knowing he would be fully visible to her. His energy had slowly returned throughout the day until he felt back to normal. So much so that he had bathed in the stream earlier that evening.

'You knew it was me?' Her voice was hushed, like the night, as she stepped into the circle of light cast by the flames. Her pale dress shimmered in the firelight. Her gaze locked on to his naked chest and the heat in her eyes—flecks of pure emerald sparking in their mossy depths—sent desire spiralling through him. Pure animal lust pooled hot and heavy in his loins.

'I hoped. And Myrtle knew.'

She hesitated then and he could see her uncertainty. He went to her and halted before her, willing his hands to remain at his sides. There were things to say before he touched her. Because once he touched her...

Her gaze roved his face. 'You are better?'

'I am.' He sucked in a breath. 'Why have you come?'

A fleeting frown flickered. 'Should I go?'

'No. That is not what I meant.'

'I came to give you warning.' She paused.

'About?'

'I cannot come to you tomorrow and neither will Anna. Lord Kilburn intends to bring you provisions and he will order you to leave.'

Anger twisted his gut. He was a free man. He took orders from no one and he needed no help. Especially not from a bastard like Kilburn. He masked his rage and instead he simply shrugged.

'This is not his land.'

She frowned fully now. 'You and I both know that will not stop him evicting you. I have brought you more food. You should leave before Kilburn comes. It is not worth the risk that he will remember you from…from…before.'

He heard the question in her voice, but he ignored it. She wanted to know. He was not ready to tell, not ready for his secrets and his shame to be exposed.

'And if I choose to stay?'

She placed her hand on his chest and his breath caught at her touch. 'I do not want you to get hurt.'

Zach stared over her head into the darkness, remembering. She could have no concept of how much he had already been hurt. He felt again the searing agony as the red-hot iron pressed against his buttock; smelled again the stench of burning flesh. His mother's screams shrieked through his memory. His half-brother, Thetford, and his men, holding him down. And Thetford's close friend, Kilburn—who had helped Thetford make Zach's life a misery throughout his boyhood—wielding the branding iron with relish, treating a boy no better than the beasts in the field, branding him with the letter *G*, laughing at his tears and his pain.

No wonder his mother had insisted they leave. No wonder she had sought sanctuary with her own family. No wonder he had chosen to continue with this life rather than return.

Seeing Kilburn again had brought it all back.

Bitter rage swirled deep inside, but he knew he must let it go. What was done was done. Revenge would change nothing.

Sheer male pride prevented him from telling her the truth. He could not reveal his shame…his weakness… his failure…to his perfect lady. She had already seen him weak and sick. He could not bear for her to see him as a victim as well.

'I promised his lordship I would not come here tomorrow. I made no promise about tonight. I needed to be sure you are well. I wanted to say goodbye.' She smiled. 'Again.'

He touched her now, cupping her chin, capturing her gaze.

'Is that all, my dove?'

He registered the movement of her pale throat as she swallowed. 'No.'

She stepped closer and the warmth radiating from her skin caressed him as her scent filled him. She was sweet apple blossom, warm sunshine, desire and need.

'He kissed me.'

Three simple words, but their impact was akin to a knife in his heart. 'Then why are you here?'

She ignored his question. 'He will call at the Grange tomorrow and I suspect he will make his offer.'

'And what will your answer be?'

'I am still undecided.' She turned from him and he saw her shoulders tremble. 'He took me to meet his children today.'

He waited, sensing her inner struggle.

'Thomas—Kilburn's son—he is confident. Strong. But the two little girls—Kilburn has no patience with their timidity. They need a mother.'

'But that is no reason to wed a man, especially not a man like Kilburn. What about you and your needs? What about what *you* want?'

He reached out and caressed her shoulders. She leaned back into him, for a fleeting moment, before spinning to face him again.

'It is not just because of the children. I cannot end up like my aunt's companion. I simply cannot.'

'But *you* will not be poor. You will be in your brother's home.'

He cupped her shoulders again, but she shook him away and paced to the far side of the fire.

'I know that is the case now. But in thirty years' time? Forty? The person I am now will be lost in the past—forgotten in the bustle of family life. To future generations I will simply be a distant great-aunt who is fortunate enough to live in their home. And I shall feel myself obliged to prove my usefulness. And, before you suggest it, I cannot bear the thought of living alone, with maybe a companion of my own. I cannot bear to think of my life and my identity—my *purpose*—dwindling and fading into nothing, living in the hope that every knock on the door heralds a visitor.' Her fierce gaze pierced him. 'I want—I *deserve*—more than that.'

He went to her. 'You deserve *everything*, my perfect lady.' A lump swelled in his throat as emotion threatened to overwhelm him. 'If only I were the man able to give it to you.'

*If only there was a way...*

Her eyes, glinting green in the light of the flames, softened. 'In another life, mayhap,' she whispered and rose on her toes, and pressed her lips to his.

For an instant, he succumbed. Then he gripped her shoulders and set her back, away from him.

'Did you enjoy his kiss?' The words tore out of him, angry and rough. But he didn't care. Jealousy was a novel emotion for him. He could not bear the thought of any man touching her. Having the right to kiss her, fondle her, *swive* her. His fingers flexed, biting into her soft flesh.

Her eyes widened. 'No. I did not.'

He continued to search her expression.

'Have I shocked you? Coming here like this?'

As he went to answer her, she put her fingers to his lips. 'Shush. Do not say anything. I want to kiss you again. I want to know how I should feel—how I *could* feel. I want the memory of you in my future.'

A deep groan tore at his throat and he pulled her into his embrace, wrapping his arms around her as though he would never let her go. How he yearned to keep her with him for ever. She melted against his body, every delicious hot, soft curve cushioned against him. His blood scorched through his veins as he plundered her mouth, tasting her sweetness, exploring, sinking deeper and deeper under her spell.

He stroked and caressed her, some distant corner of his mind registering that she wore no corset. He traced the delicate bones of her spine and the ladder of her ribs, down past the dip of her waist, then cupped her bottom, succulent as a ripe peach. His blood surged anew, driven by the thumping heat of desire and he flexed his hips, trying to ease the almost painful throb of his erection.

*God, how I want her.*

The agony of wanting her and of not having her threatened to break his control. He released her bottom to caress her smooth, delicate fingers before sliding his palms up her silken arms to her neck. Cupping her face to hold her still, he plundered her soft mouth, tongues tangling, breathing in her honey-sweet breath. Seemingly of their own volition his hands moved to her lush breasts, caressing and squeezing, and teasing her taut nipples until she moaned into his mouth.

Reality impinged.

*She said a kiss. Can she know where this could lead?*

He tore his lips from hers. 'You should go.'

She grabbed his head, one hand each side, and kissed him fiercely.

'No.' Her tantalising breath whispered across his sensitised lips and he seized her mouth once more, losing himself in her.

His perfect lady.

Cecily plunged her hands through Zach's locks, relishing the smooth slide of his curls between her fingers. She buried deep any whisper of doubt. There was just this moment in time. This perfect moment, with its promise of delights she had never before experienced. The promise of passion. The future would happen, come what may, but now—here—was about her listening to her heart. It was about admitting the love she felt for this man and expressing that in more than words, even though it went against every single precept of her upbringing.

Tomorrow could take care of itself.

She pressed closer, committing to memory the feel of his solid yet supple contours. She stroked the heavy muscles of his shoulders and arms, tracing the rock-hard bulges and indentations as his muscles flexed. He was so big. So strong. All male. She traced the landscape of that perfect chest, that same glorious sensation she remembered from before gathering between her thighs.

Delicious anticipation. Urgent promise.

He swung her into his arms and carried her to his pallet, following her down, lying full-length beside her, half-covering her, and their kiss turned even more hot and demanding as his tongue plunged into her mouth and then withdrew, only to penetrate her again, the visceral rhythm driving her wild. His hard thigh pushed between hers and she squirmed at the delicious pressure, unconsciously tilting her hips, frantic to ease that place between her legs where all these new, exciting sensations coalesced in a vortex of need.

Zach softened the kiss then, easing back, and she felt his smile just before his lips slid to her ear. His tongue probed and she squirmed with delight, then his lips were on her neck…her collarbone…and he tugged at her neckline to expose her breasts.

'Ohhhhh.' She tipped back her head, arching her back, as his teeth grazed her nipple and then lightly nipped. She squealed.

'You like that, my little dove?'

'Ohhhhh, yes…'

He moved on to her other breast and her words drifted into silence. He explored without haste, his fingertips drifting along the sensitive skin of her inner arm, from wrist to elbow, raising shivers in their wake. He pressed hot, open-mouthed kisses—accompanied by appreciative murmurs—from breast to neck. Desire gathered, like a bud swelling, the pressure building deep inside her, and she closed her eyes—reaching,savouring every minute, every second, aware of nothing but him.

Zach.

The feel of him, the weight of him, the scent of him.

Intoxicating, evocative, manly.

His body was all heat, a solid pressure over her and against her, and yet not heavy. She raised reluctant lids—watched his almost fierce expression as he concentrated on her…on her body…on giving her pleasure—and her heart blossomed with a feeling like nothing she had ever known. Then he looked up, capturing her gaze, and—with a wicked smile—he pressed high with the leg that parted her thighs. High and hard.

That swelling bud of anticipation—deep inside her core—grew tighter…impossibly, gloriously tight. Then his hand was on her leg, stroking upwards with a delicate, knowing touch. She moaned as he reached the slick folds between her thighs and her breathing fractured as he played—stroking and swirling. One finger invaded her and she froze but, as he penetrated deeper, and stroked inside, she welcomed the feeling of him inside her and when he withdrew her body clenched helplessly around the sudden void.

Then he touched her again. Pressed. And she arched, crying out as that bud finally flowered and pleasure exploded, streaking through her. She collapsed back, every muscle and bone in her body turned to water, and then she was drifting on a lake of serenity, in a dream, aware only of the pulsations of that tender flesh, slowly diminishing.

Zach murmured low and deep in that musical language she did not understand. He gathered her to him, then he settled down, with her in his arms. Safe. Gradually, her breathing slowed and steadied. He watched her closely, his dark eyes enigmatic.

'I gave you pleasure, little dove?'

She smiled and reached to brush his hair back from his brow. 'You did. Although…' She felt her brows knit. 'We did not… You did not…'

She knew there was more, but she could not bring herself to speak the words. She knew how the animals mated. He kissed her—a slow, drugging kiss that melted her insides anew and stirred her desire. She kissed him back, hard, hooking her hand behind his head, feeling that sense of urgency build again. It was Zach who broke that kiss.

'If you cannot be mine, *gadji*, I will not take your innocence.'

Cecily absorbed those words and a great sadness invaded her. *If you cannot be mine…* And she could not. Of course she could not.

She eased from his arms and forced herself to sit up, folding her knees sideways under her so she faced him.

'I am thirty years of age. It is way beyond time I should be called an innocent even though, in truth, I am.'

'Nevertheless…' He said no more, but she could hear both his regret and his resolve.

She sighed. She could not fault him, or disagree. 'You are right. If I wish to marry, whether it be Kilburn or another, then I should go to him whole.'

Her conscience—her moral compass—would allow nothing less.

'You must not choose him. I cannot bear the thought of you with him.' He stroked her cheek, brushing strands of hair back from her face.

She stared up at his grim countenance. 'What are you not telling me?'

He frowned, then shook his head. 'I am asking you to trust me. He is a cruel man. Do not accept him, if he asks again. He is not worthy of a passionate, loving woman such as you. Choose another man for your husband—a good man.'

He levered himself up on to one elbow, his stormy gaze searching her expression. Her heart squeezed and regret scoured her.

'Choices are few for a woman of my age, Zach. I want

a family and Kilburn is my best hope. Tell me *why* he is not a good man. Give me a reason to refuse him.'

He sighed, his gaze lifting to stare into the flames. Again, she had the sense of him waging some inner battle. Then his lips firmed, he sighed again, and he returned his eyes to her.

'I knew him. When I was a boy. He and—'

He paused. Sat up and wrapped his arms around his bent knees, staring once again into the flames. Cecily sat up, too, and put her hand between his shoulder blades, circling, soothing.

'He made my life hell when I was a boy. Him and one other. I have seen neither of them since I was sixteen years of age.'

Cecily hesitated, fearful of saying the wrong thing. But there were too many anomalies for her not to question him.

'When you were sixteen,' she said, 'he must have been—'

'Twenty-four. Yes. Old enough to know better.'

'Better than what?'

He shook his head again. 'I have said enough. You do not need the details—'

'But…it makes no sense. You are constantly on the move. You cannot have come into that much contact with him.'

His eyes were bleak when he turned to her. 'The contact was sufficient for me to know the truth of him. You do not know him. I have never lied to you, dove. Trust me. Please.'

She shook her head in frustration. 'You ask me to make a decision about my life and my future based on the vaguest of accusations. Wedding Lord Kilburn would be no different for me than for countless other women of my class—a marriage of convenience with advantages for both sides. Were you and I two different people, from similar backgrounds, I could love you, Zachary Gray. But we are not and, having met you, I now find myself…strangely indifferent about my choice of husband.' She swallowed the tears that filled her aching throat. 'Being unable to choose you will be the biggest regret of my life.'

She rose to her feet, and straightened her clothing. Every inch of her yearned to stay with him despite knowing she could never embrace the Romany life. And duty…family…expectation…drove her on. She must return to her life as the perfect lady. Zach had risen as well and he folded her into his arms. His body shook, as though he reined in some strong emotion—or perhaps it was the trembling of her own body she could feel, vibrating through him and back into her. His warm breath stirred the hair at her temples as they stood, holding one another, for the longest time. Eventually, she stirred. His arms tightened around her as she leaned up to kiss him.

'I cannot stay. We both know that.'

He released her then and let her walk away but, when she looked back, he was following. He would not allow her walk back alone, she knew. But she understood it was too hard for them to walk together. She walked on, back to Leyton Grange and to her life of duty, restraint and respectability.

Zach heard them coming early the next day. Men on horseback. At least four of them. He stood tall and straight. Outwardly relaxed, but holding himself ready.

Five men rode into the clearing, Kilburn at their centre. The others—and Zach breathed a sigh of relief—had the look of labourers and grooms. Not a posse of vigilantes then. No self-righteous crowd of townsfolk, eager to chase the thieving gipsy from the area.

'Good morning, gentlemen. To what do I owe the pleasure?'

The surprise on each face gave him some satisfaction. Let them wonder at this gipsy who spoke like a gentleman.

Kilburn nodded at one of the men, who dismounted, a basket clutched in one hand.

'I promised Lady Cecily I would bring you provisions for your journey,' Kilburn said.

The man crossed the campsite and placed the basket on the ground.

Zach inclined his head. 'I am grateful for the provisions, but I fear you labour under a misapprehension, my lord. I plan no journey.'

Kilburn's eyes narrowed and he nudged his horse forward until the beast was standing right alongside Zach, who did not move. He stared up at Kilburn, his arms folded across his chest.

'If you know what is good for you, gipsy, you will go. Today.'

'And why, my Lord Kilburn, are you so very keen to see the back of me?' Zach described a sweeping arc with one arm. 'What harm am I doing? What possible threat am I to you?'

'Threat?' Kilburn barked a laugh. 'A common gipsy is no threat to *me*. But I do not appreciate your association with my betrothed. I want you gone.'

'Your betrothed?' Anger throbbed in his veins. The man lied. 'If the Lady Cecily is truly your betrothed, then you can have no reason to threaten me. One word in her ear will be sufficient to ensure she confines herself to the Leyton estate.'

Too late, Zach realised his recklessness in challenging Kilburn, and far too late he registered the light of recognition dawning in those deep-set eyes. Kilburn's brows beetled over the bridge of his nose and he peered closer at Zach, who held his gaze, head high. He would not back down, even though he now teetered on the edge of a precipice.

'I know you,' Kilburn said slowly. He peered closer. 'But where—?' His jaw dropped. He turned to his men and waved them away. 'Get back to work.'

Kilburn did not speak as he watched his men ride out of sight, giving Zach a few minutes to realise that the other man did not want anyone—even his own servants—to discover Zach's true identity. Kilburn slid from the saddle and faced Zach.

'Graystoke?' He sounded incredulous. 'Zachary Graystoke? What…?'

Zach waited.

'Does Cheriton know? Or Lady Cecily?'

'Do they know what?' Zach turned to feed another log to the fire, his mind racing. Where would this lead? What would it mean, for him? For his future? 'Do they know that my brother drove his stepmother and his sixteen-year-old half-brother away in defiance of our father's dying wish that he protect us?'

Kilburn paced across the camp and back again. 'Do they know who you are?'

'That,' said Zach, 'is none of your business.'

'By *God*, you have a nerve, sir. Charming your way into the life of a trusting lady such as Lady Cecily. I suggest you leave and leave today. You can be certain I shall write to apprise your brother of your deceitful attempts to inveigle an acquaintance with the Beauchamp family. If you refuse to leave at *my* command, you will not dare defy your brother.'

Zach allowed a slow smile to stretch his lips, relishing the fury it prompted in Kilburn's expression. 'You forget

I am no longer a stripling with no power to withstand my brother, Kilburn. I am a man grown. And if I choose to remain here, in this place, then neither you, nor Thetford, nor even the Prince himself, will change my mind.'

'My letter shall be sent by the swiftest means possible, Graystoke. *If* you are so unwise as to remain in the area, you may expect a visit from Thetford within the next two days.' He thrust his face close to Zach's, a sneer twisting his mouth as he said, 'Do you still have your mark, gipsy boy? Perhaps you wish for another? Heed my advice. Leave, while you have the chance.'

Zach watched Kilburn strut away, his mind full of the plan that had begun to take shape in the hours since he had seen Cecily safe back to the Grange. He had inherited a small, unentailed estate—Edgecombe—from his father, and it had been under his control since his twenty-fifth birthday. His brother—his *half*-brother—no longer held the purse strings. What if he and Cecily were to marry? He would at least have something other than the Romany way of life to offer her. She had said herself that she did not much care for London and society—they could settle at Edgecombe, hidden away from the damning eyes and opinions of the *haut ton*. They could keep the whole world at bay.

But would she agree? Or would the risk of being estranged from her family, as well as society, be a step too far for her?

## Chapter Fourteen

The enormity of what had nearly happened hit Cecily as she waited, sick with nerves, for Kilburn to call. She would have given herself to Zach, seized with a kind of madness that drove her on, reaching for the promise that seemed to flutter just out of her reach. It was Zach who had shown restraint. Even now that same restless yearning toiled deep inside her as though trying to find its way out of her body. Just the thought of him set her pulse skipping and her heart lurching. Then she thought about doing those same unimaginably intimate things—and more—with Kilburn and her stomach clenched.

*But it will be different with Kilburn. It will merely be breeding, like the animals in the fields.*

She must simply learn to separate her mind and her feelings from the physical process. It was no more than many a wife must do when she harboured no tender feelings for her husband. But when she relived last night—how Zach had made her feel and how she felt *now*—she felt even less ready to accept Kilburn even though her head still told her it was the right path to take, despite the misgivings fuelled by Zach's warnings.

She paced the salon to the window that overlooked the

carriageway. She wished Kilburn would make haste—she could not abide this waiting. She looked at the clock on the mantel. Almost noon. He must have visited Zach by now. What was keeping him? Had Zach gone yet? Did Kilburn force him to leave? Her throat thickened and she diverted her thoughts. Waiting. Waiting.

The door opened. Parker entered and bowed.

'Lord Kilburn is here, milady.'

'Thank you, Parker. Please show him in.'

Now the moment had arrived she felt strangely calm. This was her choice. She yielded her hand willingly when he carried it to his lips.

'Lady Cecily, I trust you are none the worse for your adventure yesterday?'

There was no hint of nervousness on his face, just supreme confidence and an abundance of male satisfaction. He was utterly assured of his own worth and that she would accept him.

'I am indeed none the worse,' Cecily said. 'And might I enquire whether you delivered adequate supplies to Mr Gray this morning, as promised?'

His lips tightened a fraction. 'Why is it you are still concerned with his welfare? You saw for yourself yesterday that he was recovering.'

'I should like further reassurance, however, my lord, for my brother will certainly wish to know his friend was in good health when you saw him. You *did* visit him?'

'Yes, I did, first thing this morning, as promised. I then had urgent correspondence to send via the London mail coach, or I should have attended you earlier.'

She reined in her irritation. She couldn't care less about his correspondence. 'And did you find Mr Gray well?'

'I did. His camp was all packed up and I watched him leave. You will not be troubled by him again.'

Her heart cracked and pain ripped through her at the thought of never seeing Zach again, never feeling his arms around her; his lips on hers. She gritted her teeth and stood straight, folding her hands before her. To reveal any emotion at this news would only raise Kilburn's suspicions.

'I am pleased to hear of his recovery and I know Vernon and his new wife will also be relieved. Thank you.'

'Now, enough of that heathen. I believe you know the question I am about to ask you.'

Cecily lowered her eyes as he once again took her hand.

'Lady Cecily Beauchamp, will you do me the great honour of being my wife?'

Cecily willed herself to remain calm, her years of experience in navigating awkward social situations coming to her aid. She lifted her gaze to his. There was no ardour in those grey eyes, merely the light of lasciviousness as his own gaze dropped to her décolletage, followed by a hint of impatience as it rose again to meet her eyes.

'I am sensible of the honour you do me, sir, but before I give you my answer, I have a request of you.'

His expression turned stony. 'And that is?' He released her hand and took a turn about the room, halting again before her. 'I trust you are not playing fast and loose with my affections, madam.'

'That is not my intention. But you know—you must know—after all, I refused your offer earlier this year, so surely we can dispense with any pretence that this would be a love match?'

His eyes narrowed. Then he inclined his head. 'Go on.'

'It is a practical arrangement—one that suits us both. I should rather have that openly acknowledged between us before we proceed. You require a mother for your children.'

'And another son. At least.'

'I understand. And I, for my part, wish for the status of a married lady and a house and a family of my own.'

'Then what is there to discuss? We are agreed, are we not?'

'We are, but my request is that we delay our formal betrothal until the end of the month. In the meantime, let there simply be an understanding between us. I should like the opportunity to tell my family in person and, as you know, Vernon is currently on his honeymoon.'

'When do you expect his return?'

His impatient tone, and a hint of desperation, puzzled her. She had glimpsed the same after she refused his original proposal. She caught her bottom lip between her teeth. Kilburn's gaze dropped to her mouth and lingered there, making her feel a little sick. She released her lip and strove to keep her voice level.

'Vernon and Thea will arrive in London in a few weeks, before travelling on to Brighton for the race meetings. Once I have told them, our betrothal may be announced.'

'Can you not write to them?'

'I should prefer to tell all my family face to face. And no doubt you will also wish to discuss the settlements with Leo first? There is surely no need for an unseemly rush?'

A muscle tightened in his jaw, suggesting there was something of which she was unaware—some reason why he wished to wed her sooner rather than later. Could it be that Vernon was right and his debts were bigger than was commonly known?

'And I do not wish for any hint of our understanding to reach my aunt, if you please,' she added, 'for she will be certain to announce it to all and sundry before I have the opportunity to inform my family. As we both intend to return to London shortly, we can discuss the matter with Leo then.'

Surely, this would afford her sufficient breathing space to put Zach behind her and to get accustomed to the idea of her new role.

Kilburn bowed. 'Very well. I see I have little choice but to accept, but do not keep me waiting too long.'

Was that a hint of a threat? No. It could not be. She was growing fanciful—looking for reasons not to trust him. At least this way she could learn more about her husband-to-be and, hopefully, become reconciled to her fate.

He reached for her hands and, before she realised his intention, his lips covered hers and his tongue was in her mouth. She kissed him back, mirroring his movements, but it felt all wrong. Unnatural. Kissing Zach had been effortless. She didn't once have to think about how to kiss him, it just happened. Instinctively.

She waited until the door closed behind him before rubbing her mouth dry with the back of her hand.

That evening, Aunt Drusilla retired early with a headache and Cecily and Miss Fussell sat together in companionable silence as the day dimmed to twilight. A book, resting open on Cecily's lap, held no interest for her. She could not even recall the title. Her mind was miles away, with Zach and his animals. Where was he now? Would he return to his family? Was he thinking of her? Would she ever see him again? She knew the answer to that. No. Marrying Kilburn would place an insurmountable barrier between them.

*Oh, and the fact that he is a Romany and you are the daughter of a duke is not an insurmountable barrier?*

She pushed that snide inner voice aside.

She wanted him. She longed for him. But she could not deny that her brief taste of the Romany way of life had been long enough to dispel any romantic, fanciful notion that she might relinquish her home comforts and be happy with a life under the stars.

But, oh, how her heart ached for him.

'Are you feeling quite the thing, my dear?' Miss Fussell's timid enquiry brought Cecily back to the present with a start. 'You look rather peaked, if you do not object to me saying so. And you have not turned a page in the past half-hour.'

Cecily set aside her book and sighed. 'I am quite well, thank you, Miss Fussell. I confess to a certain restlessness of spirit, however. I wonder—would you care for a turn around the garden before it gets fully dark? It is a beautiful evening and so very warm.'

Miss Fussell smiled, a little anxiously. 'I should enjoy that, if my company would be agreeable to you?'

Cecily rose to her feet and smiled warmly at her aunt's companion. 'I should not have asked you if I deemed your company unwelcome, Miss Fussell. Come. I do not think we shall require shawls, do you? There is not a breath of wind out there.'

They strolled through the garden, the scent of flowers heavy in the evening air. There were so many questions Cecily longed to ask Miss Fussell, but she feared any attempt to equate their positions might prove offensive. She, after all, was not impoverished. And she did have a choice, even though the idea of remaining a spinster held no appeal. Children—both Lord Kilburn's children and, hopefully, her own—would surely provide adequate compensation for any compromise in her choice of life companion.

'Forgive my boldness, Lady Cecily, but you must know... That is, your aunt—she has hopes of a match and we did think, when his lordship called this morning...well, that he might have—' She took a deep breath. 'I beg your pardon, but you seem unhappy. It is not my place to offer,

I know, but if you did wish to speak of it—I can keep a confidence, my lady.'

Cecily touched Miss Fussell's shoulder. 'Thank you. I—'

Miss Fussell emitted a squeak of alarm as a ghostly form swooped low over them before disappearing into the gathering gloom. Cecily's pulse leapt, sending the blood singing through her veins.

'Do not be alarmed.' She marvelled at how very calm she sounded. 'It was a barn owl. Was it not a beautiful sight?'

'Why, yes. Of course, I knew what it was, it simply took me by surprise. Look.' Miss Fussell clutched Cecily's arm as she pointed. 'There it is again.'

Again, the owl—and she was certain it was Athena—flew towards them. On impulse, Cecily held her arm aloft, as Zach had done. The bird descended, slowing, its wings widespread, its legs thrust forward but then, at the last minute, it rose again, effortlessly it seemed, and continued its flight without touching Cecily.

'It is fortunate, my lady, that she did not land on you.'

The deep voice came from behind them and Cecily twisted around to face the tall figure that emerged from the camouflage of the dark mass of hedge behind him.

Zach.

Calm descended, surrounding her, and she only then appreciated how tightly strung her nerves had been since the moment Kilburn told her Zach had gone.

'Mr Gray. I am pleased to see you. His lordship said you had gone.'

She was conscious of Miss Fussell's grip having tightened on her arm. A quick glance revealed wide eyes above an open mouth, but then Miss Fussell looked at Cecily and the understanding and compassion in her gaze thickened Cecily's throat. Was she that transparent? She returned her attention to Zach.

'Why is it fortunate Athena did not land on me?'

'Your skin is unprotected.' He brushed his forefinger from elbow to wrist, raising shivers in its wake. 'Her talons would bruise you. Maybe even break the skin. And his lordship was mistaken.'

'Mistaken? Or—?'

He silenced her with a gesture, his gaze flicking to Miss Fussell. Cecily introduced them, emphasising that Zach was a friend of her brother's.

'There is something I have neglected to tell you, my lady.' His dark eyes bored into hers. Intense. Trying to convey a message to her. 'Something of great importance. If Miss Fussell could find it in her heart to allow us—'

'Oh. I am sure—that is, I *am* a little weary, my dear Lady Cecily. If you do not object, I shall sit on this bench for a few minutes to rest while you and Mr Gray enjoy the flowers.'

The romantic gleam in those old eyes spoke volumes and gratitude for Miss Fussell's discretion flooded through Cecily.

'Thank you,' she said.

Miss Fussell sat down, arranging her skirts, and Cecily turned to continue along the path with Zach. As soon as they were out of earshot, he halted.

'What did you wish to say to me, Zach?'

*It can make no difference. Even if he does declare his love—*

'I love you,' he said.

Her heart twisted and a great sadness welled up within her. It was still impossible.

Zach took her hand and placed it over his heart. 'I told myself I should go. That I must leave you to your chosen future and that I must continue to follow my own path through life. But my heart—' he pressed her hand tighter to his chest, so tight she could feel his pounding heart through the coarse cloth of his shirt '—my heart tells me otherwise. My heart tells me to admit the truth to you and to try to find a way. I will fight for you, my perfect lady. I will fight.'

There was much she did not understand. 'What is the truth? That you love me?' She raised her other hand and brushed it through his disordered curls, searching his stormy eyes. 'How *can* that be enough, Zach? I love you, too, but I cannot live the life you live. I cannot.'

His chest rose as he hauled in a deep breath. His arms came loosely around her.

'I do not ask you to live that life. I would not see you living the travelling life—you are used to the best. Although I cannot offer you the luxury you are accustomed to, I *can* offer you a home. My mother, she was a Romany—that is the truth—but my father...' His chest heaved again, as though he were in the grip of intense emotion. 'I lived as a *gadjo* for the first sixteen years of my life. My father was the Earl of Thetford and he saw to it that I was educated in a manner befitting the son of an earl. Until he died.'

An earl's son? Hope surged even as Cecily puzzled over the bitterness of those last three words. 'But—forgive me, but you have a brother, then? The current Lord Thetford?'

'He is my half-brother. After his first wife died, my father met my mother quite by chance and they fell in love. They married, but they were never fully accepted into society. I am surprised you have never heard of that scandal.'

Cecily shook her head, her thoughts whirling. 'I did not know. But I would have been a child when your parents married and, when your father died, I would have been ensconced at Cheriton Abbey raising my brother's children. I rarely visited London after my come out, particularly in the years when the children were small.' She sensed there was more. 'Why did you not stay at your family home?'

'My brother drove us out.'

'Your father left no provision for you? For your mother?'

'Oh, yes!' The bitterness was back, more intense than ever. 'He left provision, but he appointed my half-brother as my guardian. And *he* made it impossible for us to remain at Thetford Park. But I have been in control of my inheritance since my twenty-fifth birthday and Thetford no longer has any say over my life, Cecily. Do you see?

'I own property. It is but a modest estate in Hertfordshire, but it is enough to provide for a family. We have no need of the rest of society—we can live at Edgecombe, far away from their prejudices and their superiority.'

A dream come true. A way for them to be together.

But...

And why must doubts arise now? Why could she not just embrace that dream with a joyous heart? Why must her conscience whisper all the very real reasons why the dream was still impossible?

Torn, she stared at him hopelessly. Would her family—Leo, Vernon, Leo's children—accept her decision? Would they be happy for her? What if, by choosing to be with the man she loved, she became estranged from them? Could she bear it?

And what of Zach? Could she really ask him to give up his way of life? He had *chosen* the Romany way—at last she understood his choice of that word. Would he truly be happy giving that up, or would he grow to resent her? What if he should change his mind and hanker after the travelling life again? What would happen then? She had no doubt the Romany life was not for her.

'Cecily, I cannot bear for you to be with a man such as Kilburn.' His hands moved to her shoulders and his thumbs brushed her throat. 'He is one of Thetford's closest friends and I have witnessed the true nature of the man. They made my boyhood hell and he helped Thetford drive my mother and me out. And, besides…I love you.

'Say you feel the same. Say you will marry me, my love.'

Cecily cradled his face, searching his dark eyes, his soul. She needed time to think things through, even though her heart urged her to take that leap of faith and to accept him regardless, to forget common sense and to ignore the consequences.

'I do feel the same, Zach. You cannot doubt it. I love you, so very much, and I want nothing more than to accept you. But—you have taken me by surprise. You announce you are the son of an earl—I never imagined… I cannot quite…'

'You need time to think, time to adjust.'

'I do—and not only that. I now have an understanding with Lord Kilburn and, for decency's sake, I should release myself from that obligation first.'

She put one finger to his lips, which parted. He grazed her fingertip with gentle teeth and a shiver of awareness snaked down her spine as a fire ignited deep in her belly.

'I understand.' His voice was gravelly with disappointment. 'You would not be the lady I love—the person of integrity I know you to be—if you were prepared to do anything else. I shall wait for you. Take as long as you need, my dove.'

Cecily tiptoed up and pressed her lips fleetingly to his. 'We must return to Miss Fussell. I do not believe she will betray our meeting, but every minute we remain here adds to the risk. His lordship agreed to delay our formal betrothal until I can tell my family in person. He is to call upon me tomorrow, however, and I will ask him then to release me.'

Even as she spoke the words, doubts still raged within her. Zach's announcement seemed to offer the perfect solution, but was it too good to be true? Was love enough? She still—desperately—needed time to think.

## Chapter Fifteen

Cecily didn't know whether to be relieved or disturbed that Aunt Drusilla declared herself too unwell to leave her bed the next day. She welcomed the fact that she did not have to face her aunt—and the doctor's visit certainly distracted her from her endlessly circling thoughts and from the tension that assailed her whenever she thought of the coming interview with Lord Kilburn—but there was no doubt that she would miss her formidable aunt's presence when Kilburn did finally come to call.

The day dragged and it was late afternoon by the time the clatter of hooves and the rattle of carriage wheels on the gravelled forecourt finally announced Kilburn's arrival. Cecily was so nerve-racked she was drying her damp palms on her handkerchief as the door opened to admit Parker.

'My lady—' he began, but he got no further.

A familiar tall figure, with a face like thunder, entered the room on his heels.

'No need for the formalities, Parker,' Leo said. 'My sister knows very well who I am.'

Cecily started to her feet. 'Leo!'

About to hurry across the room to greet him, she hesitated. He looked tired and unusually dishevelled. 'Wh-what is wrong? Is it Olivia? The boys? Are they all well?'

He did not reply, but continued to regard her from under frowning brows as a muscle bunched in his jaw.

'Leo? You are making me nervous. Is someone ill?'

He drew in a long breath, then released it with a huff. 'They are all well. Although I'd have preferred not to leave Livvy at the moment—she is up to something, I am sure.'

Cecily forced a trill of a laugh. 'When is she not up to some devilment or other?'

Her attempted jest failed to raise a smile. Leo stalked towards her and her breath caught. Somehow, he knew. She could see it in those knowing silver eyes of his. She felt her colour rise until her cheeks burned. He stopped before her, looking down at her, and she forced herself to hold his gaze.

'I had a visitor last night. Late. Tell me, Cecily—why is Lord Thetford warning me to watch out for your reputation?'

The softer Leo spoke, the angrier he was. And those words were *very* softly spoken. Cecily swallowed and she tilted her chin.

'Th-Thetford?'

Her voice emerged as a squeak. She had no fear of her brother. He was no ogre. But she *was* scared—so very scared that whatever decision she made as to her future would result in heartache for her, one way or the other.

Leo released another sigh and swept one hand through his hair. 'There is no point in us tiptoeing around one another, Cecy. I have been travelling since first light and I am in no mood for prevarication.' He indicated a chair. 'Sit down.'

She did as he bid and he followed suit. In the silence she could hear the sound of her own heart beating and the sound of her blood rushing through her veins. She folded her hands in her lap and waited.

'Graystoke followed you here. I know it, so there is no point in denying it.'

Her spine stiffened. 'I have never lied to you and I am not about to do so now. I presume by Graystoke you mean Mr Gray? We are in love, Leo. I know my own mind—I am thirty years of age, not a naive young girl.'

'In *love*?'

'Yes.'

'But—I was told you are betrothed to Kilburn.'

'How would Lord Thetford know that?'

She knew the answer before the words left her mouth. Kilburn had agreed to delay their betrothal, but for Thetford to know of it and for Leo to arrive here so speedily...

She recalled Kilburn's words from the day before: *'I had urgent correspondence to send via the London mail coach, or I should have attended you earlier.'*

Anger spiralled from deep down, burning inside her chest.

*Was he so certain of me—so sure I would accept—that he wrote to Thetford of our betrothal before he even asked me?*

It was clear that he had.

'Lord Thetford is mistaken,' she told Leo, acidly. 'We are not betrothed. Indeed, at the time Kilburn penned his letter to Thetford he had not even made me an offer. Even now, there is merely an informal understanding between us.'

Leo took her hand. 'If you are absolutely determined to wed, Cecy, Kilburn would be a decent enough choice.'

She stayed silent, gazing at their joined hands through blurred eyes.

'If you are thinking of Graystoke…it will not do, my dear. You *know* that, deep in your heart.'

'He is the son of an earl.'

'But his mother was a gipsy—'

'A Romany, Leo.'

'It makes no difference what you call him, Cecy. You will be ostracised. Your children will be shunned. Is that what you wish?'

'But if *you* were to accept us, Leo, it would make all the difference.'

He stared at her in silence. She waited. Then, with a muttered oath, he surged to his feet, sweeping his hand through his hair. He strode to the window where he stood staring out, his shoulders square, back stiff. Still she waited, understanding the war that was going on inside him, silently praying that he would see things her way. That he would give her his support.

When he finally faced her again, she knew by his expression that she had lost and her throat constricted as her heart splintered.

'I cannot. It is too much, Cecy. I am sorry, but I cannot condone such a match.' He crossed the room to sit beside her and gathered up her hands. 'You appear to have endless faith in my ability to dictate society's opinion, but I doubt even *my* approval would prove sufficient to stop you and your children being rejected by many in the *ton*.'

'Not by our true friends. It would only be by some people and I do not care about them.'

'But I do care, my dear. I care very much what might happen to you—and the strains it would put on any marriage—if you are rejected by any in society.' He laid his hand against her cheek, regret in his eyes. 'I also must consider the impact on the rest of the family, Cecy. In case you have forgotten, it is not only Olivia's come out, but Nell's, too. Rosalind has high hopes of her sister making a good match and she is already anxious about her own background tainting the family name. And there are the boys to think of as well. Dominic, I know, wishes to look high for a bride.' He hesitated, then said, very deliberately, '*He* knows his duty to the family.'

Resentment at that unfairness scoured her throat. 'I have *always* put our family first, Leo. You know I have. What about Rosalind's background? And Thea's? They are hardly from the upper echelons of society.'

'That is different. A wife is elevated to enjoy the status of her husband. You know that. Besides, Graystoke is but six-and-twenty. He is too young for you.'

'Young?' She had barely considered the age difference. 'It is only four years. There are ten years between you and Rosalind.'

'That is entirely different. I am a man. I am the head of the household.'

Cecily leapt to her feet and crossed to the window. 'That is a ridiculous argument. If Zach and I do not regard the difference in ages, what possible business can it be of anyone else's?'

She leant her forehead to the cool glass. Her breath misted the pane but she did not care. If the glass was smeared, let someone else worry about it. The choice she must make ripped at her and only with the strongest effort did she keep her tears at bay. What Leo had *not* said was as clear as what he had, but she nevertheless must ask that fateful question. With dread pooling in her stomach, she turned to face him. He was watching her. There was a gleam of sympathy in those silver eyes, but also an implacable determination. Her courage almost deserted her. Almost. But she must know for sure. Only then would she be certain that her choice was as stark as she feared.

'Let us be clear, Leo. If I choose Zach, do I lose my family?'

The look on her brother's face was answer enough and she fled the room.

Zach had waited all day, hoping Cecily would come to him, but there was no sign of her. There was, however, a visitor to the Grange in the middle of the afternoon. He heard the sound of a swiftly moving vehicle and he ran up to the road to see a chaise and four turn in between the stone pillars of Leyton Grange. And he was in time to catch a glimpse of the sole occupant. The Duke. Cecily's brother. His coming could mean only one thing and it was only by the strongest effort of will that Zach did not chase after the vehicle as the sweating horses galloped up the carriageway. He knew why the Duke had come: it had Thetford's grubby fingermarks all over it. Rather than come here himself, and face the half-brother he despised, he had involved the Duke—no doubt to remove Cecily from Zach's contaminating influence.

Cecily's response to Cheriton's arrival would tell Zach all he needed to know. He wanted her to choose him of her own accord and so he resisted the urge to stride up to the Grange and hammer on the door and demand admittance. But he could not resist keeping watch from the cover of the nearby wood.

He saw Kilburn arrive and depart, but he was too far away to decipher the man's expression and to guess at what decision, if any, had been reached. Had Cecily asked Kilburn to release her? Had she been able to withstand her brother's inevitable opposition to her marrying Zach? Or was duty so deeply ingrained in her that she would bow to her brother's edict and conform to society's mores rather than follow her heart?

It was only then, his heart sinking as he watched Kilburn ride away from the Grange, that Zach started to doubt his strategy. It was important to him that Cecily's choice was hers and hers alone and he had stayed away to avoid pressuring her. The cards had been dealt. He had placed his bet last night and today he had given her brother time and space to play his hand. But, in so doing, had he been too honourable? Cecily loved her brother dearly and he exerted enormous influence over her. Whatever persuasions the Duke employed to sway her would be reinforced by thirty years' of shared history and the very real sense of familial duty that was instilled into any lady of high birth.

Cecily loved him. He did not doubt it, for otherwise she would never have been prepared to give herself to him. But did she love him enough to turn her back on her family, if that stark choice was the only choice on the table?

He left the cover of the trees and strode purposefully across the lawn and up to the front door. The butler, as behoved any servant worth his position, started to shut the door in Zach's face as soon as he saw him upon the doorstep. Zach stepped forward and placed his foot in the diminishing gap.

'I have come to speak to Lady Cecily Beauchamp. Be so good as to inform her that Mr Zachary Graystoke is here.'

The butler thrust his face into the gap. 'Get you gone, gipsy. We don't welcome your sort here.'

It took less than a second to make up his mind. He must get past the man, and do it quickly before he could summon reinforcements. Zach put his shoulder to the door and barged through. The butler was no match for him; Zach strode past him into the panelled hall.

'Where is she?'

The butler's face was mottled with rage. 'Simpkins! Acton! To me! Now!'

The last was a roar that echoed up the huge, open stairwell, bouncing between the walls and the high, ornately plastered ceiling and a nearby door flew open, revealing the figure of the Duke of Cheriton. Zach met his glare with a steely look of his own. He cared nothing for the man's rank. Any respect for the aristocracy had long ago been ripped from him, after his experiences at his halfbrother's hands.

'Where is Cecily?' He shook off the butler's restraining hand and strode towards the Duke.

One dark brow rose and the Duke stood aside, indicating with a sweep of his arm that Zach should enter the room, as he said, 'There is no need for you to concern yourself, Parker. You may safely leave this with me.'

Cecily was by the fireplace, her face pale, hands clasped before her. The door clicked shut behind Zach as he went to her, searching her expression as he neared her. He delved deep into the mossy depths of her eyes and he read desolation within. And he knew.

'Follow your heart.' He touched her clasped hands, felt them tremble. 'You will not be happy with Kilburn. Take courage and do as you *wish* to do, not what you are expected to do.'

Her lids lowered. 'I do not wish to prolong this, Mr Graystoke.' Her voice was level. Devoid of feeling. The only indication of repressed emotion was the rapid rise and fall of her bosom. 'I have valued our friendship and I am relieved you are now recovered from your illness, but I regret I must end our association forthwith.'

'I will give up the travelling life. I have told you. We can settle at Edgecombe. I have enough income for us to live comfortably…to provide for our children. We do not need the rest of society.' He snatched her hands, gathered them to his chest. 'Cecily, I lo—'

'Graystoke!' The Duke came between them, easing Cecily back before facing Zach. 'My sister has given you her decision. She wished to do so in person and I—reluctantly—agreed. But I expect you to respect that decision and her feelings. I will not stand by and listen to you attempt to coerce her into changing her mind.'

Zach advanced, chest to chest with the Duke.

'Her decision or yours?' He held the Duke's gaze. 'Have you even considered what your sister really wants and how she feels, or are you just concerned with what others might say, or think? Isn't her happiness important to you?'

'Her happiness is my *only* consideration. Do *you* really believe she will happy buried on some minor estate with you, estranged from her family and friends, from the whole of society?'

'Stop it!' Cecily grabbed her brother's arm and tugged him away. 'Do not make this harder than it already is. Zach…' The look she sent him—brimful of regret—made his knees buckle and only by sheer force of will did he lock them straight. She turned to her brother. 'Leo. Please. Allow us to talk in privacy.'

The Duke's brow lowered but, to Zach's surprise, he nodded and went to stand by the window.

'Zach.'

Her look, the love shining from her eyes, melted his heart. But the regret was still present. And heartache. Then his throat thickened as he recognised her resolve. As much as he wanted this to be entirely the fault of her brother, it was *her* decision to choose her family over him.

'I hoped…' Her voice was low—too quiet to reach her brother, whose narrow-eyed gaze never wavered. 'I did hope, when I knew your past, that we might find a way, but I think I always knew it was hopeless. We would *both* have to give up so much—too much.

'I would lose the family I love and the society of my friends. I do prefer country living, but if, by choosing you, I am *never* able to see my family, to go to Town, or to socialise with my friends, I suspect that I would soon hanker after the very thing that is barred to me.' A smile flickered. 'We always desire that which we cannot have. Is that not true?'

'Your brother has influence. If *he* were to accept us, then enough others would follow his lead.'

Her lips firmed briefly before parting on a sigh. 'It is not that straightforward, although that is true. He has responsibilities and he must make his decision on what is best for everyone. He has the rest of the family to consider. A daughter and a stepdaughter both in their first Season and a son and heir who wishes to make an advantageous match.

'But, Zach—' she laid her hand against his cheek '—what of the sacrifice *you* would have to make? You would have to give up the life you have chosen to live for the past ten years.'

He opened his mouth to reassure her, but stayed silent in response to a touch to his arm.

'Please. Allow me to finish. I have thought this through. Very carefully.'

She emitted a little laugh that turned into a choked-off sob and he fought the urge to take her in his arms; to comfort her.

'I have thought of nothing else since last night,' she whispered. Her eyes brimmed with unshed tears. 'I thought about you—the man I met at Stourwell Court. The man I fell in love with—your love of nature, your instinctive understanding and your natural wisdom. I know you had little choice but to embrace the Romany life at first. You were young and you and your mother had nowhere else to go. But—your mother has gone and this past year, since your twenty-fifth birthday, you have continued the Romany way of life even though you could have returned to take your rightful place in society. You *chose* not to return.

'I thought, too, about any children we might have. Without my family's support, we would remain for ever at Edgecombe, condemned to living a half-life. Neither belonging nor fully accepted in my world or yours. Look at your experience. You said yourself you are *tolerated* by your mother's people—not fully welcomed, other than by her immediate family. I cannot see a contented future for us.

'I do not want you to be forced into changing your life. I fear you would grow to resent me. And I would grow to resent you for taking me from my family. My choice is clear—become estranged from everyone I love or to lose the man I love.

'I am sorry, but I choose to stay with what is familiar. I am not brave enough to take that leap into an unknown future.'

'You have made this decision with your head. What of your heart?'

She smiled sadly. 'I have to make my decision based on fact. We do not live in the pages of a romance novel. This is real life and love does not always transcend practicalities. And if saying that makes me sound boring and sensible, then so be it. Maybe that is the person I am, the person I was brought up to be.'

Her logic was unarguable. But he did not want to hear logic. He wanted passion. He sensed the tight control she had over her emotions. If only her brother was not in the room, watching their every move, he would…

*Would what? Take her in your arms and seduce her into submission? You would pressure her to submit to your will, yet you afford the beasts and the birds the choice to remain with you or to leave?*

He bowed his head as his heart broke.

'I respect your decision.' He owed her that.

He captured her gaze, losing himself one last time in those green depths, desperately trying to convey his love without words. Her face softened, those perfect lips parting as though to receive his kiss. He blinked fast, to stem the tears that gathered.

'Goodbye, sweet dove.'

He held her hand, raising it to his mouth, and caught a restless movement out of the corner of his eye. Well, to hell with the damned Duke. He pressed his lips to her silken skin, breathing deep of her evocative apple-blossom scent. Never again would he be able to smell that flower in the air without remembering his perfect lady. A tear trickled free and landed on her skin. He wiped it with his thumb and straightened, releasing her hand. He turned and strode for the door. The Duke, as he had guessed he would, followed him outside.

'It is for the best, Graystoke.'

There was even a gleam of sympathy in the man's eyes. Every fibre of Zach's being hardened. His hand clenched into a fist and he yearned to plant it in the Duke's hypocritical face. But he fought that urge. It would resolve nothing and would only cause more pain to Cecily. He had learned long ago it was senseless to rail against the prejudices of society—anger and confrontation would never change people's minds, but only confirm their preconceptions.

'I disagree. I love your sister. She loves me.'

'And we all know that is not enough. Understand me well, Graystoke. I have my sister's best interests at heart. She is the daughter of a duke. I cannot stand by and see her throw her social standing away on a whim. You hardly know one another. You will soon forget.'

*What does he know of love? What does he know of heartache?*

'She knows me better than she knows Kilburn.'

'They will have time to become better acquainted in London before they are formally betrothed.'

Bitterness scoured Zach's throat. Any man could conceal his true nature during courtship. The thought of Cecily with that bastard sent waves of helpless fury crashing through him.

'Stay away from my sister if you know what's good for you, Graystoke. You really do *not* want to get on the wrong side of me.'

'You cannot intimidate me, Cheriton. My father—'

'Your *father* lived to regret his mésalliance with your mother, according to Thetford.'

'And that, your *Grace*, is a damned lie. They were happy together.'

One dark brow arched and again Zach battled the urge to punch the smug superiority from the man's face.

'You've lost, Graystoke. Take your failure like a man and leave my sister to continue with the life she was born and raised to enjoy.'

He clenched his jaw so hard it ached, but he realised there was nothing to be gained in prolonging the inevitable.

'The possession of a title does not make Kilburn a decent man, Cheriton. He has a rotten core and your sister deserves better.' He held the Duke's gaze as he silently debated with himself. 'He's cruel, Cheriton. I have a brand burnt into my arse to prove it. Even you will have no power to protect her once they are man and wife.'

He twisted on his heel and strode away.

His camp was packed up in record time, rage driving him on, the busyness stopping him from dwelling on his pain. He was on the road within the hour. He turned Titan's head to the west and rhythmic clop of the horse's hooves steadied his racing heart and soothed the turmoil battering his soul but he could no longer hold his thoughts at bay. And through the heartache crept a growing realisation and, finally, full acceptance.

He steered Titan in a half-circle and sent him to the east. To Hertfordshire.

Cecily had been right. She could not ask him to sacrifice the life he had chosen. But he could make that sacrifice nevertheless. He must choose henceforth to embrace the *gadje* world. He must take his place in society and face up to the inevitable challenges if he was to have any chance of winning the hand of the woman he loved.

His Lady Perfect.

# Chapter Sixteen

*Beauchamp House, Grosvenor Square, London*

'Will you not tell me what is wrong, Olivia?'

The dark circles beneath her niece's eyes and her uncommon listlessness troubled Cecily. Something was undoubtedly wrong, but all her efforts to uncover the reason behind Olivia's low mood had failed. When she was out and about she hid her melancholy very well and was her usual vivacious self, but at home there was no disguising her gloom. Cecily empathised, for was her behaviour not similar? And she suspected the cause might also be similar—Olivia's unhappiness bore all the hallmarks of a broken heart. At least the worry over Olivia helped to consign Cecily's own misery to the back of her mind.

'It is—'

Olivia fell silent as the parlour door opened and Grantham entered. Cecily had rarely seen their stiff and exceedingly proper butler look so flummoxed.

'Yes, Grantham?'

She tried not to reveal her exasperation at the timing of his interruption. So many minor irritations these days seemed to try her temper in a way unheard of in the past and she had caught more than one member of the family casting her a puzzled look when she overreacted.

'A gentleman is demanding to speak with you, my lady.'

'A gentleman? At this hour?'

It was only ten o'clock. No gentleman—or lady, come to that—would pay a social visit so early in the day.

'I suggested he might leave his card, but he is most insistent. He refuses to leave until I have given you his name.'

'Well? Who is it, Grantham?'

'Mr Zachary Graystoke.'

The air whooshed from Cecily's lungs and, even though she was seated, she felt herself sway. The moment she had both longed for and dreaded. What did he hope to achieve by prolonging the agony and the heartbreak for them both?

'Aunt?' Olivia was by her side, holding her hand. 'What is it? You've gone white.'

Cecily bit down hard on the inside of her cheek and the sharp pain steadied her spinning head. 'Show him into the salon, please, Grantham. I shall be there directly.'

The butler's mouth thinned in clear disapproval, but he bowed and left the room.

*Thank goodness Leo is not at home.* And Rosalind and Nell were out shopping. Olivia had declined to go with them and Cecily had opted to stay with Olivia, to try again to get to the bottom of what ailed her.

'Who is Mr Graystoke, Aunt? I do not recall ever having met him.'

'He is Lord Thetford's half-brother and a friend of Aunt Thea's brother.'

'And you met him at Uncle Vernon's wedding? And now he is calling on you. Oh, how romantic! I bet he's *much* more suited to you than that Lord Kilburn.'

Not for the first time, Cecily marvelled at Olivia's quickness of understanding: she saw things and made connections that passed other people by entirely. She directed a quelling look at her niece.

'Is that not just like you, Livvy? You hear one snippet of fact and you weave an entire story around it.'

But at least this had ignited a spark of interest in her formerly lethargic niece. Olivia jumped to her feet.

'But I am right. I can see it by the look on your face. Are you in love with him? Is that why you did not come home after the wedding? Is that why Papa was in such a foul temper when he went to Great-Aunt Drusilla's to fetch you home?'

'Olivia! Please. It is most unbecoming to bombard a person with so many personal questions. Now sit down and wait for me here.'

But as Cecily reached the door, Olivia was on her heels.

'Livvy…'

She put as much menace as she could into that one word, but Olivia merely cocked her head and smiled.

'You cannot meet with a gentleman caller unchaperoned, Aunt. That is what you always tell me.'

'It is different for me. Please, do not be so exasperating and wait for me here.'

'I shall come with you and I shall sit at the far end of the room so you may speak privately, and then I won't feel duty bound to tell Papa of your scandalous behaviour.'

She couldn't help it. Cecily laughed. Olivia, irrepressible as ever. It was good to see her niece exhibit some semblance of normal behaviour.

'Very well,' she said, with a shake of her head. 'You may come with me.'

*It may ease the awkwardness when we meet.* Her heart rose to crowd her throat. *Zach.* He was here. She had thought she might never see him again. Her legs trembled; her stomach churned; her pulse skittered and jumped all over the place. Her very nerviness confirmed his hold over her was as powerful as it ever was, but it changed nothing. How could she bear to no longer be part of her family's lives? She buried her pain and turned to Olivia outside the salon door.

'I shall expect you to be quiet and discreet, Livvy. And you *must* stay out of earshot. Is that clear?'

'Of course, Aunt Cecily.'

Cecily walked into the salon and stopped short. He stood by the fireplace, but he was not the same. This... this...

Her legs moved again of their own accord, carrying her closer as her eyes devoured the perfect gentleman standing before her. Spotless cream breeches moulded to his muscled thighs before disappearing into shining Hessian boots sporting gold-coloured tassels. She remembered picturing him wearing tight breeches, but the reality was so much more. Her pulse quickened as she took in the rest of him. His broad shoulders filled a form-fitting, exquisitely tailored black tailcoat and his snowy neckcloth was tied in a perfect knot. His dark curls had been trimmed and his face was freshly shaved. His cologne, subtle and spicy but somehow earthy, like him, weaved through her senses.

A slow smile—loving, tender—curved his lips and he held his hands towards her.

'Cecily.' His dark eyes swept her features as she placed her hands in his. His strong fingers curled around hers and her heart appeared to perform a slow somersault within her chest. 'I trust you have no objection to my calling upon you so early in the day?'

Even his voice was that of a cultured gentleman, but its deep rich tones still curled around her, warming her as tingles raced across her skin.

'No. I am pleased you did.'

She recalled Olivia as his gaze slid sideways to her niece, now by her side. As his head moved, she caught the glint in his ear and pure happiness washed through her. He hadn't fully conformed to society's rules and she was glad.

'Mr Graystoke, may I introduce my niece, Lady Olivia Beauchamp.'

Olivia's silver eyes—so like her father's—gleamed as she dipped a curtsy.

'I am delighted to meet you, sir. My aunt has told me so much about you.'

Zach glanced at Cecily, clearly startled. 'She has?'

'No, she has not,' Cecily said. 'Olivia, you are a minx.'

Silver-grey eyes wide with innocence, Olivia said, 'You did not have to *speak* for me to understand, Aunt Cecily.'

Cecily felt her brows rise. For such an impetuous young woman Olivia could still surprise her with her sensitivity. She could only hope she might discover the cause of Olivia's troubles before too long.

'Please recall your promise and go and sit quietly by the window, Livvy.'

'Oh, very well.'

To Cecily's relief, Olivia did as she was bid. She realised her hands were still cocooned within Zach's and she withdrew them.

'When did you arrive in London?'

'Last night. I have taken rooms in Jermyn Street. Are you formally betrothed to Kilburn?'

She looked away. 'No. As you are aware, however, we have an understanding.'

'Why the delay?'

She sat on the sofa and gestured for him to sit by her side.

'His lordship agreed to wait until I could tell Vernon and Thea of my decision in person and Leo…'

She hesitated. Leo, since their return, had encouraged her to delay. From telling her Kilburn would be a decent choice of husband, he now seemed less keen. He had even put forward two more names for her consideration—other widowers he knew to be interested in remarrying.

'Leo wishes me to consider other possible husbands.'

'Then I am not too late.'

'Too late? Zach—'

'No. Do not object before you hear what I have to say.'

She bit her lip, but nodded. She folded her hands in her lap and waited for him to speak and made sure to keep breathing evenly. She'd had much practice—too much practice—in concealing her inner turmoil since her return from Leyton Grange.

'I have come to fight for you, Cecily.'

Tears sprang to her eyes. 'I cannot.' Her voice choked, her throat clogged with tears. 'Zach…I cannot.'

He placed his hand over hers. Large. Warm. Comforting. Peacefulness spread from deep within her core, stealing through every nerve and fibre of her being. She knocked his hand aside as she snatched her hands from beneath his. She must not let her guard drop.

'Cecily—I will prove myself to you. Promise me—'

'Zach! Please say no more. Town clothes do not change the man you are inside.'

'Nor my breeding?'

The bitter undertone was barely detectable, but it was there and Cecily railed silently at the unfairness of it all. His half-blood made no difference to her, personally, but it *was* a consideration.

'*That* was not uppermost in my mind. I referred to the way of life you have chosen. The Romany way. But your mother's heritage does have consequences—like those ripples in that pond—and they are consequences I cannot ignore.'

'And if I tell you...'

He paused and a frown knit his brow. His chest swelled as he inhaled, then he shook his head and one ebony curl tumbled across his forehead. She tightened the grip of her hands, lest she succumb to the urge to brush that stray lock back.

'I am unused to long speeches.' A rueful smile quirked his lips. Cecily tore her gaze from them, forced the memory of his kisses to the back of her mind. 'But I have come to speak and speak I shall. I am not here to beg, but to tell you the facts, as you are determined to decide your future with your head instead of your heart.'

His smile melted through her, softening and relaxing every tightly strung nerve and every rigid muscle and every bone in her body. Her insides swirled and swooped. She gritted her teeth. She could think of nothing he could say to change her mind. Her choice was still stark—between the man she loved and the family she loved.

'The life I have led till now means nothing without you. And I now understand that my decision to remain with my mother's family after she died was no decision at all but, rather, a *lack* of decision. I chose the easy and the familiar. Now I have an incentive to return to society—to confront my half-brother and force him to acknowledge my existence.'

'But—Zach—I—'

'Hush.' He brushed her cheek with one long finger, raising shivers in its wake. 'Do not say anything. Not yet.'

He nudged her chin, encouraging her to meet his gaze and her heart broke at the sincerity and the love that shone from his eyes. If only...

'But, Zach—you are still—'

'I am still half-Rom, yes, but I feel no shame and I will not apologise for it. It is who I am. I shall no longer hide myself away. I will not be welcomed everywhere. I may very well be shunned by some. But those people are unimportant to me. Those who acknowledge me and who stick by me will be the important ones.'

'Well, I can promise you that I shall acknowledge you. As for anything further…' She could not finish, her whisper choking off.

'That is all I ask, dove. For now. But I hope you will soon see that there is a middle way and that you will feel able to stand by my side and face society with your head high.

'Promise me you will not sanction any announcement until you have thought about what I've said. I must go. I have much to do and many people to meet.'

'I promise,' she said, but her throat ached with the sadness she fought to conceal. How could this change anything?

Zach glanced over at Olivia. 'How I wish your niece to Jericho,' he whispered. 'I long to kiss you.'

His words, and the look of intent in his dark, stormy eyes, set her blood pumping and a flush rose to heat her skin. She could not tear her gaze from his.

'You must not say so.'

He dipped his head and she thought, for one frantic moment, that he would kiss her regardless. But he put his lips close to her ear. 'I am the *only* man who should have the right to say those words.'

He rose to his feet, bowed, and then again to Olivia, and he left.

He'd done as much as he could do, for now. Seeing her again had just strengthened Zach's conviction that they were meant to be together. Cecily knew it, too, in her heart, but she was afraid and he understood her fears. It was up to him to show her that middle way. Edgecombe was now his home, but he would not hide away there—he would take his place in society and he would renew his acquaintance with old friends from his schooldays. Some of them, he was certain, would stand by him. And, in time, he was certain he would be accepted by Cecily's family.

His biggest fear—did he have *enough* time?

It didn't take Zach long to decide on his next course of action. He'd be damned if he was going to wait until he met Thetford by chance. His half-brother was in Town—that he knew—and so, once he left Beauchamp House, he strolled across Mayfair to Curzon Street. The red-brick house, with its front door flanked by Ionic columns, looked unchanged. Zach rapped on the door. It was opened by a stranger who, after a swift scan of Zach—whose new gentlemanly guise clearly passed muster—bowed.

'Good morning, sir.'

'Good morning. I wish to speak to Lord Thetford.'

'Might I ask your name, sir?'

In answer, Zach handed his card to the butler, whose brows rose when he read Zach's name. But his expression remained open. He appeared unaware that Zach was his master's despised Romany half-brother. He showed Zach into the downstairs reception room.

'I shall inform his lordship of your arrival, Mr Graystoke.'

'Thank you—?'

The man bowed. 'Catchpole, sir.'

'Catchpole. Thank you.'

He didn't have long to wait. The ring of boots on the tiled floor of the hall announced his brother's approach. The door flew open and Zach faced the brother he had not seen for ten years. He was shorter, and slighter, than in Zach's memory, but that was probably because Zach had grown. He now topped Thetford by a good four inches and, were he assessing his chances against this man in a fist fight, he would experience no qualms.

*It is fortunate I am a peaceful man.*

He bit back his grin as that thought surfaced. He would attempt to keep this encounter amicable, but he would no longer take any abuse from his brother. He would stand up for himself, as he wished he could have stood up for his mother all those years ago. That shame—that he had failed her—still burned in him.

'I have come to inform you that I have taken up permanent residence at Edgecombe and that I shall now take my proper place in society. I have every intention of visiting London whenever I wish.'

*Do not let me see you around decent people again if you know what is good for you.*

The snarled words from ten years ago echoed through him.

*Thetford is closed to you. London is closed to you. Stay away and don't make me repeat this lesson.*

He felt again the agonising pain as the hot iron seared into his flesh, remembered the lingering, festering wound that became infected and threatened his life, and he controlled his rage. Rage would not help now. He would take his cue from Thetford's behaviour towards him in the coming days.

He recognised the caution in his brother's expression. The careful way he held himself told him that Thetford feared him—physically, at least, and here, where it was just the two of them. But it was how his half-brother behaved in public that would reveal what their relationship might become. Never friends. Zach neither looked for nor wanted that. But if they could remain distantly polite he would count that as a success. And he would do that for Cecily's sake. Revenge was not part of his plan.

'Kilburn said you've been sniffing around Cecily Beauchamp. I presume that is why you are here? To pursue your suit? You waste your time. She's all but promised to Kilburn.'

'That is not what I've heard. And she is not a possession to be *promised* to anyone. It will be her decision.'

'The Duke—'

'Is having second thoughts.' The news that Cheriton was actively considering other potential husbands for Cecily had aroused the hope that he had taken Zach's warning about Kilburn seriously. 'He has made enquiries about your friend and he is not happy with what he has found.'

'And he told you this himself? The Duke of Cheriton is as high as they come. He will not welcome a gipsy into his family.'

'And yet he has married the daughter of a common soldier and his brother has recently wed the daughter of a glassmaker.'

'And you imagine a gipsy is the equal of them?' Disdain peppered his words.

'*Half*-gipsy.'

'He still will not stoop to contaminated blood and you had better—'

It was simple to silence his brother's vitriol by closing the gap between them. Thetford stepped back, sweeping his straight brown hair back from his forehead. His hand—to Zach's quiet satisfaction—trembled.

'I have neither need nor desire to discuss my future with you.' Zach stared into the cold eyes. 'I have come here out of common courtesy, to apprise you of my presence here in

Town. Having done so, I shall take my leave. I hope when we meet in a social setting we can at least remain civil.'

He nodded, pivoted on his heel and left the room.

He returned to his apartment on Jermyn Street to find a note awaiting him. He broke the seal with a puzzled frown at the unfamiliar feminine script on the outside. Cecily was the only lady he knew in Town and he was filled with a sense of foreboding. He could imagine no good reason for her to write to him, other than outright rejection. He skimmed down the page to the signature. Lady Tubthorpe. His racing pulse steadied, although he was no wiser. A quick scan of her words revealed an invitation to a soirée, that evening, at the residence of Sir Henry and Lady Tubthorpe in Seymour Street. His uneasiness dissipated. Not a letter of dismissal, but he sensed Cecily's hand behind this invitation nevertheless and hope blossomed.

He rang for Tatler, the man he had engaged upon his arrival in Town. It went against his nature—to hire another man to care for him—but Tatler had been turned off from his previous position when the family returned to the country and he'd had a look of hunger in his eyes. Zach assuaged his conscience with the memory of that look. He could afford a man's wages and he needed someone to take care of his meals, his room and his clothes if he were to seek acceptance as a gentleman within society. And Tatler—who had declined to live in, as he had a wife and child—had been embarrassingly grateful.

Tatler soon appeared. 'Yes, sir?'

'That note was an invitation from a Lady Tubthorpe to attend her soirée this evening. So I shall need my evening clothes laid out ready.'

'Shall you require assistance to dress, sir?'

'No, I... Actually, yes. You may help me tie my neckcloth.' Zach tugged at the neckcloth that had taken him a dozen attempts and much swearing to get right that morning before he called upon Cecily. 'Any skill I once possessed in the art appears to have deserted me.'

He grinned and Tatler smiled in return.

'Also, what can you tell me about Sir Henry and Lady Tubthorpe?'

'Sir Henry Tubthorpe? A cit, sir—he's high up in the Bank of England, I believe—but Lady Tubthorpe, she's from an old family, sir, and they're accepted by most in society. They have a son and a daughter, whom they've launched into society this year.'

'Thank you, Tatler. That will be all.'

## Chapter Seventeen

That evening Zach walked into the soirée with his head high, knowing that if Thetford or Kilburn were present his half-Romany status would quickly spread around the room. And he had concluded that the best way to deal with any ensuing gossip was to be completely open and unapologetic about his heritage. Then people could either take him or leave him. He would not be ashamed of his family. They had treated him with far more compassion and acceptance than Thetford, a peer and a so-called gentleman.

He approached his hosts. Sir Henry, his stomach straining the buttons of his waistcoat, shook his hand vigorously.

'Graystoke, eh? I remember your father. Yes, yes. Good of you to come at short notice. My dear?'

He turned to the rotund woman by his side. Her rosy cheeks quivered as she smiled at Zach, her round eyes inquisitive, her head cocked to one side.

'My wife, Lady Tubthorpe. Mr Graystoke.'

Zach bowed.

'I am delighted to meet you, sir.'

'Thank you for the invitation, my lady.'

'I understand from Lady Olivia that you are newly arrived in Town?'

'Lady Olivia?'

'Why, yes. She sent a note to our Lizzie—that's our daughter, they're great friends, you know—and asked if we might send you an invitation for this evening.'

'I see. I shall have to thank her when I see her.'

So this invitation had not been prompted by Cecily, eager to see him again. His spirits dipped, but only fleetingly. After all, he had not yet begun his campaign to change her mind and, if Cheriton was harbouring doubts about Kilburn, he at least had more time to make his case.

'The Beauchamp party have yet to arrive but, in the meantime, perhaps you will allow me to introduce you to one or two people?' Lady Tubthorpe said as she ushered him towards a crowded room. 'There will no doubt be dancing here in the salon later, but there are card tables also set up in the book room over there—' she waved her arm, indicating a room on the opposite side of the hall '—and the sitting room is for those who wish to sit and talk.'

She halted suddenly. 'I should perhaps make you aware that your brother is already present, Mr Graystoke, and if it will set your mind at ease, Sir Henry and I discussed Olivia's request before I sent your invitation. We both remember your father's second marriage, the ill will towards your mother and how you both vanished after his death. Lord Thetford has never been forthcoming about what became of you both, but I am delighted you have decided to return.'

'I think not everyone will share your delight, ma'am.'

They continued towards the salon. 'That is true. But I faced censure when I married Sir Henry—he was plain Henry Tubthorpe then, not even a sir, and a vicar's second son with a need to earn his living—and I was snubbed by many former friends. The *ton* can be exceedingly unforgiving. Since that experience both Sir Henry and I have taken care to draw our own conclusions about people. And I understand you are a friend of Lord Vernon and his new wife—that is a good enough recommendation for me. I have yet to meet Lady Vernon, of course, but for a woman to capture such a wily rake—' She laughed merrily. 'Oh, yes. She has my unquestioning approval.'

Zach couldn't help but like her ladyship as she rattled away. She led him to the largest group and introduced him before saying, 'I shall leave you to become acquainted. I have guests to greet.' She patted Zach's arm before she left. 'You are very welcome here, Mr Graystoke, unless you should prove yourself unworthy of our friendship. But I do not believe you will.' And she bustled away.

Zach received a mixed reception from his fellow guests. No one challenged him outright about his heritage, but he was aware that curiosity about this stranger in their midst did not equate to approval, or even acceptance, and it would not prevent every salacious detail of his past spreading from mouth to mouth behind his back.

And then he saw Thetford, with Kilburn, at the centre of a small knot of guests on the far side of the room. The censorious glances from that group left Zach in no doubt as to their topic of conversation and he turned his back, attempting to concentrate on the conversations going on around him. But in reality his main focus was on the salon door...waiting for the moment Cecily appeared. It soon became apparent, however, that more and more of the guests—even those who had previously treated him with civility, if not warmth—were deliberately shunning him. Thetford and Kilburn were doing their job well.

And, at last, Cecily was there, wearing a shimmering, gauzy gold-coloured gown that draped her curves, making his blood hum with appreciation. Her chestnut hair was caught back with a bandeau of burnished steel, in the style of a Roman goddess, with ringlets falling from a knot on top of her head and a few curling tendrils framing her face. She looked utterly gorgeous. He couldn't wait to hold her in his arms again, to kiss her, to love her. Her pull was magnetic, but he kept his expression blank and commanded his legs not to move in her direction.

By Cecily's side was Lady Olivia, her raven hair coaxed into ringlets, plus another young lady—very beautiful, with her silver-blonde hair piled on to her head and threaded through with pink ribbon—and a formidable-looking older woman, dressed from head to toe in rich purple, leaning heavily on a cane and inspecting her fellow guests through a lorgnette. And, behind them, the Duke and Duchess. Any temptation to go to Cecily withered. There was no point in inviting trouble. He would remain where he was and continue to mingle with the other guests, where possible. Much as he longed to be with Cecily, it was the rest of society, including her family, that he needed to win over.

The volume of chatter in the room made his head ring as the room grew ever more crowded and his thoughts turned wistfully to the peace of his own campfire. But his discomfort vanished when he finally came face to face with Cecily and her companions. The Duke and Duchess were no longer among their number and a quick scan of the room revealed Cheriton talking to Thetford and Kilburn. Every sinew of Zach's body hardened. No matter what poison Thetford spread, he would fight for Cecily. Without volition, he pushed his tailcoat aside and ran his fingers over his buttock, feeling the indentation of that brand. He would never allow her to be under the control of the man who had wielded that red-hot iron.

Never.

He switched his attention back to Cecily and bowed. 'I am delighted to renew our acquaintance, Lady Cecily.'

Cecily bobbed a curtsy. 'As am I, Mr Graystoke. Might I introduce my companions?'

'Please do.'

'Lady Glenlochrie, Lady Olivia Beauchamp, Lady Helena Caldicot—this is Mr Graystoke, the brother of Lord Thetford.'

'Half-brother,' Zach said.

The two young ladies bobbed curtsies, but Lady Glenlochrie merely inclined her head, her mouth a thin line, before saying, 'Nell. Olivia. Be good enough to assist me to the sitting room. The noise in here is quite intolerable and my legs grow weary.'

Zach caught the disapproving glance she directed at Cecily.

'I apologise for Lady Glenlochrie's abruptness,' Cecily said. She opened her fan and plied it to cheeks flushed a delicate pink. 'She is something of a stickler and takes her role as Nell's official chaperon very seriously.'

Zach scanned the crowds. Many people watched them avidly, but quickly averted their eyes as they met his. He failed to spot Thetford, Kilburn or the Duke during his sweep of the room. Over the rise and fall of chatter and laughter he caught an occasional melody from a pianoforte.

'There is no need. I am grateful you are prepared to talk to me so openly.'

'Well, you will be pleased to learn that Vernon and Thea arrive tomorrow and Daniel, too, so you will have others to champion your cause.'

'Thea and Daniel, maybe, but I cannot see your brother feeling any more kindly disposed towards me than the Duke.'

Her green eyes clouded. 'It is not that they do not like or respect you, as a man. They are worried about me. Leo is afraid people will cut me. If you put yourself in his place, would you not behave the same?'

'So Cheriton knows I called on you this morning?'

'He does. And he is unhappy, but he cannot dictate to whom I speak. He did, however, order Olivia to do no more than briefly acknowledge you if you should meet again.'

'And yet—' he silently blessed Cecily's niece '—it was she who prevailed upon the Tubthorpes to invite me here tonight.'

Cecily shook her head with an exasperated laugh. 'Why does that not surprise me in the least? She is not a wicked girl, but she is stubborn and determined and she has a knack of reasoning that I suspect she uses on herself as well as others—reasoning that overrules any whispering of her conscience. She generally manages to persuade herself that what she *wishes* to do will, in the long term, be for the best.'

'The end justifies the means?'

'Yes. Precisely. I fear her unshakeable belief in her own abilities will lead her into trouble one day.' She scanned the crowd. 'Tell me, have you met with Lord Thetford yet?'

'I called upon him immediately I left you this morning.'

'And...?'

He shrugged. 'I informed him I intend to take my place in society. He was not pleased. We have not spoken this evening.'

'No.' Worry knotted her brow. 'I saw him and Lord Kilburn speaking to Leo earlier. I suspect they will do what they can to blacken your name and your character.'

He failed to suppress his grin. 'They need do nothing to achieve that, my dove. My parentage is known well enough to convince most people I am a man to be regarded with suspicion and avoided at all costs. The gossip will spread with little help from either of our brothers or from your erstwhile swain.'

She lifted her chin. 'He is not—yet—my erstwhile anything. I have still to decide what I shall do.'

'You will choose me.'

Her eyes flashed. 'That assumption is exceedingly arrogant, sir.'

He lowered his voice and leaned close to speak in her ear. 'We are meant to be together—you cannot deny it.' He registered the fine shiver that racked her as his breath caressed the sensitive skin of her neck. 'Have you sought out Kilburn this evening? Have you yet to even acknowledge his presence?' He knew she had not, for he had been watching her. 'No, but you *are* here, with me, playing with fire by talking openly with a half-blood Romany, my sweet, brave dove.'

With one fingertip he stroked the bare skin of her inner arm: that sensitive area that lay exposed between the top of her glove and her sleeve.

'Stop. People are watching.'

He straightened. If he followed his instinct, he would sweep her into his arms and carry her away, far from these censorious people with their rules and their pomposity. But he had returned to re-establish his place among them, for Cecily's sake. And for his own sake, too, he realised, as he caught sight of Thetford and Kilburn approaching. It felt good to finally confront his former tormenters. He had allowed them too much power, for too long, over the path his life had taken.

They stopped in front of him and Cecily. Zach bowed. 'Thetford. Kilburn.'

Thetford frowned, but nodded. Kilburn failed to acknowledge Zach's presence, going immediately to stand on the far side of Cecily. The music came to an end.

'Play something lively,' a female voice cried out. 'Let us have dancing.'

A chorus of voices joined in approval and the pianoforte started up again with the opening bars of a country dance. People began to clear the centre of the room, where the carpet had been rolled up in readiness for dancing.

'Shall we have a little entertainment first?' Kilburn's voice carried as he stepped forward into the clearing space. Zach tensed and he heard Cecily's horrified gasp as the voices around them hushed and the music faltered. 'We have a newcomer in our midst. A *gipsy*, no less—a breed famed for their flamboyant behaviour, among other things.' He pivoted smoothly and bowed towards Zach, sweeping his arm around in an extravagant gesture. 'Unfortunately, he is masquerading as a gentleman this evening, but I feel certain we can all imagine his normal colourful costume. Graystoke—' his eyes glittered with malice '—do oblige us with a jig, or whatever you call your heathen dances. It is a shame you do not have a gipsy wench here with you, too, to delight and scandalise the audience with her wanton ways.'

Titters and whispers hissed through the air and every face appeared focused on him. But Zach was aware that, in among the contemptuous looks at him, there were also shame-faced expressions—including, intriguingly, Thetford's—and one or two hard glares of disapproval directed at Kilburn. He walked forward until he was face to face with Kilburn and he bowed. He did not want this. Had not asked for this. But he would not allow Kilburn to intimidate him. He pivoted in a circle and spoke clearly as he did so, addressing every corner of the room.

'I am, as you are all aware, half-gipsy—or Romany, as my mother's people prefer to be called. I am not ashamed of that and it is not my intention to renounce it now I have returned to claim my inheritance from my late

father, the fourth Earl of Thetford.' He faced Kilburn
again. 'If your goal was to cause me humiliation, Kilburn, you have failed. As I informed you before, I am no
longer a young boy to be persecuted by his older brother
and his cronies. I am a man and I know my own worth.
*I* have no need to belittle and humiliate others in an attempt to prove my superiority. As my father—an honourable man—used to say: blowing out another man's candle
does not make yours shine brighter.'

He turned on his heel and strode from the floor, re-
joicing in the approval that illuminated Cecily's smile—a
balm to his raw feelings. At least it had not been his brother
who had tried to humiliate him so publicly and for that he
was thankful. Thetford was still standing by Cecily and
Zach saw a glimmer of respect in his half-brother's eyes.

*Wonders will never cease.*

'Lady Cecily.' Kilburn had followed on Zach's heels.
'May I claim your hand for the first dance?'

Not by a flicker did Cecily reveal either approval or disapproval for the man and what he had done. Lady Perfect
was securely in place.

'Thank you, sir, but I do not dance this evening. May I
suggest you seek a partner elsewhere?'

Kilburn scowled, but made no move to do as she suggested and they remained in an unlikely grouping, none of
them, seemingly, willing to walk away. Many couples were
already taking the floor and lining up but, all around their
little group, people had edged closer, eager to see and hear
what might happen next. Zach felt no compulsion to speak
or to act, content to wait, but he sensed the inactivity needled
the other two men and, despite their outward elegance, the air
around them seemed to resonate with suppressed violence.

'Might I escort you to your brother, Lady Cecily?' Thetford proffered his arm, which Cecily ignored with a chilly smile.

'I thank you but, no, sir. I am more than content to stand here and observe the dance. If I wish to find my brother, I am more than capable of doing so without assistance.'

'You will ruin Lady Cecily's reputation, Graystoke, if you remain so pointedly by her side,' Kilburn then growled. 'Do the honourable thing, and remove yourself from her sphere. You are not welcome here. Are you so very insensitive you cannot recognise the hostility that surrounds you?'

'I recognise *your* hostility, Kilburn.' He turned pointedly to Cecily. 'Would you care for a turn around the room, my lady?'

He did not proffer his arm. They could stroll side by side. There was no need to push her too hard. Too fast.

'I should—'

Zach never learned what Cecily's answer would be. The people around them were parting to allow the Duke and Duchess to pass through, the volume of their chatter fading as the Duke levelled a stony stare at Zach.

'I had no expectation of our meeting again so soon, Graystoke.' The tone was mild enough, but no one could mistake the steel underlying his words.

'Nor I,' said Zach, holding his gaze. 'And yet here we are.'

Out of the corner of his eye he could see the Duchess murmur into Cecily's ear, following which the two women walked away arm in arm. He took a minute to appreciate the sway of Cecily's hips in her golden gown, before wrenching his attention back to the Duke, whose glare was unmistakable.

'If you will excuse us?' Cheriton spoke to Thetford and Kilburn, one brow raised authoritatively.

They nodded and walked away. Cheriton then sent his

silvery gaze around the bystanders closest to them and, with one accord, they too moved away.

'I will not pull my punches, Graystoke. I am conscious of the debt certain members of my family owe to you, but that does not award you entry into society through any association with my name.'

Zach smiled. 'Your name is of no consequence to me, hard as that might be for you to believe. I seek neither your approval nor your permission, Cheriton. I plough my own furrow.'

A muscle leapt in the other man's jaw. 'Not with *my* sister, you don't.' His voice was menacingly quiet. 'Not only is your breeding far beneath hers, I am now informed you are not even legitimate.'

Shock ripped through Zach. Not legitimate? He looked across the room to where his brother and Kilburn were once again surrounded by avid listeners.

*That bastard.*

If he wasn't so bloody furious he would laugh at the irony of thinking of his brother in the same terms he had labelled Zach. A bastard! Rage knotted his gut. How *dare* they malign his mother's memory?

He controlled his fury. 'You have the reputation of a fair man, Cheriton, and you are old enough to have known my father in person. He was a man of honour, yet you are ready to believe that he deliberately tricked society by introducing as his countess a lady to whom he was not legally wed?'

'I have the word of two gentlemen…two *noble*men… that it was so. Are *you* able to prove otherwise?'

Zach ignored his question. 'I have warned you before not to be taken in by men's titles, Cheriton. I told you what Kilburn is capable of. I would not willingly allow him anywhere near *any* decent woman, let alone a member of my family. He has a cruel streak and men of that ilk always revert to type eventually.'

'Kilburn's lack of suitability does nothing to improve *your* acceptability. I have protected Cecily from the question about your legitimacy, but I say this to you: if you feel anything for my sister—other than that stir in your breeches—you will not further tarnish her name or her reputation. In future, I expect nothing more than a nod of acquaintance from you should you happen to meet *any* member of the Beauchamp family. Have I made myself clear?'

He did not wait for Zach to reply, but stalked away and the Beauchamp party left soon afterwards.

## *Chapter Eighteen*

The following day, having consulted with Mr Leeds, his late father's solicitor, and urged on by a little devil inside, Zach joined the promenade of the great and the good in Hyde Park at five o'clock. At his heels lurched Myrtle, the only one of his animal companions he had brought with him to Town. He imagined, with hidden amusement, what reaction Sancho Panza might have prompted from the fashionable crowds. Myrtle attracted enough attention, ranging from the sympathetic to the horrified. More than one lady, upon spying the ungainly gait of the terrier, swept her skirt aside with a moue of disgust. Zach didn't care. It soothed him to have Myrtle by his side and she needed the exercise. Although not on a lead, she stuck close to him— unused to so many people, horses and carriages—and he matched his gait to hers.

One or two familiar faces from his schooldays nodded a greeting, but he guessed from their uncertain expressions that they had not quite placed him and so he did no more than nod in reply. The few people he recognised from the night before cut him direct. Hardly a surprise, with the lie Thetford had spread about him—a lie he would expose when the time was right.

Finally he spied Cecily and his heart turned in his chest. She was every inch the perfect lady, stylishly gowned in primrose yellow with a dainty midnight-blue hat perched atop her shining chestnut hair and holding a matching parasol. She was utterly gorgeous and every fibre of his being yearned to snatch her into his arms and carry her away.

She saw him and her eyes lit up as a smile curved those luscious lips. He stopped before her and bowed.

'Good afternoon, Lady Cecily.'

She dipped a curtsy. 'Mr Graystoke. It is a pleasure to see you again.'

He was delighted to see Thea's friendly face and welcoming smile among Cecily's companions. The Duchess—her expression a touch anxious—was there, too, together with Lady Olivia and the Duchess's stepsister, Lady Helena, and he greeted them all, together with a child who was introduced as the Duchess's adopted daughter, Susie. The final member of the group was a young man, a stranger even though clearly a Beauchamp, who was holding tight to the straining lead of the tallest dog Zach had ever seen. He recalled Cecily mentioning the Duchess's dog. This, no doubt, was him—and he was clearly eager to meet Myrtle.

'I do not believe you have been introduced to the younger of my two nephews, Lord Alexander Beauchamp?'

'I have not.' The two men bowed in greeting.

'You're that fellow that's set 'em all on their ears.' Lord Alexander's laconic drawl earned him a sharp look from his aunt. 'Well,' he protested, 'everyone knows what's goin' on except me. I'm only askin'.'

'If you spent more time at home, with the family, you would know very well what is *going on*, as you put it, Alex.'

He shrugged. 'What's your dog's name? What happened to its leg?'

'Myrtle. She was caught in a snare.'

'One of yours? You're a gipsy, ain't you?'

Zach sensed the uneasiness of the others around them, but the questions did not irritate him. It was refreshing to be able to talk about the subject that everyone else carefully avoided.

'My mother was a Romany, yes. And no. I never set snares. I can't abide them.'

Lord Alexander hunkered down and held his hand out to Myrtle who, cautiously, reached forward and inspected his fingers, her tail low but slowly wagging. The other dog—a shaggy, fawn-coloured hound—took the opportunity to examine Myrtle. When Alex stood up again, he grinned at Zach and said, 'Hector needs to run off his energy.'

With that, he slipped the collar from the dog and set him free.

Zach bit back a smile at the Duchess's expression of pure horror as Hector gambolled in a huge circle around them, followed by Myrtle, keeping up as best she could. Muted shrieks sounded from passing walkers, who were stopped in their tracks as they found themselves in the middle of a canine game of tag.

'Alex! Go and catch Hector immediately.' Cecily looked no less horrified than the Duchess while Thea, Olivia and Helena stifled giggles behind their hands.

'They're doing no harm,' Alex said, with a wink at Zach.

'Myrtle. Come here, girl.'

The terrier hopped over to Zach and panted up at him. Hector followed, and Zach took the collar and lead from Alex and secured the huge hound. He then handed control of the dog back to the young man.

'Why not take them across there where they can run without scaring everyone half to death?'

Cecily's warm smile was worth the scowl he received from her nephew before he slouched off with the two dogs, Susie skipping after them.

*Might as well grasp the nettle*...

'Does the Duke intend to join you in the Park this afternoon, Lady Cecily?'

'They are already here,' Thea said, in her gruff voice, 'but on horseback. Do you mean to avoid them, Absalom?'

'Absalom?' Lady Olivia said. 'Why do you call him Absalom, Aunt Thea?'

Thea blushed fiery red. 'Should I have said Mr Gray?'

She glanced anxiously at the Duchess, who said, 'No, Thea. Do not fret. As you and Vernon have only just arrived in Town, we have not yet had the opportunity to tell you the latest news. It transpires that Absalom's real name is Zachary Absalom Graystoke and his father was the Earl of Thetford.'

Thea's eyes sparkled. 'An *earl*?' She smiled widely as she looked from Zach to Cecily and back again. 'Why, that is wonderful news.' Her smile faltered as she took in Cecily's expression. 'Oh.'

Cecily swallowed past the painful lump that had formed in her throat. She put no blame on Thea for not understanding that Zach's paternity would make little difference—her father was a manufacturer and she was unused to society and its ways, having never set foot in London until this morning.

Why did life have to be so complicated? Cecily's jaw ached with the effort of keeping tears at bay. She was aware Thea still stared at her, her expression puzzled, but there was nothing she could say to explain.

'It is because I am still half-Romany,' Zach said into the sudden silence. 'That is enough to keep me isolated from much of society. But not all, I hope,' he added, flicking a glance at Cecily.

She felt her cheeks heat.

'Well, not from me,' Thea declared. She put her hand on his arm. 'I shall never forget you saved my brother and you will always be a welcome visitor to my home.'

'Thea—that may not be wise.' Rosalind exchanged an anxious glance with Cecily. They both knew Vernon might have something to say about that.

Thea sniffed, tossed her head—causing two wayward curls to tumble and bounce around her ears—and stuck her nose in the air. 'Abs—*Zachary* saved Daniel. I shall not turn my back on him. In fact…we are throwing a party tonight to celebrate our marriage and to introduce me to some of Vernon's friends. It's not formal, not like a ball,' she added hastily. 'I should not enjoy that, one little bit, not yet any-way. It is at our house in South Audley Street and it would give me great pleasure if you will come, Zachary. Daniel will be there—he is due to arrive in London this afternoon.'

'Thank you.' Zach bowed. 'I am honoured.'

He slanted a glance at Cecily, and her insides melted at the heat in his eyes. Vernon and Thea's party suddenly held much more appeal than it had five minutes ago. They started to stroll once more. The number of hostile looks they attracted was noticeable and Cecily's heart sank as she realised that many in the *ton* had already turned against Zach.

And then, visible in the distance and heading in their direction, she spied Leo and Vernon. Her heart plummeted to her toes. Leo had been clear—none of the family were to engage with Zach beyond a polite greeting and yet here they all were—his wife and daughter included—walking out in public. Although Rosalind remained steadfast in her backing of Cecily in private, she would never defy Leo in public and Cecily knew she must be worried about being with Zach now.

Cecily had challenged Leo and he had cited the attitudes of many of the people present at the Tubthorpes' soirée last evening.

*'A too-close association with a man like Graystoke will only harm your chances of a decent match, if you are still set on marriage.'*

The attitude of many of their fellow walkers towards Zach confirmed Leo's fears and Cecily felt sick to the stomach at the barely veiled animosity on display. Thetford had done a fine job of hardening attitudes against Zach. She was ashamed to be a part of such a bigoted society and she was aware her own attitude was hardening, too—but against her own 'kind', as so many people termed it. And that scared her. She looked at Zach…drank in his tall manly form, his dark good looks, his air of calm. She loved him and she wanted him, but had she courage enough to go against every precept of her upbringing and follow her heart? Could she really alienate society and turn her back on her beloved family?

Or could that flicker of hope—that her family and others in society would one day accept Zach, now that he had returned—grow into a flame?

Of one thing she was certain, though. After his nasty display at the soirée, she had finally determined to reject Kilburn. All she need do now was to tell him tonight, at Vernon and Thea's party.

Her brothers rode ever nearer, wearing identical expressions of disapproval. Leo, she knew from past experience, would not hesitate to exert his authority. Another glance at Zach heightened her sense of unease. His attention was fully focused on Leo, and Cecily had no doubt he would resist any attempt to coerce him. Olivia and Nell—both of them wide-eyed with curiosity—were also watching the men's approach and that only added to Cecily's disquiet.

Before she could say anything to the girls, however, Rosalind said, 'Go after Alex, girls, if you please. He is in need of your help to keep the dogs from bothering other people and to look after Susie.'

'But—'

Cecily found her voice. 'Livvy. Go. Please.'

Cecily turned to Zach, aware of a crowd gathering at a discreet distance, watching and whispering.

'Please leave before they get here, Zach. No good can come of a public confrontation.'

Zach studied her. His dark brows twitched and one corner of his lips quirked. Exasperation joined the agitated mixture of emotions that swirled and spiralled through her. The dratted man was trying not to laugh. She longed to throw her hands in the air and walk away and leave these stubborn men to their inevitable clash, but she remained rooted to the spot.

'I intend no confrontation, dove. I merely wish to put your brother straight on a particular matter. And here is as good a place as any. In fact, it is perfect. It is far better for these people—' he indicated the onlookers '—to hear the truth direct rather than some third-hand account that has been falsely embellished by every person who passes it on.'

Cecily lowered her voice. 'I do not know the matter to which you refer, but this is unwise, Zach.'

'Not to me. The truth is never unwise—especially when so many people are happy to peddle the lies Thetford has told about me. I will not hide away in corners waiting for the truth to spread piecemeal.'

Leo and Vernon reined to a halt a short distance away. Leo dismounted, handed his horse to Vernon and strolled towards them, stripping off his gloves. There was a collective gasp from the gathered crowd. Cecily's insides lurched and then roiled alarmingly. She moved to intercept him.

'Leo! What… Why do you remove your gloves? Y-you will not—surely you do not intend to—' She could not finish her sentence.

Leo halted, glanced down at the gloves he now carried, then back at Cecily. His silver eyes gleamed. 'Cecy,' he said, in a low voice, 'do try not to be such a goose. I am hot, that is all. If I decide to call him out, I would not do so in public. Now, please—' he moved her to one side '—allow me to pass.'

She watched helplessly as he strolled on past her and stopped in front of Zach. 'Good afternoon, Graystoke.'

Zach nodded. 'Cheriton.'

'Was I not sufficiently clear last night? I do not wish any members of my family to associate with you.'

'You were clear. But you were not clear as to whether your *request* stemmed from the fact that my mother was born a Romany or your belief that my parents were unwed.'

Cecily gasped. Unwed? Was it true? Her thoughts tumbled. *This* was what Leo had been at pains to protect her from yesterday? She had suspected there was something. This—*this*—if true, it placed Zach even further beyond her reach.

'Either one of those is sufficient. Together—well, I shall allow you to draw your own conclusion as to my opinion on that subject.'

Zach's lips firmed. 'I will not be ashamed of my Romany blood. *That* side of my family behaved with compassion and generosity when my mother and I had need of their help, unlike my brother—a so-called gentleman. But I shall defend my parents against Thetford's slur. They were married legally and I have the proof. After my father's death, the relevant page was ripped—by *someone*—from the parish register at Thetford in an attempt to deny the marriage ever took place. However, I have here my mother's copy of the marriage lines and I have today been handed further proof by my late father's solicitor.'

He reached into his inside pocket and withdrew two documents. He handed them to Leo and then looked around at the people nearby. He raised his voice.

'The second document is an affidavit, sworn by the vicar who married my parents, and signed by my father. It confirms the marriage. Condemn me if you will for my Romany blood, but do not sully the memory of my father or my mother by believing lies.'

He reached to take the documents from Leo. 'Will you confirm that what I have said is the truth, Duke?'

Cecily held her breath as Leo eyed Zach. She knew her brother very well and her heart lifted as she recognised the glimpse of respect in his eyes.

'I will,' Leo said. He spoke as loudly as Zach had. 'They were legally married.'

'And my brother—a gentleman who, in his own estimation, is worth so much more than me—told a blatant lie.'

Leo's jaw firmed and he took Cecily by her arm. 'It makes little difference, Graystoke. Come, Cecily. Let us go.'

On the brink of snatching her arm away, Cecily caught sight of Rosalind's troubled expression. She couldn't do it. Too many eyes were watching and she would neither humiliate Leo by publicly opposing him, nor give rise to even more malicious gossip about the Beauchamps and lowering standards. Rosalind already had concerns that any hint of scandal attached to the Beauchamps would be laid at her door and at Thea's.

And Cecily still could not quite bring herself to choose her own happiness above that of her family, even though her love for Zach burned brighter than ever.

The understanding in Zach's eyes as he watched her almost changed her mind.

Almost, but not quite.

'Get used to seeing me around, Cheriton.' Zach faced Leo, relaxed and yet, somehow, alert at the same time. 'I am a patient man. In fact—' one dark brow lifted '—I shall see you again tonight.'

He bowed, winked at Cecily and strode away in the direction of the Serpentine, where Hector could be seen protecting a terrified Myrtle from an attack by an enraged swan.

'Tonight?' Leo growled.

Vernon nudged his horse with his heels, moving closer before dismounting. 'Thea? What have you done?'

She cast a conspiratorial glance at Cecily before saying, brightly, 'I invited Mr Graystoke to our party tonight. He is my friend and he saved Daniel's life. Why would I not invite him?'

Vernon held her elbow and spoke in a quiet voice. 'You should have asked me.'

Thea stuck her nose in the air. 'Should I consult you about every decision I make, Husband? Which gown I should wear? Which street I might walk down? *You* failed to warn me that Mr Graystoke was even here in London— let alone that, for some reason, you now disapprove of a man you formerly liked. Therefore, as I see it, you cannot blame me for my spontaneous invitation when I met with an old friend. And Daniel arrives today—he will *certainly* wish to see Mr Graystoke.'

If her own worries were not playing such havoc with her nerves, Cecily might have laughed at the look of helpless exasperation on Vernon's face. It appeared that Thea's outspokenness was not dimmed by being in Town for the first time. This time, not even Leo's presence had cowed her strong spirit. How Cecily wished for some of her sister-in-law's courage to rub off on her.

## Chapter Nineteen

'Cecily.' Thea tugged Cecily to one side as she arrived at the house in South Audley Street that evening. 'I am sorry, but I could not stop Vernon from calling on Zachary and withdrawing my invitation.'

A wave of desolation washed over Cecily, catching her off guard, and Thea gasped.

'Are you all right? I am so sorry to tell you bad news. Really, I am so cross with Vernon, he simply *would not* listen to reason. Stubborn man. Daniel is furious with him.'

Cecily quashed her own feelings and patted Thea's shoulder. 'Do not allow this to come between you two, Thea. Leo and Vernon are protecting me, as they see it—conforming to society's mores is in their blood. I doubt they would behave like this towards Zach if it were not for the—the friendship he and I share. Now, let us forget all about this silly squabble and enjoy celebrating your marriage, for that is what tonight is all about.'

She fell back into habit: behaving and talking, laughing and dancing by rote. She had done this most of her life and she did not need conscious effort to maintain outward appearances. Inside, though, her emotions and her thoughts had free rein as she waited for Lord Kilburn to arrive, knowing she must tell him tonight that their understanding was at an end.

Following her meeting with Zach in the Park, she had done much soul-searching. She could no longer deny the truth. If she were to wed any man other than Zach, she would never know true contentment. A part of her heart would always be empty and a part of her mind would always regret. She would always yearn for him.

It hurt that neither of her brothers seemed to care about her feelings. About what she truly desired. All they cared about was that she remained Lady Perfect, as she had always been. Resentment had mushroomed inside her, no matter how she tried to suppress it, until she had felt ready to explode.

And she had, finally, realised what she must do. What she *chose* to do.

Kilburn arrived and immediately tried to claim a dance. Rosalind, at that moment, was by Cecily's side and, feeling she must prepare herself for the forthcoming interview, Cecily nudged her sister-in-law's hand before saying, 'I must decline, I'm afraid, my lord. I have this minute agreed to accompany her Grace on to the terrace. It is exceedingly hot in here and we are in dire need of cool air.'

'Indeed,' Rosalind said. 'And I'm afraid I fully intend to hold Lady Cecily to her promise. I suggest you try again later, sir.' She smiled graciously and tucked her hand into Cecily's elbow. 'Come, Sister. I have a private matter upon which I need your advice.'

Outside, Cecily crossed to the stone balustrade that surrounded the terrace and gazed out over the walled garden to the mews beyond. Rosalind joined her and touched her forearm.

'I shall not presume to offer unsolicited advice, my dearest sister,' said Rosalind, 'but the truth is—I wish you might reconsider this plan to marry. We do not want to lose you.' She raised her hand as Cecily made to reply. 'I *do* understand your reasons for exploring such a path. I suspect I might do the same were I in your shoes.' Her arm slipped around Cecily's waist and she pulled her in for a hug. 'I wish I could help—I know where your heart lies—but...Leo...'

The aching knot that filled her throat had become so familiar that Cecily barely noticed it any more. She tilted her head to rest briefly on Rosalind's shoulder.

'You cannot become involved, Ros. I realise that. I expect nothing more from either you or from Thea. It does help, knowing that you understand.'

'Will you marry Lord Kilburn?'

'No. And I shall tell him so tonight.'

Rosalind hugged her again. 'I am relieved,' she whispered. 'I cannot like him after the way he behaved last night and Leo has uncovered some unsavoury details about him. He is far deeper in debt than anyone realises, you know. Leo suspected you intended to refuse his lordship anyway and he wanted you to make your own decision.'

*If only he was happy for me to make my own decision to marry Zach.*

Cecily did not quite dare tell Rosalind of the decision she *had* reached, however. A decision made with both heart and mind. For the first time in weeks, calmness descended and her soul expanded as she inhaled and tipped her head back to gaze up at the stars. She would inform Lord Kilburn of her decision and then she would tell Leo and the rest of her family that she intended to accept Zach. They would be unhappy, but she hoped in time they would come to accept it and that she would not be estranged from her family for very long. The alternative was to condemn herself and the man she adored to a life of misery apart. And that was a future she was no longer prepared to contemplate.

Hard grey eyes bored into hers. 'I *beg* your pardon?'

Lord Kilburn glanced around the room, then gripped Cecily's upper arm and guided her forcefully towards the open window and the terrace beyond. Cecily complied. This needed to be done and she did not entirely blame his lordship for being angry with her. She had, after all, led him on, albeit unintentionally. Outside he released her arm, almost thrusting her away.

'You have played fast and loose with my affections, madam.'

'Fast and—?' She laughed. 'Really, sir. Such a claim is unworthy of a man of your intelligence. Our conversation at Leyton Grange confirmed affections were not engaged on either side, so it is of no use invoking them now.'

Beads of sweat glistened on his brow and any humour she'd found in the situation evaporated as she recognised again, and more forcefully this time, his air of desperation. And at last she understood the reason for it and the reason for his continued pursuit of her. A thirty-year-old spinster with a large dowry must be close to a rock-solid certainty for a man as deep in debt as Kilburn.

'I apologise, sir. I did not intend to sound as though I were mocking you, but you have never led me to believe that your affections were engaged. Now, if you will excuse me, I should like to return to the house.'

She went to step past him, but he grabbed her arm and propelled her along the terrace to the end, until she was effectively trapped in the corner of the surrounding stone balustrade.

'Is it the gipsy? Is he the reason you have again refused

my perfectly respectable offer?' A bitter smile twisted his lips. 'There is no future for you with him, my dear.'

He pressed closer, crowding her. The edge of the balustrade dug into the small of her back as she arched back from him. Why had she allowed him to steer her outside without protest? She'd had no inkling that she would lose control of the situation in this way or that he would behave in such an ungentlemanly way. Had her own behaviour encouraged such disrespect? She feared the answer must be affirmative.

'Say you'll marry me, Cecily. You'll be a countess. A mother. There are already mutterings about your friendship with that gipsy…'

*Yes. Thanks to you.*

'Your reputation is sullied and you may never receive another offer.' He stared down at her. 'And do not—ever—doubt my desire for you.'

He bent his head and her stomach churned as she realised his intention. She twisted her face aside and brought her hands up between them in an unsuccessful attempt to push him away.

One hand framed her jaw, tightening painfully as he jerked her back to face him. 'You kissed me eagerly enough in Oxfordshire. And tonight you willingly came outside with me…what is a red-blooded man to expect? The Beauchamp name and status has already suffered after your brothers' recent alliances. Is it your wish to add to your family's fall from grace by gaining a reputation for being fast?'

'If the Beauchamp name is so sullied and my own reputation so suspect, I wonder at your still wishing to ally yourself with our family at all, Lord Kilburn. I wonder you do not look elsewhere for a bride.'

His brow darkened and his eyes narrowed, but Cecily

was beyond caring as rage erupted through her. How dare this…this…*pipsqueak*…malign her beloved family? Recklessly, she carried on.

'Or could it be that your need for my dowry outweighs every other consideration? I—'

She ceased her diatribe as a shadow fell across them. Daniel Markham stood silhouetted in the open doorway to the terrace. Kilburn stepped back as Mr Markham raised his voice, to be heard above the music in the room behind him.

'Lady Cecily, my sister is looking for you. Might I escort you to her?'

She heard Kilburn's growl of frustration as she moved away from him and towards Mr Markham.

'Thank you, sir. That is most kind of you.' She took his arm and he led her back inside the house, dipping his head to speak low into her ear.

'I spied you from my bedchamber window,' he said, 'as did a mutual friend of ours. I fear that if you do not reassure him *in person* and *immediately*—his words, not mine—that you are unharmed, he will not hesitate to seek you out himself, without regard to the consequences.' He flicked his head towards Vernon, currently partnering Thea in a country dance.

'Zach is here?' Joy and fear intertwined. What if Leo or Vernon should see him?

'He is. And he wants to speak with you. Come.' He led her to the door and out into the hall. 'He awaits you in the morning parlour. No doubt you know the way.'

She flashed a smile at him. 'Thank you, Daniel. You will not tell anyone?'

He laughed. 'You can be sure I shall keep your secret, my lady—I value my skin too highly to reveal this or my part in it.'

She sped to the parlour and straight into Zach's arms,

seeking his mouth with hers. Her fingers dug into the fine cloth of his sleeves as his smooth, warm lips parted and his tongue caressed hers. She felt as though she was melting into him, the strong frame of his embrace all that stopped her from sinking to the floor. His scent weaved through her senses and desire sizzled, igniting every nerve ending she possessed. Her breasts swelled within the constraints of her corset, her nipples ached with pure need and the heavy weight of desire gathered in her core. A low moan hummed in her throat and was answered by a groan that she felt rather than heard as it vibrated from his chest direct to hers.

She released his arms and thrust her hands through the satiny warmth of his hair, feeling the weight of his thick curls slip and slide between her fingers as she pressed her mouth even closer to his, drinking in the sweetness of his kiss, savouring every moment. It was Zach who ended the kiss. Her tiny protest prompted a gruff laugh from him as he dropped a kiss on the tip of her nose.

'I dare not carry on, sweetheart, or I will end up pleasuring you on the floor.'

She clung to him. 'At least we will be indoors this time and not under the stars.'

His eyes gleamed as he returned her smile. 'This is your brother's house. No matter how I am tempted, I would not abuse his hospitality. Even,' he added, as she opened her mouth to point out that Vernon was unaware of Zach's presence under his roof, 'if it is unwitting.' Then he sobered. 'Are you hurt? I will kill him.'

'No, I am not hurt. But never mind me—why are you here? Why take such a risk?'

His heart felt full to bursting with love for her as he gazed down into her treasured face.

'I have come to tell you what I could not say earlier. I

will wait for you, sweetheart. I will wait for as long as it takes for you to choose your path and only if your choice is not me will I give up hope.'

She laughed, her lips—swollen from his kisses—parted to reveal pearly teeth, her honey-scented breath wreathing through his senses. Excitement radiated from her and pure love shone from her eyes.

'You will not have long to wait, for I have made my choice. I have refused Lord Kilburn and I am ready to follow my heart.'

The breath he had held released in a silent sigh of joy. Cecily touched his temple, then traced his cheekbone and around the line of his jaw, as her soft green eyes searched his. 'I shall hold my head high and stand proudly by your side, if you are certain that is still your wish?'

'Can you doubt it, my sweetest, dearest love?'

He gathered her into his arms and held her tenderly as he pressed his lips to her hair, breathing in her evocative scent: woman and apple blossom. He grew hard again, just holding her. She leaned back against his encircling arm and laughed up at him, her eyes sparkling with mischief as she pressed her hips into him.

'I doubt it no longer.'

She wriggled free of him and then took his hands in both of hers. Faint strains of music drifted through the open window and she tilted her head to one side.

'Listen. That is the newest dance, brought over from Paris. It is called the waltz.' She swayed in time to the melody. 'It is still viewed as scandalous by some, but I think it romantic. I should like to teach you. I should like to dance with you.'

He caught the rhythm from her; found his body swaying, too, of its own accord. 'If it is so scandalous, my perfect lady, I wonder that you even know the steps.'

She stepped closer. 'I learned it at home, but I have yet to dance it in public. If I am going to set society on its ears by marrying you, I cannot baulk at dancing the waltz with you. Only you.'

She tiptoed up to press her lips to his and he caught her in his arms, holding her hard against him as he kissed her again, with a demand that she responded to with a sigh and a quiet moan, sparking trails of fire that scorched through his body. He took his time, exploring her mouth, nipping her lips and feathering kisses over her silken skin, until she brought her hands between them and pushed his chest.

'Dance.' It was an order. She placed his right hand firmly at her waist, put her left hand on his upper arm and held his left hand in her right. 'It will not be as good on the carpet as on a ballroom floor, but at least we will not slip—and dancing will distract you…us…' She twinkled up at him and he found himself smiling again as she went on to say, 'Now, concentrate, if you please.'

He dipped his head to whisper in her ear, 'I might change my mind, if you are to be this dictatorial, dove.'

He felt her quiver and he licked her lobe before nipping it in his teeth. Cecily giggled and pulled away. 'That tickles! Come, now, I long to dance with you. Please?'

*How can I resist?*

She taught him the gliding step and the dips and the sways and how to twirl her around and then take her in hold again and, gradually, he lost himself in the music and in the heady feeling of holding the lady of his dreams in his arms as they moved around the floor. The music finally ended and their steps slowed, and he held her even closer, reluctant for this sensual experience to end.

'That,' he whispered into her ear when they at last came to a stop, 'did nothing to distract me.'

She pressed closer, her lips to his jaw, then stepped out of his arms, gazing into his eyes, her own full of regret.

'I must go. I will be missed and I do not want someone to catch us.'

He caught her to him and kissed her. 'Does it matter if we are to be wed anyway?'

She pursed her mouth, a fine line etched between her brows. 'It matters to me. I want to declare our love to the world and to prove this is my choice. I have no wish for any whispers that we have only wed because we were found in a compromising position.' She stroked his hair back from his brow. 'This is a love match, my darling, and I want the whole world to be in no doubt.' She backed away from him, her hands clinging to his until the distance became too great. 'I shall tell Leo of my decision as soon as we return home.'

Fear clutched him at her words. Before she could open the door, he seized her by the shoulders and embraced her, holding her close to his heart.

'How shall I sleep tonight, dove?' He pressed his lips to her hair. 'Your brother is a persuasive man. What if—?'

'Hush, my love.' Her arms encircled his waist and she hugged him. Hard. 'I shall not change my mind. I promise. But I must leave now.'

He nudged her chin up and kissed her.

'I shall see you tomorrow and we will make our plans,' he said, as he released her. 'But I shall not rest easy until we are wed.'

She slipped from the room, leaving him hardly able to believe his good fortune. His perfect lady was to be his.

# Chapter Twenty

'So.' Leo opened the door to the first-floor salon at Beauchamp House and ushered Cecily through. 'What is it you wish to discuss? Does it concern your refusal of Kilburn's offer?'

Olivia and Nell had been sent off to bed as soon as they all arrived home from the party. Rosalind, after a few seconds' hesitation, joined Leo and Cecily in the salon and sat quietly at one end of the sofa while Cecily settled in a chair.

'Indirectly, yes.'

'Well, I cannot pretend I am not relieved you have decided against him.' Leo sat next to Rosalind. 'Are you still adamant you wish to wed? I do not know what else there is to discuss—you have rejected my every suggestion of other prospective suitors, all of whom would prove eminently acceptable husbands.'

'They are no more acceptable to me than Lord Kilburn was.' Cecily hauled in a deep breath. 'I intend to wed Mr Graystoke.'

Leo surged to his feet. 'No! I forbid it.'

Cecily forced herself to remain seated, folding her hands in her lap as she tilted her chin.

'It is not in your power to forbid it, Leo. I am sorry if you feel my choice will reflect badly on the Beauchamp family name, but—for once—I intend to follow my heart. I love Zach and he loves me. And, as *I* advised *you* not so many months ago, it is no simple matter to change your heart.

'Rosalind, I am sorry. I know you have qualms about this fuelling the gossip about your family connections, but my decision is made. I told Zach tonight.'

'Tonight? I did not see him at the party.' Rosalind stood up, and went to Leo, taking his hand. 'And please do not worry about me. I admit I was concerned initially, but who are we to stand in the way of true love?'

'Rosalind. I think it is time you went to bed,' Leo growled.

She smiled at him, and kissed his cheek. 'I shall wait for you, my sweet.'

She put her lips to his ear and whispered something that brought a gleam to his eyes and a quiver to his lips. Their intimacy brought a lump to Cecily's throat. *This* was what she desired. *This* was what she and Zach would share. She would never enjoy that sort of closeness with any other man.

Rosalind spoke to Cecily again. 'Any gossip will be short-lived and last only as long as it takes the next scandal to emerge. And Leo—*if* he chooses to do so—is capable of dealing most effectively with anyone unwise enough to besmirch the Beauchamp name.'

'Thank you, Rosalind. I am grateful.' Cecily stood, smoothing her hair, and walked over to stand in front of her brother. 'I hope you can find it in your heart to at least accept our union, Leo, if not approve it wholeheartedly. I have supported this family all these years and I have done so willingly. Happily. But, for once, I should like someone to consider my *feelings*, not just my duty.

'I shall say goodnight.'

\* \* \*

In her bedchamber, she dismissed Anna as soon as her gown was removed and her stays unlaced, hearing again and again Zach's last words. His fears. She had let him down before, at Leyton Grange, even though she had made him no promise at the time. If Leo hadn't arrived when he did, would she have accepted Zach there and then? She did not believe so. Not at that time. The hope raised by him admitting his father's identity had not been enough to persuade her to entirely turn her back on the life she had known. But now that Zach had faced his brother and taken his place in society, he had given her the courage to accept him. Together they would face the snubs and the criticisms and, in time, she was confident they would be accepted by her family and those whose friendship mattered to her.

She understood, though, why Zach would be plagued by doubt and her heart ached at the thought of the long night ahead of him.

So she sat in a chair, in her shift, and waited until the house grew quiet. Lady Perfect was about to throw caution to the winds. Her words to Leo had sparked a rebellion deep inside her. She *had* always behaved properly. Done what was expected of her. Now…it was time to take charge of her own life and to grasp happiness.

She picked a simple yellow-sprigged muslin gown— with the fewest possible fastenings—from the wardrobe and quickly dressed, reaching awkwardly behind her neck to do up the buttons, before bundling a hooded cloak and a black veil under her arm. Snatching up her reticule and checking she carried enough money for a hackney, she quietly left her bedchamber and headed for the back stairs. A footman remained on duty in the hall all night, but there would be no one to see her slip out of the kitchen door.

Once outside, she donned the cloak and draped the veil over her hair and face before pulling up the hood.

She walked swiftly until she spied a hackney and, by half past one in the morning, she was standing outside the house on Jermyn Street where Zach rented his rooms. Now she had reached her decision, she did not want to wait any longer to be with the man she loved. She felt no guilt at her actions. No shame. Love was not shameful.

At her soft knock, a bleary-eyed night porter opened the door.

'Mr Graystoke's rooms, please,' she whispered, keeping the hood low over her veiled face. She fumbled in her reticule and took out a crown. The man's eyes widened and he accepted the coin with a bow.

'Up the stairs, second floor, madam.'

On the second floor, she pulled down her hood and stuffed her veil inside her reticule. A light shone beneath a door and she knocked lightly. She heard the creak of the floorboards as he crossed the room. The door opened and, for the second time that night, she walked into his arms. He held her to his chest, the steady thump of his heart loud in the hush of the night as he stroked her hair.

'Do not doubt that I am pleased to see you, my dove, but…how did you get here?'

She leaned back against the circle of his arms to look at him. 'I came in a hackney.'

Disapproval etched his face. 'Alone?'

'But of course. You do not think I would bring Anna to a—an *assignation*?'

'An assignation? Is that what this is?' His lips quirked, but only fleetingly. He shook his head. 'What am I to do with you? It is one thing wandering around in the countryside, alone and after dark. But—here? In London? When I think of the dangers…'

'Zach.' She framed his face, searching his dark, stormy eyes. 'I have told Leo we are to be married. And, yes, he did try to change my mind, but he was unsuccessful. I wanted to set your mind at rest. I shall stay true to my promise. My decision is made.'

The harsh planes of his face softened as she drew him to her for a slow, sensual kiss, tasting of brandy. She explored his mouth and her confidence grew as he allowed her to set the pace. She worked on the fastenings of the floor-length banyan he wore. She pulled it open and slipped her hands beneath. And stilled. Beneath his robe he was stark naked—all hot, hair-roughened skin. She tore her lips from his and stepped back, unable to keep her gaze from dipping down, feasting on the heavy muscles of his chest, his flat stomach, and—she paused again as her eyes locked on to his manhood and she felt them widen.

She looked up. Met his gaze.

'This is what you want, my dove? Tonight?'

'Yes.'

He smiled as he shrugged out of the banyan. Of its own volition, her gaze again swept his body.

Fully naked, fully erect, he was magnificent.

She stepped closer and pressed herself full length against the man she loved more than life itself, her arms around him, her hands roaming his muscled shoulders and his smooth, broad back as their kiss turned urgent, molten. Boldly, she slid her hand between them, closing her fingers around his staff, marvelling at the feel of silken skin sliding over hot, hard flesh. Zach groaned, growing harder and thicker as she held him, then he pulled away. She went with him, murmuring her protest into his mouth. But he lifted his lips from hers and, firmly, he turned her. His arms came around her, his hands seeking her breasts as he nibbled her neck. She tilted her head, sighing her pleasure.

Then his hands were on the buttons of her dress, releasing them, moving slowly but with purpose from one to the next. A shiver chased across her skin as warm breath caressed her nape, but she was not cold. She was shivery with heat, shivery with need, shivery with wanting as he raised gown and shift over her head, stripping her in one swift movement.

He turned her to face him, his dark features intent, his concentration fierce and her insides—already a maelstrom of boiling, urgent need—erupted at the wonder on his face. Her breaths came quick and shallow with the urge to rush him and she clutched at his shoulders…his arms.

'Please.'

He shook his head, his hot gaze locked on to her nipples, now so hard they ached.

'No, dove.' He clasped her hips, his hands hard and calloused, yet gentle, and held her still. 'I will make this a night to remember, for us both. And that will not be by speed.'

He dipped his head.

The slide of his tongue around her nipple was pure torture. The nip of his teeth and the pull of his lips had her gasping for more. Her fingers tangled in his hair, holding him tight to her breast as she succumbed to the feelings swirling around inside—tipping her head back, closing her eyes as every nerve in her entire body flamed. And then they were on the bed, skin to skin, and those swirling feelings wound tighter, spiralled higher, as the torture started again: her breasts, the sensitive skin of her inner arms, her legs, her toes. He raised her leg, licking behind her knee, then running his teeth along her inner thigh to…

At the first probe of his tongue her eyes flew open, but she saw nothing. Her hips bucked and he held her still as he licked into her most intimate place, teasing, sucking lightly. He held her hips captive and she clutched mindlessly, first his hair and then, as he continued, the coverlet on which she lay.

She arched as a hot tide of passion seized her, consuming her as it swept her away, lifting her higher—and higher—and then his weight was on her, between her thighs, and she could feel him nudging at her entrance. Instinctively she tilted her hips and then, slowly, he filled her, stretching her. He withdrew and entered her again, once, twice and then, a sharp pain—gone as soon as it registered—and he was buried inside her, deeper than she thought possible.

Then he began to move.

Deeply. Relentlessly. Powerfully.

And she rode that wave of passion once again until, this time, it peaked and she cried out as her world shattered into bone-melting pleasure. As she floated in ecstasy, she felt Zach grip her, felt the force surge through him as he drove into her and then he, in his turn, cried out and she felt the warmth of him deep inside her.

The tears came then. Crowding her throat, seeping from her eyes, dampening her cheeks, as she gloried in the feeling of his weight on her, and in the feeling of him still deep inside her and in the heady sensation of feeling truly alive for the first time in her life.

No longer a perfect lady, but a woman.

He raised his head, and frowned, his eyes heavy-lidded. Dazed. He brushed her cheek with his thumb.

'Why the tears, dove?' His voice low and raspy.

She shook her head. 'Happy tears.'

He kissed her then—tenderly, lovingly—and withdrew, rolling on to his back, settling her into his arms, her head on his chest, holding her as they slept in one another's arms.

* * *

They stirred at first light and made slow tender love, reaching their fulfilment together. Then Zach, with a final, searing kiss, threw back the covers and arose.

'Come, my dove. We must get you home before you are missed.'

Cecily rolled over to admire his naked body, then gasped at the sight of a deeply grooved letter G on his right buttock. Zach turned at her gasp, a look of resignation on his face.

'What—?' Hot anger curled deep in her belly. 'Is—is that a *brand*?'

Zach nodded, then grabbed a pair of breeches from a chair and pulled them on.

'But—' Cecily sucked in a breath, her thoughts whirling. 'Who did it? Tell me.' But she was afraid she already knew the answer.

'Thetford and Kilburn. It was their idea of fun. Actually—in the main—I believe it was Kilburn. He was always the stronger of the two of them. The leader.'

She pressed her hand to her mouth. '*Kilburn?* B-but I—I might have—'

He sat on the bed and pulled her into his arms. 'I would have stopped it, dove. Trust me. You would not have married Kilburn while I drew breath.'

'Does it hurt?'

'No. But it did at the time. Now, come. It is time you went home.'

Hatred for the men who had inflicted it spiked through her and her fingers crooked into claws. If only she could get her hands on them—but she must just be grateful she discovered the truth about Kilburn in time to stop the biggest mistake of her life. She shuddered at the thought of being under his control.

Reluctantly, she left the warm bed, shivering a little in the early morning chill. She found her shift and pulled it on, followed by her gown.

'I shall go to the bishop for a special licence this morning and make the arrangements at St George's,' Zach said.

They had agreed their betrothal and wedding would be done properly. They would not sneak around as though ashamed, but neither did they wish to wait three weeks for the banns to be called. They wished to be wed as soon as possible.

'As soon as all is arranged, I shall call upon you at Beauchamp House to confirm the details of our wedding.' He grinned then—full of enthusiasm—and caught her to him, swinging her around. 'I cannot wait until you are Lady Cecily Graystoke.'

Their lips met in a fiery kiss, but Cecily soon pulled away, her arms still around his neck.

'I shall be happy to be plain Mrs Graystoke,' she said, smoothing his hair from his face until his earring was exposed. She tightened her arms to pull herself up and took his lobe between her lips and swirled her tongue around the diamond. 'If my family refuse to accept our union— accept *you*—then I shall no longer use my courtesy title. I shall want no part of the Beauchamps.'

She said the words with bravado, but a lump of dread settled in the pit of her stomach. She could not imagine the future without her family. But she'd made her choice and she would look forward, not back.

Zach hugged her close, then lowered her to the floor and pressed his lips to her forehead. 'I know it is hard, but let's see what happens first,' he said. 'Maybe—when your brother sees how happy we are—'

She pulled away from him.

'Yes. Let us see what happens,' she said.

The night porter was nowhere to be seen when they reached the entrance hall. The front door was unbolted and they left the house and walked along the road until they saw a hackney and flagged it down.

Back at Beauchamp House, Cecily crept in through the kitchen door and then slammed to a halt as she came face to face with Michael, one of the footmen, still in his shirt-sleeves, his hair tousled with sleep. His shocked expression said it all but, of all the servants—apart from Anna—she was relieved it was him.

'Michael, please, I beg you—' she pulled open her reti-cule and felt around for another coin '—do not tell anyone you have seen me.'

'N-no, milady.' His cheeks bloomed scarlet, but his trou-bled expression transformed into a grin as she pressed a shilling into his palm.

The clock on the mantel in the salon of Beauchamp House showed half past three. More than ten hours since Zach had escorted Cecily home. Ten hours of silence. Her stomach churned and her throat choked with suppressed fear.

*Where is he? He* promised *to call this morning.*

Doubts—insidious and pervasive—crept through her as the minutes ticked by. If there had been a delay in see-ing the bishop, surely he would have sent word and not left her in silence? She had given herself to him, against every principle by which she had lived her entire life—because she loved him; she believed in him; she *trusted* him.

But what if...? Her throat clenched even tighter and tears scalded her eyes. What if, having succeeded in bed-ding her, he had changed his mind? It was the warning all mothers and chaperons impressed upon their young

charges—give a man what he wants before he puts a ring
on your finger and he never will.

What if he had decided to return to his former life
with his Romany family after all? Leo's words ricocheted
through her memory: *Who knows what tricks and wiles a
man like Gray has up his sleeve?*

*Have I been too stupid, too naive to see the truth? No.
I will not—*cannot—*believe such a thing of Zach.*

*Can I?*

*How well do I truly know him?*

She had even sent a note to his lodgings, but there had
been no reply. She paced the room, feeling caged. In time,
though, an image arose in her mind's eye, slowly calming
her increasingly frantic thoughts. The memory of Zach,
telling her about when he'd found Athena—that protective gesture, the unconscious cupping of his hands. *That*
was Zach. That was not a man who would trick a woman
in order to seduce her.

*But if that is the case, where is he? Why has he not
called or sent word? He must know I am waiting.*

And suspicions grew. Zach had enemies. Thetford and
Kilburn had gone to extreme lengths to get rid of Zach
and his mother in the past. What if they tried something
similar again?

*And Leo and Vernon?*

Her brothers were opposed to her plans, but would they
resort to underhand methods to split her and Zach apart?
She did not want to believe they would, but once the doubt
entered her head it was hard to dislodge it. Leo, Vernon,
Dominic and Alex were all away from home. They had set
off early that morning for Buckinghamshire to inspect the
Foxbourne estate—a horse-breeding enterprise recently
purchased by Leo. He had formed the intention of settling

it upon Alex in the hope it would help his youngest son to settle down and reform his wild ways.

What if they had snatched Zach? Taken him with them by force?

But surely they would not—what could they hope to achieve by it?

The door opened and her gaze snapped to it. Olivia entered, becomingly attired in a sprigged-muslin walking dress and pink spencer, with a jaunty pink hat on her ebony ringlets and carrying a matching parasol.

'Aunt *Cecily*. You are not even changed yet. We are all ready to go to the Park.'

Cecily had agreed to accompany her two sisters-in-law, plus Olivia and Nell, for a walk in the Park that afternoon. She could not continue to sit here and wait and hope. If she went out and Zach arrived, he would either wait here for her or he would follow. And, if anything untoward had happened, she was more likely to learn of it in the Park than sitting here on her own.

'I shall be but five minutes,' she said to Olivia before hurrying upstairs to change her gown.

# Chapter Twenty-One

Day by day the company in London had thinned as many families returned to their country estates and nowhere was that sparsity of numbers more visible than in Hyde Park during the promenade hour. Cecily's hope that Zach might be exercising Myrtle was dashed when she entered the Park and scanned the walkers. There was no sign of him. Her insides continued to roil with nerves and those earlier doubts re-emerged to nibble away at her, even though she had previously dismissed them.

And then, in the distance, Cecily saw Lord Kilburn strolling alone, swinging his cane as though he hadn't a care in the world. He spied her and immediately headed towards their little group, which included Thea's brother, Daniel, who had agreed to escort the ladies.

Kilburn halted, raised his beaver hat and smiled.

'Good afternoon, ladies, Markham.' He bowed and each member of the group bowed or curtsied in reply.

'Good afternoon, Lord Kilburn.'

It was Rosalind who spoke, her voice cool. Cecily had confided in her about Kilburn's behaviour the previous evening. Both Rosalind and Thea had privately expressed their support for Cecily and Zach, and both also promised to work to soften their husbands' objections to him, but Cecily had told neither of her sisters-in-law about her visit to Zach the night before, or that he had failed to call upon her as promised today. She could not bear to be the recipient of sympathy. Not until she could find out what was going on. And, she suspected, here might be her chance.

She smiled at Kilburn, who immediately said, 'May I offer you my arm, Lady Cecily?'

She inclined her head graciously. As she took his arm she shot a reassuring look at Rosalind and gave a swift nod in response to her arched brows. They began to walk, Kilburn and Cecily falling into step behind the others.

Following the briefest of pleasantries, Kilburn said, 'I must apologise for allowing my passions to get the better of me last evening, my lady. I am sure you will understand that I was overcome by disappointment and I promise you my behaviour was *quite* out of character. I can only hope you will find it in your heart to forgive me and to give me another chance?'

'Another chance, sir? Why should you imagine I have had a change of heart so soon?'

Her heart stuttered as he smiled down at her. The smugness was back, in his eyes and in the curve of his mouth. That he knew something she did not was clear and she braced herself, certain she was about to find out what had happened to Zach, fighting to keep her expression impassive, raising her brows as though she awaited a reply that had little significance.

'I do not denounce you for having your head turned by Graystoke, my dear but, now that he is languishing in Newgate, I suspect you will view your future differently. My offer of marriage—' he placed his hand on hers and squeezed '—is still open.'

The breath flew from her lungs, leaving her gasping. Kilburn appeared oblivious to her distress as he continued, 'You must not be embarrassed by your poor judgement of his character. These people, they have the inbred talent to charm and deceive. More worldly individuals than you have been taken in.'

'B-but—*Newgate*? Wh-why is he in Newgate?'

'Oh, had you not heard, my dear?' His voice dripped false sympathy as he halted, gazing down at her with hard eyes. 'How very remiss of me to blurt out such shocking news without first preparing you. I am so sorry to be the bearer of bad tidings. Zachary Graystoke has been arrested for an unprovoked attack on Lord Thetford that left him close to death.' He tutted and shook his head. 'His own brother! Poor Thetford has yet to regain consciousness. One can only hope he survives such a brutal attack.' He patted Cecily's hand. 'You need not fear, however, my dear. The scoundrel has been sent to Newgate to await trial. I doubt we shall see him again. It'll be the rope or transportation for him and good riddance.'

It took several minutes for her confused brain to make sense of Kilburn's revelation. Then her stomach clenched violently, forcing its scalding contents to invade her gullet. Only by dint of swallowing repeatedly did Cecily avoid disgracing herself in the middle of the Park. Her legs trembled and her eyes blurred.

'I do not believe it, sir,' she said when she at last had that nausea under control.

Her hand was still on Kilburn's sleeve and, aware she was clutching the cloth so tight it was in danger of becoming wrinkled, she released her grip and withdrew her arm from his. She clenched her jaw hard and concentrated on slowing her rapid, shallow breaths. Rosalind and the others had seen that she and Kilburn had stopped and were retracing their steps. Rosalind was soon by Cecily's side, linking arms and looking daggers at Kilburn.

'Are you quite well, Sister? You look pale.'

Cecily shook her head. She could not bring herself to say the words out loud. But Kilburn had no such compunction. He announced, in a very loud voice, the news of Zach's arrest.

'Well, there must have been a mistake,' Thea said, stoutly. 'Mr Graystoke would never do such a thing.'

'One can only applaud your loyalty, Lady Vernon, but I am afraid there is no mistake. I saw him myself, stooping over his brother's inert body, stealing his valuables.'

A gasp sounded from those walkers near enough to hear his words and a scowling Daniel added his growled denial to Thea's. Rosalind clamped Cecily's arm hard between her own arm and her body, offering her silent support as Cecily's head whirled, grasping at ideas to help Zach.

'I am a little weary,' she announced. 'If you will kindly excuse us, Lord Kilburn, it is time we returned home. Come, girls.'

She steered Rosalind in a tight circle and they began to walk briskly towards the Park gate. Once they were outside, on Park Lane, Cecily halted, a plan forming in her brain.

'Thea, may I accompany you to your house? I feel a little shaken still and it is nearer than Beauchamp House.'

'Of course,' Thea said.

'We can summon a hackney—'

'No!' Cecily cut Rosalind short. 'I thank you, but I shall be perfectly all right after a cup of tea to revive me.' She smiled at her clearly worried sister-in-law. 'Daniel will escort me home later, I am sure. You take the girls on home and I shall see you at dinner.'

* * *

At Thea's house, Cecily waited until tea was served and the door closed behind the maids.

'It cannot be true.' Cecily sipped at her tea. 'Kilburn is lying.'

'I do not trust him,' Thea said. 'He has a shifty look about his eyes. Oh, I *wish* Vernon was here.'

'I need to find out exactly what happened, but if you feel unable to help me, Thea, I will understand. I know Vernon will disapprove and I have no wish to come between husband and wife.'

'Well, I owe no such allegiance to Vernon,' Daniel said. 'I owe my life to Zach and I am ready to help in any way I can.'

'As will I,' Thea said, resolutely. 'I do not believe that Zach would attack anyone, even his horrid brother.'

'What can we do, though?' Daniel asked. 'Will they allow me to visit him in the prison?'

'I am not sure,' Cecily admitted. 'I do not know how one might go about gaining permission. The first action we must take is to find out if Lord Thetford has regained consciousness and then go to speak to him.'

'The servants might know,' Thea said, jumping up. 'Vernon told me Thetford only lives around the corner and you know how servants gossip.' She hurried from the room.

'I will escort you,' Daniel said. 'Anything to find out the truth and help Zach. We could also go to his rooms—he has taken lodgings in Jermyn Street. Someone there might have more information—his man or the doorman or a neighbour.'

'Myrtle! We must rescue Myrtle, too. She will be frantic with Zach gone like this.'

Thea returned. 'The news is already widespread,' she

said, gloomily. 'It is true. Lord Thetford was struck from behind and then robbed. He did regain consciousness, but his physician gave him a sleeping draught and has left instructions he is not to be woken until morning.'

Cecily's heart sank as her faint hope that the whole incident had been fabricated by Kilburn disappeared.

'We can still go to Jermyn Street,' Daniel said. 'We may learn something new there.'

Cecily hung back while Daniel rapped on the door of the house in Jermyn Street where Zach lived. She sighed with relief when a stranger answered the door, having dreaded the possibility of being recognised from her visit last night.

'Is Mr Graystoke's man in his rooms?' Daniel said.

The servant shook his head. ''E went home, he did, when 'e 'eard what happened.' He eyed Daniel and then assessed Cecily, looking her up and down. 'Who's enquiring?'

'My name is Markham,' Daniel said. 'And you are?'

'Blair, sir.'

'Very good, Blair. I'm a friend of Mr Graystoke. What exactly happened?'

''E was arrested, that's what 'appened. The Runners took 'im. Good thing, too, I say. 'E's a *gipsy*, so he is. Thieving no-goods. Got no right taking rooms in a respectable house like this and so I'll tell the landlord when I see him. I'm not paid to open the door for no gipsy.'

'At what time was Mr Graystoke arrested?' Cecily asked, moving to stand by Daniel's side.

Blair sidled across the step to stand opposite her and she recoiled from the stench of onions on his breath as he said, 'You take my advice, ma'am. You give that gipsy a wide berth. 'E's no good, I tell you.'

'When I want your advice, my man, I shall ask for it.'

Unconsciously, Cecily adopted the clipped tone her brother used when he was at his most ducal and it worked like a charm. Blair stepped back and straightened. 'Now, at what time did the Runners apprehend Mr Graystoke?'

'Just after six, ma'am. He'd only just got back, 'e 'ad—attacked his own brother, so they said. Blood still on 'is hands,' he added with ghoulish satisfaction. 'Well, they got him bang to rights they did and a good job, too.'

Cecily's heart sank. Zach had left her at Beauchamp House at five o'clock. What had he been doing until six? She still did not believe he would attack Thetford, but how could he prove it?

'Is Mr Graystoke's dog still upstairs?'

'Yes, he is. Mangy three-legged m—' His jaw snapped shut as he caught Cecily's icy glare. 'Yes'm.'

'We'll take her with us,' Daniel said. 'Have you a master key for his room?'

The man indicated a bunch of keys at his waist.

'Lead the way, then, and be smart about it,' Daniel said. He turned to Cecily. 'Come inside while you wait. It won't do for you to be left standing on your own on the doorstep.'

Five minutes later they were outside on the pavement with Myrtle between them.

'Where next?' Daniel asked.

'Bow Street, I should think,' Cecily said. 'That where the Runners are based—in the Police Office at the Magistrate's Court.'

Daniel hesitated. 'I do not think—'

Cecily glared at him, her temper on a knife's edge. 'If you are about to suggest that it is no place for a woman—'

Daniel held up both hands, palms out. 'Peace! But it *is* no place for a lady and neither is a prison. Besides, there really is no need for us both to go—I shall enquire about visiting Zach in prison and I know for a fact he will not wish you to see him in there—you know how proud he is—so there is no use you arguing with me.'

'Very well. But you will not talk me out of speaking to Lord Thetford tomorrow, Daniel, so do not waste your breath attempting it.'

He laughed. 'I would not dare, although I fail to see what you hope to achieve by challenging him. If he is determined to have his brother convicted, then I do not see how you might talk him out of it.'

'I must do *something*.'

They had been walking as they talked. A hackney bowled up the street towards them and Daniel flagged it down.

'I will drop you and Myrtle off at Beauchamp House, then I shall find out what I can at the Police Office.'

The stench was enough to slay him. The Romany half of Zach shrank from the filth—Romanies were fastidious about cleanliness and Zach had spent the past ten years following their complex rules until it was now instinctive. This place was hell on earth as far as he was concerned. He closed his eyes and tipped his head back, rubbing his jaw, wincing at the tender swelling. It had been necessary to defend himself when first he was hustled, clad in chafing leg-irons, through the damp, poorly lit maze of staircases, passages and wards by two turnkeys wielding cudgels. He had been left to find his own place in the common yards. As noxious as the yard was, it was at least better than being in the cells with their barred windows and stinking soil buckets.

The yard—where the inmates had access during daylight hours—were crowded with young and old men alike: the untried and the tried, the accused and the condemned, the first offender with the hardened criminal. They were all massed together in one seething cauldron of despair. Zach had been ready for the challenges—he was a big man and he knew there would be men who would try to assert their authority over him from the start. He soon disabused them of any such notion and now, close to twelve hours after the Runners had taken him, he was left largely alone. But he kept his back to the wall as he thought through what had happened, what he had learned about the accusation against him and what might come. He did not think of help from outside. No one, other than Cecily, would care what became of him. He must be ready to defend himself by whatever means he might, but he did not doubt that his future appeared bleak.

Thetford had been robbed. Beaten unconscious. But Kilburn had disturbed the attacker and identified him as Zach. Now, they must wait until Thetford regained consciousness in order to press charges. That he would do so, despite the fact that Zach had not carried out the attack, seemed to go without question. The delay was merely a formality. Thetford would awaken, swear a deposition, and bring Zach to trial at the Old Bailey. And Zach would be found guilty. Zach had little faith in the fairness of the judicial system, particularly with his Romany blood to stand against him.

His only defence—and it was a defence he could never, ever use—was that he had an alibi: Cecily. But his honour simply would not allow him to bring her name into the affair.

After settling Myrtle in with an overjoyed Hector, Cecily gave orders that she was to be informed immediately Mr Markham called and then she shut herself in her bedchamber to think. She paced her room restlessly. She did not believe Zach would harm anyone, even his brother,

but—he had been arrested. Surely they did not arrest someone without some evidence they were guilty?

And what about when Leo learned of the attack and
subsequent arrest? He would be delighted to be proved
right, no doubt, and he would use it as proof why Cecily
could not wed Zach. As much as her head echoed with
snide remarks that he was right and she'd been too hasty,
her heart simply could not believe that Zach would harm
Thetford. Unless—if Thetford attacked him first, would
he not defend himself? Sick dread pooled in her stomach.
Would they believe Zach, if that were the case? And what if
Thetford died? Would they hang him as a murderer? Thetford was a nobleman after all, and… Her heart seized in
terror. Zach was Thetford's heir. Any jury, surely, would
view that as motive enough to kill.

When Daniel eventually called, it was with no further
news whatsoever. His visit had been in vain. Nobody at the
Police Office was able—or willing—to answer his questions and he still had no idea how to arrange a visit to a
prisoner inside Newgate. It was one of the disadvantages
of him being a stranger to London and its institutions.

Never before in her life had Cecily so keenly felt the
restrictions of her sex.

Daniel had left soon afterwards, with the promise of
calling for Cecily the next day as soon as he heard via the
servants that Lord Thetford had awoken.

Leo had returned home late that night and Cecily did
not see him, but she knew there would be a moment of
reckoning come morning. If Rosalind did not tell Leo what
had happened, then he would for certain hear it from some
other source. She slept badly, tossing and turning, drifting in and out of a light sleep but, at first light, she was up

even though there was nothing she could do. She picked at her breakfast, her appetite flown, and—in no mood for company—she returned to her bedchamber to continue her interminable wait. Finally, after hours of indecision, she sent for Anna. Visiting Newgate was not an option, but she *could* go to Bow Street. Surely she could demand answers where Daniel could not? Being the sister of a powerful duke did have some privilege.

The chimes of the longcase clock that stood in the hall drifted through the door as Anna came into the room and bobbed a curtsy. Ten o'clock already! She wondered what Zach was doing; what he was thinking. Did he feel abandoned? Well, *she* would not abandon him.

'Anna. Make haste now, I must dress and go out. And I wish you to accompany me.'

'Milady—' Anna made no attempt to follow her bidding, but remained by the door, holding it open. 'His Grace has asked you to attend him in his study. *Immediately*, begging your pardon, milady.'

## Chapter Twenty-Two

Cecily's heart leapt up into her throat and then sank again. Leo knew. The sympathetic glow in her maid's eyes almost proved Cecily's undoing, but she had kept her emotions under control thus far and she was damned if she would appear before Leo with swollen eyes. She had more pride than that. She must hope that Leo would be able to tell her more details about what had happened.

Grantham opened the door of Leo's study for her and she walked in to find her brother standing by the window, his back to her, and a stern-faced Vernon standing by the unlit fireplace, his arms folded across his chest. Leo turned—his features as grim as Vernon's—as the door clicked shut behind Cecily and gestured to her to sit. She ignored it. Instead she crossed the study to a space where she could see both her brothers at the same time, her pulse pounding. Too late, she wished she had taken action straight away and gone earlier to Bow Street. She would rather face the court officials and the Bow Street officers than face these two in their current moods.

She seized the initiative while she had the chance.

'Tell me what you have heard, Leo, please.'

Leo's brows shot up. 'You know, then? About Graystoke?'

Cecily nodded as Vernon unfolded his arms and moved towards her.

'And here we were, worrying about how to break the news to you.'

'Please—' she looked from one brother to the other '—tell me what you know…everything you know.'

'The news is all over Town,' Vernon said. 'The servants are agog with it and it is here, in *The Times*. Every nasty detail of it.'

Cecily held out her hand. 'May I read it?'

'Unnecessary,' Leo said, 'when we have the full story straight from the horse's mouth. Kilburn called here, not half an hour since.'

'Did he tell you what happened?'

Leo frowned. 'What difference does that make?' His silver eyes softened in sympathy. 'Kilburn identified the attacker as Graystoke.'

Tendrils of anger wound tightly around her heart—a rage she welcomed, to hold secure her courage and her belief and to prevent her heart from breaking in two. She must not fall apart. Zach needed her and she would not let him down.

'I do not believe him. Zach is not a violent man. Nor is he a man to attack another from behind. He is no coward.'

Leo sighed and swept his hand through his hair. 'How can you be so certain, Cecy? The magistrate had no hesitation in refusing him bail. He'll stay in prison until he's tried. Cecily—my dear—you barely know the man. He has lived with Romanies for the past ten years—who can tell what association with such people will do to a man's character? You should be relieved you have discovered the truth about him. You have had a lucky escape. It was fortunate Thetford was quickly discovered and taken for medical attention or it might have been a murder charge.

Not that it will make much difference. Violent robbery attracts the most severe punishment. Kilburn has returned to Thetford's house in order to record what he remembers of the attack as soon as he wakes up.'

'Oh, I can well believe that.' Cecily marched across the room to the window, then twisted around to face her brothers. 'He will take the opportunity to collude with Thetford so they can be rid of Zach once and for all.'

'Cecily—' Vernon came to her, put his arms around her and hugged her to him. 'I know you're reluctant to believe the worst of him, but he was *seen*.'

Cecily shrugged him away. 'Seen by one man only—a man who has reason to hate him.' She again looked from Vernon to Leo and back again. 'He knows that Zach is the reason I refused his offer and he sees in this a convenient way of removing Zach as a rival.'

'But…Cecy…you and Kilburn…' Vernon sighed and took her hand. 'It was no love match, on either side. He is not a spurned lover. Why would he go to such lengths?'

'He is deep in debt and he needs a wife with a large dowry. Ask Leo. Plus his pride is hurt. I saw a side of him that frightened me at your party. And I know what cruelty he is capable of.'

'Frightened you?' Leo growled. 'If he laid a finger on you—'

'He did not, but he would have done if Daniel hadn't intervened. Suffice it to say that what I have since discovered is enough to destroy any lingering doubts I might have possessed. Tell me—' there was no time to be distracted by Kilburn and his nastiness '—where did the attack take place?'

'You do not need the gory details.'

Cecily crossed her arms. 'I wish to know.'

Leo held her gaze for several moments, then nodded.

'Oh, very well. Thetford was attacked in Jermyn Street after leaving his club but, as fortune would have it, Kilburn left soon afterwards and disturbed the attacker.'

*Jermyn Street?* Cecily's certainty in Zach's innocence suffered a wobble. This time it was Leo who put his arm around her.

'Cecy—my dear—I know you wish to champion the man, but Graystoke has rooms in Jermyn Street. The evidence is damning and the location itself points to a different motive than mere robbery. For such an attack to take place in such a respectable neighbourhood—'

Again, Cecily shrugged away the comfort of a brother even though a weak part of her longed to allow him to hold her. Support her. Protect her, as he had done her entire life. She must stand alone and she needed to see their faces in this discussion, not allow them to hug her and soothe her and take control. It was what they had always done—what she had allowed them to do. No longer.

'Lord Stanton suffered a similar attack at the start of the year, did he not? In Sackville Street, as I recall. It is not unprecedented.'

'That is different. Do you still protect Graystoke, even after this?'

Leo looked at her as though she were a stranger. She hated the pain she could see in his eyes. *Hated it.* But it could not be helped.

'I will never believe Zach to be capable of such a vicious, cowardly attack. He is gentle and loving—'

Her voice choked into silence, remembering their laughter as she taught him to waltz and she blinked away a sudden welling of hot tears. She thought of his tenderness as he made love to her—

Her breath hitched. Thetford's *club*? Had he been out all night? It was as though a bank of cloud parted to allow a beam of light to penetrate the turbulence of her thoughts. She frowned. '*When* did the attack take place, Leo?'

'The night before last. In the early hours of the morning. Why?'

'Did Lord Kilburn say the *exact* time?'

'He said he left White's around four, not five minutes after Thetford.'

*Four?* She frowned. Blair's account had suggested the attack had taken place just before Zach's arrest.

*Just after six—blood still on 'is hands—*

Relief—spiced with self-recrimination—flooded her, easing the vice that had seized her chest ever since Kilburn had told her the news. *Why* had she not thought to establish the exact time of the attack?

'Then Zach is innocent,' she said.

'You can be so sure?'

'Yes.' It was time to be brave like never before. She sucked in a shaky breath. 'I was with him.'

'I *beg* your pardon?'

Vernon's growl sounded somewhere to her right. She could see by both brothers' expressions that they knew precisely what she meant and she could also see neither of them were about to make this easy for her. And, after all, why should they? She was their little sister still, even though she was thirty years of age. They—Leo in particular—had spent their lives taking care of her.

Protecting her.

But they could not protect her from the scandal she was about to unleash and she did not expect them to. It broke her heart, but her choice was for love. For Zach. And she could only hope, in time, her family would come to forgive her.

She walked across the room to stare unseeingly out of the window. It took all her courage to say her next words and

she could not bear to see desolation—or, worse, disgust—
on her brothers' faces as she said them.

'I was with him. All night. Until dawn.'

'You were here. You went to bed.'

'I went out. Later. At half past one.'

'Kilburn confirmed Graystoke as the attacker.' Leo's
voice was right behind her. 'It was he who raised the alarm.'

She spun around and met his steely eyes.

'He lies. Zach was with me.'

Leo grabbed her shoulders, his silver gaze boring into
her. 'Are you lying for him? Do not act in haste and destroy your reputation unless this is the truth. You must
know that bearing false witness is a crime.'

'I do not lie. I was with him. The night porter in Jermyn
Street saw me, although I was veiled, and one of our footmen saw me return home. I begged him not to tell you. I
love Zach, Leo. I will not stand by and see him falsely accused simply to protect my reputation. If people choose
to think the worst of me, and to shun me, then that is up
to them.' She hauled in a deep breath. 'And if you—if our
family—choose to disown me, then th-that is up t-to y-you.'

Her vision blurred and she stared at the floor, concentrating on the floral pattern of the carpet. She inhaled
again and willed her voice to sound strong. Steadfast. As
she must be from now on.

'I shall go and tell the authorities,' she said. She was
on her own. For the first time in her life, she would not
have her family—Leo—at her back. She swallowed her
fear and blinked away her tears before looking up at Leo
again. 'Th-they will have to release him then.'

Leo paced the room, his brows lowered. 'It may not be
as simple as that.'

'But why should it not be? They must listen to the truth.'

'Kilburn has accused Graystoke direct and he has a

lawyer standing by so as soon as Thetford regains consciousness he can swear a deposition against Graystoke. He will then be committed for trial. It will be your word against theirs.'

Anger, peppered with fear, bubbled behind Cecily's breastbone. 'I am a lady. The daughter of a duke. My word is true.'

'And Thetford and Kilburn are peers of the realm. Their words are—should also be—true. Your words will be twisted, my dearest sister. Once someone—anyone—calls your integrity into doubt—'

'My *integrity*? My behaviour and conduct has been beyond reproach my entire life. Why should anyone now doubt me?'

'By the simple fact of your confession that you were with Graystoke that night, in his room. In his bed. They will say if a lady can lower herself so very much, how can her word be relied upon? And if Thetford decides to prosecute Graystoke, you would be called to repeat what you have said in open court. You will be depicted in every newssheet as a fallen woman, and will become an object of scorn for the caricaturists to poke fun at. Are you truly prepared for all that?'

She felt as though she'd been kicked in the stomach, knowing he was right. Her mind raced. She must find another way, but she could not think straight while she was here with them. She headed for the door. Vernon reached it before her and blocked her way.

'Where are you going?'

She raised her chin. 'I am going to my bedchamber to think about what you have said,' she said haughtily.

She saw Vernon look at Leo and give an infinitesimal shrug. Then he stood aside.

'Cecily.' She looked back at Leo and raised her brows. 'Do not go out without informing one of us first, if you please.'

*How dare he?* She had never lied to him, but she had come this far and she did not see why she must be constricted by petty notions of honesty when a man's life was at stake. She would do what she must, irrespective of any promise Leo might coax from her. She hid her hand in the folds of her gown and crossed her fingers as she spoke the lie.

'Very well.'

She left the room, anger and fear churning away inside her.

Outside Leo's study, Cecily paused, thoughts chasing around inside her head. She saw now the way forward. She could only hope an appeal to Thetford in person might work. If not, then she would take the stand in court, regardless of the consequences. With determined steps, she headed for the parlour and penned a hasty note to Daniel Markham. She would wait no longer. She left the parlour and handed the note to Grantham.

'Have a footman deliver this to Mr Markham at Lord Vernon's house, please, Grantham, and tell him he is to hand it to Mr Markham in person. If Mr Markham is gone out, then he is to enquire after his direction and follow him. Any answer is to be brought directly to me.'

'Yes, milady.'

'Thank you. And please ask Anna to attend me in my bedchamber.'

Grantham bowed. 'Yes, milady.'

When Anna entered her room, Cecily wasted no time.

'I should like you to accompany me to Lord Thetford's house, Anna. But I need you to understand—what I am about to do might very well bring disgrace upon me.'

Anna's face sagged. 'But milady...' Fear coloured her voice.

Cecily raised her hand. 'No. Say nothing yet. Allow me to finish. If you should prefer not to continue to work for a-a fallen woman—then I shall understand. Our future—whatever happens—will not be within the Duke's household and, if we are unable to prove Mr Graystoke's innocence, then I might find myself living out a life of genteel obscurity after all. The very situation I have been at such pains to avoid. There will always be a place for you within my household, but I understand if you prefer to remain with his Grace. All I ask is that you do not reveal this conversation to him.'

The maid's mouth set in a stubborn line. 'I am with you, milady.'

A warm glow suffused Cecily at Anna's words. She had the feeling she would need all the friends she could get.

'Thank you, Anna. I am more grateful than you can know. We shall ready ourselves to go out and then we must wait for a response from Mr Markham.'

Time had never passed so slowly. Every time a door closed or they heard a footstep in the passage outside, they both jumped. Finally, though, as the clock struck noon, a note was brought to Cecily's door. Daniel awaited her in a hackney coach around the corner in South Audley Street. Cecily tied her bonnet strings under her chin, picked up her reticule and looked at Anna.

'The back stairs, I think, Anna. Will you lead the way, please, and alert me should any of the family be about?'

Inside five minutes, Cecily and Anna were sitting in the hackney on their way to Curzon Street and Cecily told Daniel of the place and time of Zach's arrest.

He folded his arms across his chest as he listened to Cecily's story, his lips thinning in disapproval as she—with a hot blush—skated over how she could now prove that Zach was innocent. She could not bring herself to boldly admit her fall from grace to this man she barely knew.

*And yet I shall have to find the courage to confess it—out loud—to Thetford and Kilburn. And, possibly, in court.*

'I expect Thea to get herself embroiled in such escapades,' Daniel grumbled, once Cecily fell silent, 'but I thought you to be a respectable lady.'

Cecily sighed. 'As did I.' And he—and no doubt the entire *haut ton*—would soon know how *unrespectable* and *imperfect* this particular lady actually was. 'But I shall do whatever is needed to save Zach from this injustice and my best hope is to throw myself upon Lord Thetford's mercy.'

Daniel reached across the carriage and squeezed her hand. '*Our* best hope,' he said. 'I shall do my dam—my *utmost* to help my friend.'

The first challenge was gaining entry to Lord Thetford's house. The butler looked down his nose at Daniel, who had warned Cecily to let him do the talking and not to draw attention to herself. She had made him no promises. She would do what she deemed necessary—no longer would she be the perfect lady waiting in the background for the men to organise matters and to dictate her life.

The butler's sniff of disdain was audible. 'His lordship,' he intoned, 'is indisposed.'

The front door started to close. Daniel put his booted foot in the opening and then his shoulder to the door itself. One shove sent the butler stumbling back.

Daniel bowed. 'After you, my lady.'

Cecily swept past the butler, whose eyes widened and jaw dropped as he took in both her appearance and that of Anna, who dutifully followed her. Cecily had anticipated resistance from Thetford's staff and had dressed accordingly—in her very latest promenade dress of sea-green jaconet muslin and matching high-crowned bonnet—to emphasise her wealth and her status. That she was accompanied by her maid only added to her consequence.

'Milady! Sir!' The butler, all dignity discarded, scurried to block the foot of the stairs. 'You cannot—I have orders—' He again scanned Cecily as though he could not believe his eyes. 'It is unseemly,' he added in desperation. 'His lordship is in *bed*.'

Daniel bypassed Cecily and slung a matey arm around the butler's shoulders. 'What is your name, my good man?'

Cecily bit back her smile as Daniel eased the man away from his self-appointed sentry duty.

'C-Catchpole, sir.'

'Then, Catchpole, be a good fellow and occupy yourself elsewhere. We mean your master no harm, but we *shall* speak to him. Whether or not you nurse a bloodied nose while we do so is entirely your choice.'

He released Catchpole and smiled at him. 'And before you consider summoning help, just remember—' He put his mouth close to the butler's ear and whispered a few words that caused the man to blanch.

Catchpole visibly swallowed, and then said, 'S-second floor, first door on your left.'

Daniel slapped his back, eliciting a muffled yelp from Catchpole as he stumbled under the weight of it. Cecily started up the stairs. Daniel overtook her and reached Thetford's bedchamber door before she did. It was firmly closed and no sounds could be heard from within.

'Are you certain about this, my lady?'

'Yes. I am absolutely certain. Please, allow me to do the talking. Just be there if I need you.'

# Chapter Twenty-Three

Daniel rapped on the door and entered Thetford's bed-chamber and Cecily followed, with Anna on her heels. Contrary to her expectations, Thetford was sitting up in bed, his arms folded across his chest. A bandage around his head bore witness to his injury, but he did not give the appearance of a man at death's door. Kilburn stood by the unlit fireplace and another man, clutching a roll of parchment, hovered near the window.

'What the devil—?' Kilburn strode across the room to confront Daniel. 'Who permitted you entry, sir?' He then glared at Cecily. 'And what are you about, visiting a man in his bedchamber. Have you no care for your reputation, madam?'

'Clearly not. And I am here because I wish to speak with Lord Thetford.' She brushed past Kilburn and addressed Zach's brother. 'I was disturbed to hear of the attack upon you, sir, but I am glad to find you less gravely injured than I feared.'

'Thank you.' Thetford's chest rose as he drew in a breath and he raised his hands to massage his temples. 'You might as well give this up, Kilburn. If I wouldn't sign that deposition before, I most certainly will not sign it now.'

'Does the deposition concern your brother?' Cecily glanced at the stranger by the window. He had the look of a lawyer. 'He did not attack you, sir, no matter what you believe you saw.'

'I saw him—'

Cecily rounded on Kilburn. 'He. Is. Not. Guilty.'

'Spare your pleas, Lady Cecily.' Kilburn's gaze slid past her to the man in the bed and she read the silent warning in their grey depths. 'I saw him with my own eyes. I can prosecute him myself. I don't need you, Thetford.'

'You lie, sir!' She hauled in a deep breath. 'I can prove it.'

'Prove it?' Kilburn gripped her upper arms, shaking her. 'How?'

'I was *with* him,' she spat, glaring up into his face. 'At the time you say you saw him attack his brother. You, sir, are a liar!'

He thrust her from him. 'Better than a whore, madam.'

From the corner of her eye she saw Daniel start towards them, but it was Thetford's voice that slashed through the air like a whip.

'Enough!'

Kilburn stared at his friend, his jaw slack. Daniel backed away again, joining Anna and the third man.

'I have had enough, Kilburn.' Thetford's voice was weary. He waved a dismissive hand. 'Leave. Take your lawyer friend with you. I may not be overjoyed by my half-brother's presence in Town, but that does not mean I am willing to perjure myself or to see him hang. Get out!'

Kilburn ignored him. His eyes clung to Cecily. 'Marry me, Cecily. I am willing to overlook your scandalous behaviour. No man could be fairer than that. Say yes and I shall save Graystoke. Otherwise—'

'Otherwise,' interjected a bored voice, 'you will be exposed as the liar you undoubtedly are.'

Cecily spun to face the door, scarce able to believe her ears. But although it had been Leo's voice she heard, she had eyes only for the man who followed him into the bed-chamber.

'Zach!' She launched herself at him, touching him all over with frantic fingers—his face; his hair, damp and curling; his torso—reassuring herself that he was real and not some figment of her imagination. 'It really *is* you. How—?'

One dark brow rose. 'How do you think?' He jerked his head towards Leo and then to a scowling Vernon, who had followed them in. 'Your brothers contrived to persuade the magistrate to release me into their custody pending trial.' Zach's expression, far from appearing grateful, was the picture of disgruntlement. 'I *told* them I didn't need their help.'

'I'm beginning to wish we'd left you there to rot,' Vernon muttered. 'You haven't stopped belly-aching since and I fear I'll never get that God-awful smell out of my nostrils.'

Cecily frowned. 'Smell?' She sniffed gingerly. 'What smell?' All she could detect was her beloved Zach and the fresh scent of soap.

'He even had the nerve to insist on returning to his lodgings to bathe and change his clothes before coming here,' Vernon said.

'And it's fortunate I did,' Zach snapped. He turned again to Cecily. 'Myrtle has disappeared.'

'He's more worried about that damned three-legged mutt than he was about his own neck.'

'That's because I know I did nothing wrong.'

Cecily hastened to interrupt their squabble, fearing it might escalate into a full-scale row. 'Daniel and I took

Myrtle to Beauchamp House. She is safe there, happily playing with Hector.'

Zach did not appear placated by her words and she realised how much his pride had been dented. Vernon then switched his attention to her.

'And what, precisely, are *you* doing here, Sister?' he growled. 'You gave us your *word* you would not go out without informing us first.'

Cecily tilted her chin, hotly conscious of both Kilburn and Thetford listening to every word.

'I left you a note, informing you where I had gone. It is hardly my fault you had already left the house.' She omitted the fact she had left her note in her bedchamber so it would not be discovered too quickly. 'You should have had the decency to inform me of your plans.' She included both brothers in her sweeping glare. 'I had a right to know.'

Vernon ignored her. 'And as for you, Markham—what the devil were you thinking, aiding my sister in this piece of madness?'

Daniel stalked towards Vernon, his eyes narrow as his jaw jutted out belligerently. 'Much the same as *you* were thinking when you aided and abetted *my* sister in her recent escapade, Beauchamp—that she would have carried on with or without my help.'

Vernon had the grace to look shamefaced at that riposte from his brother-in-law as Leo grasped Cecily's elbow and smoothly manoeuvred her away from Zach.

'You need not think that our intervention to release Graystoke from prison indicates anything other than a desire to prevent an injustice from being done,' he said to her. 'Nothing has changed.'

Kilburn stirred at his words, stepping forward eagerly. 'You are right not to trust that gipsy, Cheriton. Keep your sister away from him and his contaminated blood. I can save her reputation. I am still prepared to marry her—upon the right terms, of course. It is the only way you will prevent her disgrace from dragging the Beauchamp name through the mud.'

A harsh growl erupted from Zach. He moved swiftly and hauled Kilburn around to face him, drawing back his fist before letting fly. His blow landed on the side of Kilburn's jaw and he staggered back against the bed. Cecily gasped and Zach's arms came around her, tugging her from Leo's grip as he gathered her into his chest. Then she heard a scuffle, a sharp cry of, 'Look out!' and the sound, once again, of a fist hitting flesh. She wriggled around until she could see. This time Kilburn was on the floor, groaning as he held a hand to his nose, and Leo was massaging the knuckles of his right hand. Vernon stooped to retrieve a half-drawn sword stick from the floor.

'Bad form, attacking a fellow from behind,' he murmured, with a glance at Zach. 'Seems you're in our debt yet again, Graystoke.'

Cecily felt Zach tense. 'I did not ask for your help, Beauchamp,' he growled.

She turned within the circle of his arms and laid a placating hand on his cheek. 'You will soon learn, my love, not to allow Vernon to provoke you with his teasing. Just ignore him.'

Then she turned to Leo and she quailed inwardly as his silver gaze swept over her. His expression gave nothing of his feelings away, but it was time she made clear—again—where she stood.

'You were wrong, Leo, when you said nothing has changed.' she said. '*I* have changed. I have been changing since the moment I listened to Vernon and Thea exchange their vows. And now, for the first time in my life, I choose to follow my heart and not to be the perfect lady.'

Her words warmed his heart, soothed his soul and eased his ruffled temper. Zach wrapped his arm around Cecily, fitting her close to his side, where he could feel her. Where he knew she was safe. Both of her brothers stiffened, identical disgruntled expressions on their faces, but he could not care less. She was his.

*Mine.*

*And the sooner they get used to the idea, the better.*

Thetford had been silent throughout, but his eyes were open and Zach had been aware that his brother's attention had been on him since the moment he entered the room. He met those grey eyes now. He needed answers.

'Why did you accuse me?'

Somehow—in all the history that lay between them: all the bad blood, all the rejection, all the cruelty—the answer to this question meant more to Zach than the rest put together.

'I made no such accusation. My attackers were strangers to me.'

At Thetford's words, Cecily wrapped her arms around Zach's waist to hug him and the tension seeped from him, leaving him drained. Seeing Cecily's brothers together, with their close bond and the clear trust between them, had awakened an unwelcome longing within him. His relationship with his own brother might never be close, but maybe they could look forward now instead of back.

'Thank you,' he said.

Kilburn stirred at his feet. 'You fool, Thetford,' he mumbled through the hand still clasped to his nose. 'You'll never—'

His words were cut short as Cheriton bent to him and hauled him upright by his lapels.

'Your behaviour, sir, convinces me you are no gentleman and I suggest you remove yourself from my sight before I forget that *I* am a gentleman and teach you a lesson here and now.'

He shoved Kilburn backwards, releasing his lapels. The Earl staggered in his effort to remain on his feet as the Duke straightened his coat and then brushed a hand down each of his sleeves, smoothing out any wrinkles, completely indifferent to Kilburn's glare of loathing. Zach watched this interplay with dawning respect for Cecily's brother. He brushed a kiss to Cecily's temple, murmured, 'Trust me', and, unhesitatingly, he handed her over to Cheriton. He needed to be sure she was safe while he dealt with Kilburn.

Cecily barely had time to squeak a protest before Zach grabbed Kilburn's arm and shoved him to the door.

'You and I need to talk,' he growled.

Kilburn dug his heels in. 'I don't answer to you, gipsy boy.' He shot a look brimful of mockery at Cecily. 'Did you see his brand? He'll always be marked for the gip—'

He ended abruptly on a screech as Cecily flew at him, fingers crooked, and raked her nails down his face, just missing his eye. 'You—you—'

Zach hauled her away from Kilburn.

'Shhh, my love. He's not worth it,' he whispered.

'Brand?' said Vernon.

'On his arse, like the animal he is,' Kilburn snarled. 'And he yelped like one, too. You should have smelt his flesh burn—'

This time it was Vernon who silenced Kilburn's tirade by bunching his lapels in his fists.

'Really, Kilburn,' he said, softly, shaking his head at

the Earl. 'One might have hoped a fellow of your breeding would exhibit a dash more intelligence, or at the least a smidgen of self-preservation. Do you not know when you are beaten?

'I am impressed you did not kill him the minute you met him again, Graystoke,' he added. 'I am sure I would not have shown such restraint.'

'I remember telling a cousin of mine—not so long ago—that the mark of a gentleman is manners and the treatment of others and, in particular, the treatment of those of lower birth,' Leo said. 'Good birth clearly does not guarantee a gentleman—Graystoke has exhibited far more of those qualities than you, Kilburn, despite your contempt for his breeding. I know which man I would trust more.'

'Beauchamp.' It was Thetford who spoke, his voice weary. 'Get him out of here, will you?'

'With pleasure,' Vernon replied. 'Daniel? Care to join me?'

They took one of Kilburn's arms each and bundled him from the room. Leo, after ushering out the lawyer, closed the door behind them and leaned back against it, effectively blocking Zach from following the others.

'You will gain nothing by challenging Kilburn further, Graystoke. I suggest that here is where you need to do your talking.' He nodded towards Thetford, then beckoned at Cecily. 'Come, Cecy. It is time we went home.'

'No, Leo. I—'

'She stays with me, Cheriton.'

That silver-grey gaze pierced Zach as the Duke moved between the two of them. Zach's fingers curled into a fist, but he hesitated. He owed the man a debt of gratitude.

He remembered the flood of relief as he had been released from Newgate; the carriage, complete with ducal crest on its door and its liveried coachmen; the shock at the sight of the Duke and Vernon inside; the conviction that they would somehow contrive his disappearance, or offer him a bribe to desert Cecily; his astonishment when they did not, even after revealing that Cecily herself had provided his alibi.

Oh, they had given him a hard time, but they had also brought him here to confront his brother over the false allegations. Yes, he owed a debt of gratitude, but that did not give the Duke the right to come between him and the woman he loved. Before he could speak, or act, however, it was Cecily who soothed the tension that sizzled in the air between them.

'Thank you for getting Zach released, Leo.'

His hard expression softened. 'I would never let an innocent man hang, no matter how convenient that outcome might be for me.'

'If only I had known you would put everything right.'

He pinched her cheek. 'When have you *ever* known me not to do whatever it takes to protect my family, Cecy?' Then he shook his head, a smile lurking. 'Are you telling me that if you had known I would sort this out, you would have left it to me?' He laughed then, but it was rueful laugh. 'The Cecily of old might very well have allowed me to take control, but I am not convinced this new version of my sister will readily allow *anyone* to handle the ribbons in her stead.'

He flicked a glance at Zach and he could swear it was one of sympathy.

'Cecily.' Cheriton's voice turned serious, all hint of teasing gone, and all his attention on his sister, who gazed up at him with troubled eyes. Zach tensed, ready to resist any attempt to take Cecily away. He would fight if necessary. 'Are you certain this is what you want?'

'I am. More certain than I have ever been about anything in my whole life.'

He smiled. 'Then how can I stand in your way?' He looked Zach in the eyes. 'I cannot give my wholehearted blessing, but you do have my understanding. I recognise love and I recognise a good man when I meet one.

'Now, let us leave Graystoke and Thetford to thrash out their differences.'

'Zach?' Cecily's moss-coloured eyes were wide, pleading.

'Your brother is right, dove. Go home. I will call on you later.'

'We will wait for you downstairs, Graystoke. My carriage is here, and I am sure you are eager to be reconciled with your—er—Myrtle.'

It was a flag of truce.

'Just make sure Kilburn is gone by the time I get downstairs, or I might kill him anyway.'

'That,' Cheriton murmured, as he steered Cecily from the room and beckoned to Anna, 'would be the actions of a fool. Even *I* might not be able to extricate you from Newgate twice in one day.'

The door closed quietly behind them.

Zach approached the bed. 'Well?'

His brother was still as white as the bandage encircling his skull, but he was not in mortal danger and Zach was surprised to find that he was glad.

Thetford's lids lowered as though unable to meet Zach's gaze.

'Over the years I have had cause to regret my treatment of you and your mother,' he said. 'Not enough to track you down, but—' His lips firmed. Then he opened his eyes and fixed them on Zach, sucking in a deep breath. 'I do not expect forgiveness. What we did to you was unforgivable. But my intention was merely to frighten you that day—Kilburn always did take pranks a step too far. We were foxed, hot-headed fools.' He heaved a sigh. 'When you came to Town, after our first meeting I felt...diminished. You could have wreaked your revenge on me then and there, but you did not and, despite myself, I found a grudging respect for you.

'And afterwards, I watched you and I watched Kilburn and I realised that the man with all the dignity and the integrity was not the man who was an earl, but the man who was a gip—no. A Romany. A half-Romany. And *he* was a man who made me feel shame.

'It was footpads who attacked me, and that is what I told Kilburn when he found me. This whole—' he wafted one arm '—*mess* was of his doing and I am sorry.'

He held out his right hand and raised his brows. Zach grasped his hand and they shook.

## Chapter Twenty-Four

She hadn't seen Zach in days, but the fact that Leo was dressed in his best swallowtail coat, over black breeches and black silk stockings, at ten o'clock on the morning of her wedding reassured Cecily that all was still well. Leo and Vernon had continued to give Zach a hard time every time they met, but Cecily had ceased to panic over her brothers' attitudes—she detected underlying respect in their pointed comments and jests and realised that, although neither would probably ever admit that Zach was the perfect husband for her, they approved of him well enough to overlook his mother's birth.

Dominic and Alex were less critical, saying only that they were happy for her. She had been surprised by Dominic's easy acceptance of her choice of husband—he was the one member of the family who set store by position and status—but when she had told Leo of her surprise, he had reminded her that Dominic's expectations of himself, as Leo's heir, were always the most demanding. Alex—an animal lover himself—was fascinated by Zach and as a consequence when Zach had decided he needed to travel to Edgecombe before the wedding, Alex had gone with him, as had Daniel. Cecily could only hope they would all arrive back in London in time for the ceremony.

The female portion of the family were all truly happy for her and Rosalind, Thea, Olivia, Nell and Susie now all clustered in her bedchamber to admire her wedding dress—a gown she had commissioned especially for her wedding day. Afterwards, she would have some of the trim altered so she could wear the dress again but, today, she would show her respect and her love for Zach by wearing a gown she had never worn before, unlike many brides who must walk down the aisle in their best evening dress. It was one of the privileges of wealth and she reminded herself—as she admired her image in the pier glass on the wall—that her future would be more frugal, even though she and Zach would still be rich compared to most folk. They would have a wealth of love to sustain them, though.

'You look beautiful,' Olivia breathed, standing next to Cecily and gazing at their joint reflection. 'I wish—'

Cecily saw her niece bite her lip and wondered at the sudden sadness in her expression. She had been so caught up in her own life that Livvy's troubles had faded to the back of her mind. She had already warned Rosalind to keep a close eye on Olivia. Although she had noticed no partiality for any particular young man from her niece, the highs and the lows of her moods suggested a heart that was, if not already broken, very close to being that way. She slipped her arm around Livvy's waist.

'Do not speak your wish aloud, Livvy, or it may never come true. Keep it in your heart and try to keep faith.You never know—it may all work out for the best.'

She saw the effort Olivia put into her smile. 'Oh, I want for nothing, Aunt. You need not worry about me,' and she kissed her on the cheek before moving away, leaving Cecily to tweak once again at the blush-pink roses woven through her hair. Their scent, for her, would always transport her to Stourwell Court and the rose garden where she and Zach had met in the moonlight. Her throat ached with emotion at the memory. Who could have known where that meeting would lead?

'Leave it, milady,' Anna scolded, pulling her hand away. 'You don't want them falling out as you walk down the aisle, do you?'

Cecily smiled. 'No. No, I do not.'

A knock at the door heralded Grantham. 'The first coach is ready, your Grace.'

'Thank you, Grantham. We shall come immediately.'

Rosalind took Cecily's hands. 'We shall see you in church,' she said and kissed her cheek.

Thea added, her gruff voice choking a little, 'You look radiant, Cecily. Zach is a lucky man.' She, too, kissed Cecily and followed Rosalind out of the door.

Olivia, Nell and Susie, pretty as a picture in palest-pink satin gowns, were to be her bridesmaids and they descended the staircase with her. Leo waited at the bottom, looking up, his eyes suspiciously shiny as he took in her appearance. The three girls went ahead, to travel to the church in the town coach, leaving Leo and Cecily to travel in the same barouche—drawn by Leo's matched team of six gleaming chestnuts—that had conveyed Rosalind to St George's for hers and Leo's wedding, less than three months ago.

'I don't want to lose you, Cecy,' Leo muttered, his voice catching.

Cecily blinked away her tears. 'You have only yourself to blame, Leo. Look what you started—no sooner did you finally succumb to Cupid's arrow than Vernon and I needs must follow suit.'

She went up on tiptoes to kiss his cheek. 'But you are not losing me, my darling brother. You have Rosalind, Vernon has Thea and I will have Zach—but that will enhance our family, not diminish it. We will be bigger, stronger and happier. Now, let us go. I cannot wait to begin my life as Lady Cecily Graystoke.' A moment's disquiet threaded through her. 'Have you seen Zach this morning? Is he returned from Edgecombe?'

'Oh, yes. He is returned.' There was the slightest quiver in his voice that made her look at him with suspicion, but his expression gave nothing away. 'Come. Let us go.'

The Season was over, yet many families had remained in Town to see the final member of this generation of Beauchamps tie the knot and they had gathered outside St George's in Hanover Square, mixing with the commoners who had also come to enjoy the spectacle of a society wedding. A cheer went up as the barouche drew up outside the church. It was still uncertain quite what the *ton* would make of this marriage between a duke's daughter and a half-Romany, but the people of London were thrilled by the romance of the story, the excitement of Zach's wrongful arrest and his rescue by one of the most powerful Dukes in the land. Zach had become something of a romantic hero to many of the ordinary folk.

Inside the church, the wide aisle was strewn with rose petals and there, at the front, dark, brooding and unbearably sexy in his black suit, enlivened by a red and gold embroidered waistcoat, was Zach. The man Cecily loved more than life itself. She inhaled, Leo squeezed her hand into his ribs and they began the long walk up the aisle. Daniel, Zach's groomsman, was by his side and her beloved family were all there, seated in the high-sided box pews, ready to watch Cecily and Zach taking their matrimonial vows. On Zach's side, there was only Thetford, but Cecily was delighted to see him and smiled with pleasure. The only person missing—her heart sank.

'Where is Alex?' she hissed at Leo.

'He is here. You just can't see him yet.'

Leo winked at Cecily and then it was too late to demand he tell her what was going on, because they had reached the front and Zach was smiling at her and, for a moment, everything else just disappeared. He filled her vision and her soul, and her heart overflowed with love. He took her hand and raised it to his lips, pure joy radiating from his eyes as his lips curved in a beaming smile.

The Reverend Hodgson, waiting to begin the ceremony, cleared his throat and they turned to face him.

'Dearly beloved, we are gathered together here in the sight of God...'

Cecily listened intently to the words of the service and held her breath as the rector said, '...if any man can show any just cause why they may not lawfully be joined together, let him now speak, or else hereafter for ever hold his peace.'

A tiny part of her wondered if Lord Kilburn would suddenly appear and object, but he did not. She sensed Zach tense at exactly the same point in the service and she glanced sideways at him, seeing the smile flicker over his lips, and she knew they had thought the same thing. She smiled in reply and then concentrated once more on the Reverend Hodgson's words, answering 'I will,' when required.

Then Leo, when asked, gave her hand to the rector. Zach spoke his vows firmly and clearly, and she did the same. And then the Reverend Hodgson held out the prayer book, asking for the rings. Zach nodded to the rector and smiled reassuringly at Cecily as he took her hand and turned her to face the rear of the church. At the far end stood a man with a large, pale oval shape balanced on his outstretched arm.

It took Cecily several seconds to understand what she was looking at. Alex. And perched upon his arm...surely that was…but it could not be. She looked to Zach, who stretched his own arm out sideways and emitted a low whistle.

Athena glided low and silent down the aisle towards them, to the collective gasp of the congregation. Several ribbons—pink and white—fluttered from her legs. As she neared Zach, she flapped her wings—once, twice—and rose higher, reaching with her feet for Zach's arm. Zach fed her a reward and it was only then that Cecily saw that each of the two white ribbons was threaded through a gold wedding ring. She watched through teary eyes as Zach untied the knots holding them in place and slipped them free. He raised his arm and Athena took flight again, this time heading back up the aisle to Alex.

Zach placed the wedding rings, one thick and masculine, the other delicate and feminine, on to the prayer book and the rector continued with the service as though barn owls flew inside his church every day.

Zach and Cecily were pronounced man and wife, they signed the marriage lines and then they were walking back up the aisle, between smiling faces. As they neared the church door, Zach dipped his head to whisper, 'Little did we know, when we met inside the church at your brother's wedding, that it would soon be our own wedding day.'

Cecily halted at his words. With a puzzled frown, Zach also stopped. She reached up and pushed his hair back from his right ear, and she breathed a sigh of pure happiness as his diamond earring was revealed.

'I feared…for a moment…' She stretched on to her tiptoes to kiss his lips. 'Don't ever change, my glorious Romany lover.'

He grinned at her words, a gleam of mischief in his eyes. 'Oh, I can promise you that, my dove. Come.'

He steered her out into the sunlight. The crowds cheered their appearance, but the sound was almost drowned out by the clatter of wings as dozens of white doves were released from wooden crates, taking to the skies above London.

'Oh, how beautiful!' She watched until the final bird was lost to sight.

And then she saw, behind the barouche that waited for them at the kerb, a flower-bedecked gig. Between the shafts, his plaited mane interwoven with yet more flowers, stood Titan. And, tethered behind, was Sancho Panza, one long ear flopping over his eye. Alex—grinning as he joshed with boys from the crowd—was in the driving seat.

Cecily burst into laughter.

'Hurrah for the Gipsy Lord,' yelled a voice from the crowd and the chant was taken up as Zach led Cecily to the barouche.

He turned to her as they set off on the short journey towards Grosvenor Square and on the long journey towards the rest of their lives together.

'Will you be my Gipsy Lady?'

'Yes. Always and for ever.'

They were still kissing when the barouche drew to a halt outside Beauchamp House.

\* \* \* \* \*

*If you enjoyed this story, you won't want to miss these other great reads by Janice Preston*

*SAVED BY SCANDAL'S HEIR*
*THE GOVERNESS'S SECRET BABY*
*CINDERELLA AND THE DUKE*
*SCANDAL AND MISS MARKHAM*